Fragile Courage

Fragile Courage

MARTHA E. CASAZZA

Fragile Courage

Windy City Publishers
www.windycitypublishers.com

Published in the United States of America

ISBN:
978-1-953294-14-2

Library of Congress Control Number:
2021914895

Cover Image by Zonda/Shutterstock.com

WINDY CITY PUBLISHERS
CHICAGO

In memory of my father
who inspired my love of books.
This one's for you.

To bring about change,
you must not be afraid to take the first step.
We will fail when we fail to try.

~Rosa Parks

1
Melina

Pressing her fingers hard against her cheeks to stop the tears, Melina barely made out the blurred shapes of Mamá and Papá as the bus pulled away from the station. She folded herself into the sticky, plastic seat and squinted out the rear window until they were just fuzzy specks on the horizon. At the bus stop, they seemed so small. Mamá held on to Papá as if her whole being depended on it, while Papá summoned all the strength his tired body had to offer, just to hold her up. He wore his mask of courage, the one he used when the family heard a strange knock on the door, frightened it might be the Immigration and Customs Enforcement agents. His head balanced rigidly on his narrow, muscular shoulders, and his mouth forced into a thin straight line, as if drawn by a Magic Marker. His eyes didn't betray him with tears as he stared straight ahead. Mamá and Papá seemed like one as they melted into each other for support. Neither appeared able to break away and stumble toward home.

Huddled deep inside the folds of her well-worn favorite yellow coat that Mamá mended last week, Melina touched the tiny gold cross. It was pretty much all she brought from home. A few weeks ago, after the last dinner plate was put away from dinner, Mamá took Melina's hand and led her to their usual place on the couch by Papa's recliner. Mamá bowed her head as if to pray but instead removed the delicate gold chain from around her neck and put it on Melina.

"This will keep you safe, Melina. Please keep it on and remember how much we love you." Melina knew this had belonged to Abuela and that Mamá never took it off. What would keep Mamá safe without it? Now, it was Melina's turn to worry.

Melina closed her eyes, and the last several weeks played under her eyelids like a streaming video. Concealing their fears throughout the summer had been difficult for her family, but it also provided them with special moments. Remembering the day Mamá took her shopping brought a smile to Melina's tear-stained face.

"Come on, we're going to the mall today. I've been saving a little here and there, and I want to get you some nice things for school."

They laughed together that day as they picked out a pair of new dressy shoes, two pairs of jeans and bright pink pajamas, just for fun. Afterwards, they sat in the park and shared a large glass of horchata and two tacos—one de asada, the other al pastor. Melina wanted to give Mamá one more hug and tell her how much she'd miss her, but it was too late now. Instead, she kept her eyes shut and her fingers wrapped around the tiny cross.

She remembered the day Gabriela came by, to beg her not to leave.

"Melina, I'm so lonely here, and you're the only one I can talk to. Mamá hardly lets me go outside, and when I stay home, she doesn't talk to me. She just sits in front of Chuy's altar and stares at the wall. Papá goes to work and tells me to take care of her, but I don't know what to do. You were the only one who cared about me after the shooting. I don't want you to leave."

It was true that after Gabriela's brother was killed in a drive-by a few months ago, Melina was the only one at school to sit with her. The other students shied away, as if simply talking to Gabriela made them just as vulnerable. Melina remembered the first few weeks after Chuy died. One morning on her way into school, she spotted Gabriela in a far corner of the school yard curled into a ball. She knew she would be late for her first class but instinctively joined her on the bench and listened.

"My mother stays in bed all day and doesn't talk to me. My tía comes every afternoon to light the candles for Chuy. After that, I hear them crying together behind the closed door. If I stay home, I'm sad and alone; if I come to school, I'm also sad and alone. I miss Chuy so much and don't know what to do."

On school days, Melina walked home following the route Mama carefully mapped out for her, but after Chuy's death Mamá gave her permission to go to Gabriela's house a few days every week. This continued all summer, and since Melina didn't have friends outside her family, this pushed her mind off leaving home. They laughed together while playing cards at the kitchen table and flipping through old fashion magazines, all the while keeping an eye on Gabriela's mother. They pretended they were the models in the magazines by making up weird poses and sweeping their hair into crazy shapes with the mousse they found under the bathroom sink. When it was hot, they ran to the corner for fresh horchatas, always bringing an extra one back for Gabriela's mother. She usually took a few sips to be polite, then put it down on the floor, in front of the altar. Gradually, she began to smile at them and sip a little more than the last time. Melina would never forget the last day she spent at Gabriela's. The girls hugged each other tight, and as Melina opened the front door to leave, she heard a quiet voice just behind her.

"Melina, you've always been so kind. Thank you for taking care of Gabriela and me."

All summer, Melina's cousins drifted in and out of the house to give her things they had outgrown. Most of them didn't fit, so Melina left them at home in a garbage bag under her parents' bed. Tía Rosa even brought over the old brown, plastic suitcase she used when she first came to the United States from Puebla.

"Melina, this brought me to a better place. I hope it does the same for you. I will pray for you."

Melina pushed away another trail of tears as the bus veered further from her home, and she wished she'd brought her cousins' clothes, just to feel them close by. She also worried about leaving Diego. Ever since the Kings attacked him on the way home from school, her cousin stayed in his room with the curtains taped shut. He wouldn't go to school. He blared his music all day and was too scared to talk to anyone. Melina wondered if she would ever see him again.

Her family may not have understood why she was leaving, but they were all proud of her. Just yesterday, the whole family gathered for a daylong fiesta in her honor. Aunts, uncles, cousins and all the neighbors brought food to the local park where they sang and danced. The kids happily tumbled around, and Papá played his guitar well into the night.

"For my daughter, Melina," he called out many times, "Esta canción es especial para ti."

She and her cousins danced together, holding on tight, as if they would never see each other again. No one wanted to leave, thinking that maybe if they stayed awake, tomorrow would never come. Leaving to follow her dream was harder than she thought.

In the morning, everything was different. It was eerily quiet as Melina pulled the sheets off her mattress and stuffed them into Tía Rosa's tiny suitcase, along with her new clothes. She shoved the mattress into a closet. As she carefully removed her posters from the wall and started to roll them up, Melina was startled to hear the phone, but relieved to have the stillness broken.

"Hi, Melina. This is Ms. Ingram. I just called to wish you luck and let you know that you can call me if you have any questions once you reach the university. I'm so proud of you and can't wait to hear all about it when you come back to visit."

I wish I could have brought Ms. Ingram with me, thought Melina. Just last week, they crammed together over the used laptop that Ms. Ingram managed to borrow from school for Melina. She also gave her a monthly planner and journal, as she cautioned Melina to write everything down. Ms. Ingram reminded her that at home, Melina's schedule had been determined by others, but now she would be responsible for keeping track of all her classes, assignments, and deadlines. There was so much to think about. Melina was excited and scared to death. This was her dream. She hoped she was up to it.

Papá and Mamá helped Melina carry her few things to the El, which took them to the bus stop downtown. Papá didn't go to work so he could be there. Melina knew that meant no pay for him, and less job security. He didn't say anything all morning. He kept his eyes down while Mamá chattered away. Melina had a hard time walking. Her legs felt wobbly, and a few times she was afraid she might fall. She concentrated on putting one foot in front of the other and kept silent just like Papá. Her stomach churned as they watched the bus approach. The big sign on the front announced it was going to Hamilton.

"Goodbye, Amá and Apá; I'll call you tonight. I love you both so much," she said as she hugged them tightly. They hugged her back, and then she rushed to board. Melina knew if she said anything more, she might not leave.

After three long, lonely hours at the back of the bus, where it was empty and Melina was able to curl up and stream memories under her eyelids, the bus driver called out in a raspy, tired voice, "University stop number one."

Eyes open and slowly unfolding from the safety of the sticky back seat, Melina stumbled down the aisle behind some other passengers, and followed them off.

I wonder where I am, thought Melina as she watched the others, who seemed to know what they were doing, take off in different directions. Since she couldn't afford to visit the campus earlier, she had no idea where anything was, but Ms. Ingram told her there would be plenty of people around to help her find her way. She pulled a crumpled letter from her pocket. She had read it so many times that she had it memorized:

> *Dear Ms. García,*
>
> *You are assigned to room 503 in Forbes Hall. Theresa Anders is your roommate. You must arrive on August 23rd by 3:00 p.m.*

Now what? There had been a map attached to the letter, but it disappeared after one of her nephews had eaten half of it.

Melina peered through the drizzle that had started as soon as the bus driver handed her Tía Rosa's suitcase. She was overwhelmed with excitement and curiosity but a little frightened; her legs were still weak and trembling as she tried to move forward. Melina felt she was being swallowed up by something she didn't understand, and that left her numb. *Was this her dream come true? Did she really belong here?* Her eyes grew wide at this place that stretched out in all directions. Tall buildings dotted the campus alongside pathways that crisscrossed every which way. There was lots of green space where students played ball and laughed together. Everyone else seemed to know what to do.

This was so different from the cracked, gray sidewalks and garbage-filled alleys of the neighborhood she had left behind where the right streets took you straight home.

"I wonder where I should start?" she asked herself, half out loud. As she stood there feeling very alone and wishing she had an umbrella, she heard a voice.

"You look lost. Can I help you?" Melina turned and came face-to-face with a huge smile pasted on a guy about her age who had a mass of blond hair curled into a tight bun on top of his head. His bright yellow shirt stood out with "Student Guide" splashed across his pocket in bold, friendly letters. "I'm Todd, and I'm here to help lost souls like you. I'll bet you're a freshman and want to find your dorm. Am I right?"

Melina almost melted and suddenly felt a little less lonely, and less in need of an umbrella.

"Hi," she stammered. "My name is Melina. I'm looking for Forbes Hall. Can you help me?"

Todd grinned, "You've just made one of the most common mistakes that all freshmen make. You got off at the first bus stop. Forbes is the third stop and on the other side of campus. No problem. I'll walk with you, and we can do some sightseeing on the way. Okay?"

"Sure," she said, and followed Todd through the tangled web of pathways that would soon become her new home.

As Todd walked ahead with confidence and purpose, Melina lagged behind, hugging Tía Rosa's suitcase tightly to her chest. *Why couldn't it have little wheels like all the others she saw?* Constructing a mental map to help her navigate this crazy maze on her own, she remembered walking down the streets at home with Mamá, who created "safe" maps to help guide her home from school, from the store, and anywhere else she went.

Todd burst through her reverie by calling out, "Over there is Hamilton where you'll eat, and next to it is Clawson, where you register for classes. Oh, and here is the Student Center where you'll find the worst food in the world, but you'll have fun with your friends!"

Todd ticked off names and places as if he lived here forever.

Melina assigned markers to each one: Hamilton had a bush in front that looked a bit like a hamburger from a certain angle; Clawson had a white sign that became a registration form in her mind; and the Student Center was beneath a rotunda that she envisioned as a circle of friends. Even with these visual markers, Melina became more and more nervous about finding her way back and wondered if this would ever seem natural to her. She also wondered if she would ever meet those friends Todd mentioned. She didn't have many friends at home because Mamá said it was too dangerous to hang out with anyone after school. *How would she make friends here? Was it safe?*

"And here is Forbes, on your right. This is a great dorm because everyone's so friendly, and there are lots of parties here. You're all first-year students, but each floor has a senior student advisor to help you figure things out."

They walked through the giant, revolving front doors of her new home into a lobby glistening with polished floors and fresh white paint. Everything seemed new and full of promise. Melina felt a tingling sensation throughout her body that was a combination of excitement and fear.

By now, she'd affectionately named her suitcase "Tía Rosa." As she and Tía Rosa began to stumble up the first staircase she saw, Todd called out, "You can walk if you want the exercise, but most people take the elevators. Here, I'll show you. They're right around the corner."

Melina retraced her steps and turned the corner. *Yikes!* There were three elevators with glass doors opening and closing as they swished their way upward with boxes, suitcases, and people. She could feel the energy even though getting into a tiny, enclosed space with people she didn't know was an unexpected and somewhat alarming surprise.

Mamá had always warned Melina to be careful in elevators and to take the stairs whenever possible: "You never know who might be hiding in an elevator; on the stairs there is always a way to run from any danger. Always be aware of your surroundings and have an escape plan." With Mamá's words in her head, Melina reluctantly managed to squeeze into one of these sleek boxes next to Todd. As Melina hugged Rosa even tighter, she felt another twinge of excitement along with escalating alarm bells in her head from all the uncontrolled exuberance and commotion around her. They got out on the fifth floor and made their way down the hall, nearly tripping over discarded boxes and empty suitcases that had been tossed out of rooms filled with noisy families and friends. The door to room 503 was open, and laughter came from inside.

With a crooked smile, Todd said, "Here you go! Enjoy the next four years," and he took off to help another newbie. Alone again. What should she do now? Why were there so many people in this space?

As she tentatively entered the room, a little girl ran up to Melina and said, "You look funny. Why do you have those weird boots on?" Melina looked down at her old hand-me-down boots and felt so ashamed.

Before Melina could answer, a voice called out from across the room, "Missy, that's not polite. Tell her you're sorry!"

Missy sulked and walked to the other side of the room without saying a word.

"I'm really sorry. I'm Theresa, and you must be Melina, right? Nice to meet you. Missy is my little sister, and these are my parents. They've been helping me get settled and hang some posters. I hope it's okay that I took this side." Looking over Melina's shoulder, she added, "Your parents here?"

Shifting nervously from one foot to the other and self-conscious of her boots thumping together, Melina glanced around the room. It was so big, larger than her parents' living room. There were two of everything: two desks, two chairs, two beds, two dressers and two closets. One side of the room was filled with posters, photos, a yellow flowered bedspread, fluffy pillows and dozens of stuffed animals. The other side, a blank space, was apparently hers to fill. Despite the noise and overwhelming commotion all around her, Melina felt alone. She hugged her suitcase, suddenly unwilling to put it down.

"No," she said to Theresa. "My parents are working and couldn't come today. I'll just put my suitcase over here and put my things away later."

She felt the Anders family quietly checking her out. *What were they thinking about her oversized boots and pants that might have been too tight?* Maybe it was just her imagination because Mrs. Anders seemed sincere when she said, "I'm so sorry we can't meet your parents, Melina. Maybe another time we'll all have dinner together and get to know each other."

She put an arm around Melina and offered to help her get settled, but Melina thanked her and said she was fine. Again, she felt the weakness in her legs and sat on the bare bed that was now apparently hers.

Hugging her parents as they turned to leave, Theresa assured them she was okay. Missy gave Theresa a big hug and then looked at Melina again asking in a small, squeaky voice, "Where are your boxes? What color is your bedspread?" Before she could go on, her parents told her it was time to leave. She stuck out her tongue and slowly followed them out the door.

Theresa then turned to Melina. "I'm so excited to be here! I love this room, and I just know we'll be good friends. I hope you like the colors of my bedspread. Do they go with yours? Do you like the posters? I had such a hard time deciding which ones to bring from my room at home. If you don't like them, I can take them down. Do you think we need curtains?"

Reeling from the rapid-fire questions, Melina flushed and missed the low expectations that went with her rolled up mattress now stuffed in a closet at home. She had carefully packed her plain white sheets but a bedspread? She never had a bedspread. No one told her everyone in college would have one. She wanted Theresa to like her and be her friend, but she really didn't know how to have this conversation, nor did she know how she could contribute to decorating this room.

She forced a smile and simply replied, "Everything looks great, Theresa. You've made the room look really cheerful. Thanks!"

Suddenly, three girls burst through the door, screaming Theresa's name and hugging everyone in sight, including Melina. Theresa introduced them, "Melina, these are some of my besties from high school. They're living right down the hall. Isn't that cool? We're gonna rage the fifth floor!"

One of them, Sonia, said, "Wow, this room is really glam. Love the bedspread! Can't wait to see what it looks like when it's all finished. Where're you from, Melina? We all live near each other and are so excited to get away from home. It's so stifling back there; our parents are way too strict. How about yours?"

"I live in the city, and my parents watch out for me a lot. I guess it's good to be away, but…," stammered Melina.

Cutting her off, Sonia continued "Hey, let's all get out of here and find something to eat. I'm starving. I hear there's food trucks outside with some good stuff. Who wants to check it out?" As they prepared to leave, Melina begged off.

"I need to put my clothes away, and I promised my family I'd call them tonight so they know I'm okay."

Theresa looked disappointed and quietly asked Melina if she needed any help.

"No," said Melina. "I'm okay." With that, the four girls waved goodbye as they charged out the door and left her by herself.

Sitting alone on her first-ever real bed, Melina's mind was all tangled up. *How would she fit in? She had no bedspread or posters or pillows or stuffed animals. She was used to curling up on a mattress in the back hallway at home with a few posters taped to the wall over her head. Here the clothes she brought easily fit into one drawer. She certainly couldn't afford to buy curtains, or even food from a food truck. Didn't Ms. Ingram tell her that meals were free in the dining hall? How would she explain this to Theresa and her friends? Would they be disappointed in her?* Melina was sure she didn't meet Theresa's expectations, and that she and her friends were already laughing at her. She got up and quietly folded her clothes, putting them in one drawer of her three-drawer dresser. She put her one nice pair of shoes and the red dress from her cousin Lupita in the closet. Finally, she tucked Rosa safely into the back corner, and closed it tightly so Theresa wouldn't see how empty it was.

Melina looked at the clock on the very white wall. It was 7:00. She knew her family was gathered around the tiny laptop at the kitchen table in Tía Rosa's house, anxiously waiting for her call while they talked and laughed as families do. Ms. Ingram helped Melina and her family install Skype so they could easily stay in touch. As Melina heard the laughter and screams up and down the hall, she sat alone at her new desk and opened her laptop to make the call. She would tell them everything was perfect. She would not cry.

Margot

R rrrrrr, rrrrr! *Dammit.* Rrrrr!

Tangled up in her blanket, unable to get loose, Margot fell to the floor with a thump. She'd been meaning to change that motorcycle ringtone for months. Her days of whizzing across the countryside to clear her mind were over, and her phone should reflect that. She also needed to stop napping on the couch and start acting like an adult. Should she answer?

Hmmm...not sure. She'd abruptly woken up from a dream where she was looking out over an enormous auditorium, behind an important-looking podium, at a sea of young faces, their heads nodding in appreciation of her work. Was she getting a standing ovation? Yes? Maybe? Damn...the dream was lost. Where was she? Was the phone still ringing? Rrrrr...

She untangled herself from her way-too-big and worn-out blanket, while Biko clawed up the faded and shredded red drapes that covered the drafty windows. She clambered around the piles of books and found her phone under a stack of papers by the cold, sticky coffee pot on the floor. Flicking the straggly hair from her eyes and clearing the sleepiness from her throat, Margot picked up the receiver.

"Hello? This is Margot. Yes, Ms. Munson, of course, I remember you and I'm planning to be there." Listening intently to the office manager of the Psychology Department at Balsam State, she cleared her throat again and gripped the phone tightly to make sure she heard every word.

"Yes. Tomorrow at 10:00 in Anderson Hall, room 301. Thank you so much for the confirmation."

She hung up: The second interview was really happening! Tomorrow. Ten o'clock. Now that it was official, a to-do list started to take shape in her head:

> *Reread job description for the tenth time.*
> CHECK.
>
> *Look over notes from first interview.* CHECK.
>
> *Review findings from dissertation.* CHECK.
> (Oh, where was that blasted thing?)
>
> *Find clean, professional-looking outfit.* CHECK.
> (Ooh, this would be a tough one.)

The rest should be easy, right? She knew her stuff. She was qualified, right? *But how many others were called back for a second interview? What if they were more qualified? Smarter? What if she forgot someone's names?* Clearly, a good night's sleep was a long way off and her nap was on hold. So much for that feel-good dream.

Too nervous to call anyone, she told Biko about the call. He wouldn't interrupt or give her unnecessary advice.

"Hey, buddy. Tomorrow could be a big day for us. I have an interview in the morning, and if I nail it, we can move to a new place. Replace these dreary, red curtains! Why didn't we rip them down when we moved in anyway? We'll find you some proper bird-watching windows with no obstructions! But before any of that, I need to get through tomorrow. I'll need to leave early, but don't worry; I'll put an extra special treat in your bowl first thing. Maybe some tuna? How does that sound?"

Biko deserved a treat, didn't he? All those late nights they spent together finishing that dissertation, sending resumes looking for (okay, begging for) a teaching position. Biko was there for all of it.

As always, Biko rubbed up against her ankle and listened intently to Margot's nervous chatter. He calmed her more than anyone with his empathetic purring. Much better than calling a friend whose words might jinx it. Steve would be reassuring, yes, but he would be way too optimistic. She might lose her edge. Sharon would give advice about what to wear, which would only add to Margot's anxiety, since she knew her one professional-looking shirt was currently at the bottom of her dirty laundry bag. No time to get to the laundromat to wash and iron it. Why didn't she think of that earlier? Had she really been afraid there wouldn't be a second interview? All she could think of was an earlier position where she thought she had it made, and they called to cancel the second interview. She didn't want to be disappointed again, so she stored this one far from her conscious mind.

It occurred to her that some people might call their mother with news like this. She considered it for a moment. *No way!*

With her index finger, Margot twirled a strand of hair at the crown of her head. Once it was tightly wrapped around her finger, she pulled on it and let go. Then she began another twirl and then another. This habit started in college to soothe the intense headaches she experienced before exams or important deadlines. Biko immediately sensed her anxiety and climbed into her lap, distracting her hands as he purred for a few strokes.

This was the path her parents always envisioned for her. Her mother was the first female partner in a large law firm, and now her name was on the front door too. Her father was a well-known researcher at a prestigious university who was frequently recognized with international awards. Her parents even lived separately in different cities for a while to advance their careers. They expected no less of her, and Margot, their only child, adopted their goals as her own early on.

Margot graduated at the top of her class by working harder than anyone. Whenever her friends invited her to join them at the local hangout, she'd say, "I've got a date with the library," with a shrug. She pursued her subsequent degrees in Psychology at a highly respected graduate school. She'd begun her studies to help understand herself and her family better, but she felt pressured by her advisors to conduct research in their areas of interest, which had nothing to do with human behavior and everything to do with…well, nothing relevant. Now she was on the unpredictable and tangled route to a tenured professorship with more time devoted to research, along with some teaching only when absolutely necessary. She had been trained to believe that research was far more important than working with students, and that her goal should be to get tenure and spend the rest of her life researching, speaking, and publishing. That trajectory would lead to a successful career…and happiness?

These thoughts enveloped Margot as she started down her checklist in a heavy fog that probably wouldn't lift until she made it through tomorrow. She got all the way down the list but stopped when she got to the professional outfit part. Being too tired to deal with that detail, she simply climbed into bed around midnight and prayed for some sleep.

After a fitful sleep, Margot woke up the next morning to a dreary day.

"It's raining cats and dogs out there, Biko. No offense. I hope this isn't an omen," she said as the cat sniffed the air, indeed taking offense.

He didn't follow her to the closet. He wasn't there to comfort her when a professional-looking outfit didn't burst out of the jam-packed clothing inside. He didn't rub up against her to approve the plain black jacket and skirt she chose. Margot was on her own. Her mother's voice popped into her head loud and clear:

"Top it off with my grandmother's simple pearl necklace, dear. Appear professional. The better you look, the better you'll feel." Thank goodness her mother WAS here if only in spirit.

In her early teens, Margot would stand in front of her closet door for an excruciating thirty minutes every summer morning with head and shoulders flung back at attention listening to her mother's daily lecture on how important first impressions were. She prayed to get out of these mini boot camps, but unless a client meeting took precedence, her mother was unrelenting. Margot's mother had perfected her look: Hair sprayed in place, clothes neatly pressed and matching and most importantly, shoes with no scuff marks. A tough act to follow! As much as she hated those early morning talks, Margot frequently revisited them when she needed advice.

Margot pulled her long, dark hair into a tight bun at the nape of her neck. She also slipped on a pair of black flats from the pile of shoes in her closet, quickly swiping some black marker over the scarred heels. She was tall and didn't want to tower over her potential colleagues, but she also needed to remember not to slump to match their height. Her mother always reminded her that, saying, "Slumping is a sign of laziness." Margot checked her bun again and determined this was the way to go. What better way to look professional and serious? She hoped the black marker was indelible.

Even with no soothing goodbye ankle rub from Biko, Margot graciously filled his bowl with the promised tuna and dashed out the door. Flying down the stairs, she used her app to call a cab and escape the worst of the rain. Of course, she had no umbrella! So much for looking professional.

Half an hour later, she stepped out of the cab, one foot landing smack dab in an unforgiving puddle.

"Damn!" Hopping to dry ground, she managed to keep the other foot dry as she limped toward Anderson Hall, accompanied by the rhythmic *squish, squish, squish* of her very wet shoe. The muddy water oozed right up her leg to complete the frumpy look she'd been striving for.

Damn. There was only one direction for this day to go.

At least I won't be late, thought Margot, as she nervously checked her phone for the tenth time since her mud bath. She might even be early. Ascending the steep, intimidating entry to Anderson, she repeated her personal mantra over and over, "I can do this. I can do this."

As she approached the Psychology Office, Margot wondered whether it was better to be early or to risk being a few minutes late and find a washroom where she could clean up. Caught up in her reverie, she didn't notice that she had already entered the outer office of the Psychology Department, so she was startled when Shirley, the department's administrative assistant, welcomed her.

"Good morning, you must be Margot Pearson. Welcome to Balsam State." Gently eyeing her up and down, Shirley added, "I see you also managed to find a puddle this morning. Me, too. Lucky for me, I was able to change shoes and dry off," she said as she patted Margot's shoulder. "Can I get you a cup of coffee?"

Margot was immediately envious of Shirley's dry towel and second pair of shoes. She made a mental note to remember this if she ever had an office of her own. They chatted amiably over the hot coffee, and soon Margot mostly forgot about her wet leg.

Shirley's introduction to the office staff helped put Margot at ease even though she was twirling her hair a bit, careful not to loosen her bun. What a warm, welcoming place this was. By the time Dr. Berg, the department chairperson, arrived and ushered her into the faculty interview, Margot felt right at home. *Yes, this is where she belonged.*

Six hours later, the longest day of her life was still not over because Margot was then invited to dinner with a select group of Psychology faculty and administrators.

"Margot, we hope you will join us for dinner. That will give us a chance to get to know each other better in a less formal setting. And you can see who uses the right fork," added Dr. Berg with a chuckle.

What could she do but accept, even though what she really wanted to do was go home and curl up on the couch underneath her old, worn-out blanket with Biko. She wanted to tell him how she met with ten faculty members from two departments, Psychology, and Sociology. She'd successfully navigated questions about her research and academic goals. They marveled at her past successes in finding grants to fund collaborative work, since they had a dismal record of grant awards in the department. They promised to support her, by keeping her teaching load light and student interaction to a minimum. All in all, everything lined up as she had hoped.

So now, she was headed to a social event instead of home, to the comfort of her apartment. Dinner! Small talk made Margot extremely nervous. *Who needed to know these people on a personal level anyway? What mattered was her expertise and commitment to work. Wasn't that most important?*

Suppose the conversation veered away from her research focus? Suppose they asked about her outside interests and social life? She had none. Once again, her mother's words floated through her head, "Making small talk is important for success, Margot. You must figure out how to do it."

Her mother had even given her stock phrases to use in these situations, "I just finished a book that I couldn't put down. I wonder if you've read it?" or "Last week, I went to the Sox game. The team is really strong this year!"

Neither of these activities reflected how Margot spent her free time, and she didn't know how to fake it, as her mother did so deftly. Maybe she should have put some time into figuring it out.

Margot struggled through dinner by taking on her familiar role of an active listener and asking lots of questions.

"Dr. Berg tell me about your family. How old are your children?"

"Suzanne, where was your last trip?"

"Edie, how long does it take you to get to work in the morning?"

"Rene, what is your favorite class to teach?"

By the time the first course was over, Margot learned that Robert's five children were superstar athletes, Suzanne's "amazing" partner always planned exotic trips for them, Edie lived with her parents as their primary caretaker, and Rene not only enjoyed teaching, but he found his students inspiring. Margot felt for Edie with her long commute but didn't really care where she lived, or how long it took her to get to work. And even though she couldn't possibly imagine being inspired by undergraduate students, she enjoyed listening to Rene. He seemed the most enthusiastic and interesting of all the faculty. When he told a truly convoluted story of a student who insisted his roommate had thrown his final paper in the garbage, Margot genuinely laughed out loud, despite her nerves.

Margot eventually arrived home, thoroughly exhausted and still a bit muddy. Active listening is no easy matter. *Pay attention. Ask relevant questions even when you really don't care.*

As these thoughts rambled through her head, she glanced appreciatively down at Biko who greeted her by arching his back and rubbing up against her ankle. How often had he nuzzled her attentively and pretended to listen, when all he probably wanted was food in his bowl? As she tossed her jacket toward a nearby chair and fell onto the familiar, lumpy couch, Biko scrambled for her lap seemingly eager to hear about her awfully long day.

"Biko, you're such a good listener," said Margot as she unconsciously tangled her fingers in his long coat and scratched behind his ears. "I just did it for eight straight hours! How do you do it? Why don't you run and hide under the couch when you hear me coming?" Then she laughed and told him all about the faculty and their boring stories.

"But, Biko, here's the best part. Just before dessert Dr. Berg offered a toast. You know what he said?" She cast her mind back, and repeated verbatim,

> "To the newest member of the Psychology Department! We've been looking for someone just like you, Margot, who will develop our research arm and help us write successful grant proposals. The university has made it a priority for each department to strengthen its publication record and bring in additional funding through grants. I spoke to the provost yesterday and after reviewing your credentials, she gave me permission to offer you the position if today's interviews went smoothly."

She smiled. "Our first full-time job, Biko; mission accomplished! Let's go tear down those red curtains."

Melina

Melina slowly closed her laptop afraid that if she did it too quickly, she might lose her family forever. She closed her eyes to hold on to them for a few minutes more. How she loved hearing their voices and seeing their faces! Even though they all talked at once and asked lots of questions she couldn't answer, it helped her forget how far away she was. The nephews she took care of every morning before school made silly faces and threw paper airplanes at the screen. She missed them already. *Who is watching them now?* Her cousins wanted to see her room, so she twirled the computer over her head to show them. Mamá sat quietly behind Tía with a tight smile pasted across her face while Papá was sitting off to the side with his head down. *Was he asleep or just angry at Melina for leaving them?*

As always, Tía was in charge and asked most of the questions.

"What is it like? Where will you sleep? You have your own room? Wow! Did they give you a mattress? Did you lock the door? How is the food? You won't go out at night, will you?"

Melina opened her eyes and looked around the room. *Did she deserve this? Would she get used to sleeping in a real bed? And the carpet! Her feet wouldn't be cold in the mornings. She ran her hands across the desk, her own desk. It was so clean and free of the usual stuff. Her desk at home was the kitchen table with its plastic cover where she did her home-work after the dinner dishes were cleared and the bills pushed aside. She* had learned to block out Papá's TV with its constant soccer games just a few feet away. Would Theresa be noisy? Would they get along?

Just then as she was sorting things out, the door burst open. Theresa and her friends were back, and they had a pile of styrofoam cartons, red and green sauces dripping down the sides. They dumped them on Theresa's desk and looked over. "Hey, Melina, we brought you some food. Hungry?"

The inside of Melina's head had felt like a collision course all day. Bumper cars battled each other for dominance, each carrying a different emotion ranging from fear to loneliness to excitement. She forgot to eat! But it was a little more complicated than that. She was hungry but didn't know where to look for food. And after Mamá's tortillas at breakfast, she paid more attention to the rumbling in her head than the one in her stomach. She realized now that it was grumbling, loudly. Embarrassed, she felt her hand instinctively cover it and answered, "Sure! I'd love some. What do you have?"

Theresa answered enthusiastically as she spread the wet cartons out across the desk. "The trucks had lots of good stuff! We grabbed some burgers and ate them outside, but then Sonia saw a taco stand, and we thought of you immediately. We brought back a few with ground beef to share and even found one with crispy onion rings on top. Oh, and we have some chips and salsa. What do you think?"

Melina hid her disappointment as she remembered Mamá's kitchen with the smells of tacos de asada or al pastor. She never saw onion rings, whatever they were, on any taco in her neighborhood. And chips and salsa? How about hot chips with lime juice? She pushed these thoughts deep down as she forced her lips into a smile and reached for a taco. "Thanks, everyone. This is just what I needed."

Theresa's crew spread out on both beds and started asking Melina questions about her family and where she came from. She was happy they cared and as she described her neighborhood, Sonia jumped up and said, "I know Villacito! I did a community service project there last year. It's a Mexican community with lots of kids who need help in school, right? I tutored at Obregon High School in a special English Language program. It was kind of a creepy place with a security guard at the entrance and crackled brown linoleum floors up and down the hallways. The kids were nice, but I felt sorry for them and was a little scared every time the bus dropped us off. My mom told me it was a good experience for me to see how others lived and to help. Our high school was so different. She also told me to be careful and not to wander away from the group. Do you know it, Melina?"

Of course, Melina knew it; it was her school. But she faked it and told Sonia she had heard of Obregon but didn't know anyone who went there. The heat from her face betrayed the lie, and she tried to cover it up by putting her head down to reach for more chips and salsa.

Sonia missed Melina's embarrassment and chattered on to say, "It always smelled so good there. The bus driver let us roll down the windows a little, not too far, so we could really understand the neighborhood. I'll bet the street food in Villacito is awesome, and the music must be rad! Hey, with Melina we'd be safe. What do you all say we take a road trip there, and she can show us around? Okay, Melina? You can show us the clubs, teach us about the food, introduce us to your friends, and maybe some cute guys. I can borrow my dad's car sometime when we have a long weekend with no classes."

Before Melina could answer, Theresa sensed her discomfort and quickly changed the subject. "Who wants to take a walk and see what's going on? Somebody around here must be having a party tonight, and it would be nice to meet some people."

The girls, led by Sonia, jumped up and ran to be first at the mirror Theresa had hung on her closet door. Deciding they all needed to fix their hair and freshen up before going out, they disappeared through the door and down the hall to their room. "We'll be right back," yelled Sonia as she tore off her green sweater to trade it for a new one. "Wait for us!"

Relieved by the sudden quiet, Melina started to clean up the mess from all the food on Theresa's desk. She felt bad about throwing away food, but she didn't see any place to store it. *If only Mamá were there, she would know what to do.* She started to wipe down the surface with her only towel and jumped when she felt a hand on her back. Melina forgot she wasn't alone.

"Melina, you don't have to do that. We'll all help with it later. Right now, let's get ready to take that walk. I think I'll change clothes. You?"

"I don't think I'll go, Theresa. I'll stay here. I'm pretty tired. You go ahead."

"Melina, if it's about Sonia, I want to apologize. She's an old friend, but she can be insensitive like she was a few minutes ago. She gets excited and doesn't always think. I'll talk to her, and don't worry we won't take a road trip to Villacito. I'll bet Obregon is your high school. Right?"

Melina dropped her head to again hide her shame, not about Obregon but about how she had lied. "Yes, it is. I shouldn't have lied about it, but I didn't know what to say. It wasn't a great school, but I don't want people to think my neighborhood is a scary place." She was blinking hard to stop the tears she knew were coming.

Theresa sat down and gave her a hug. "Melina, I'll take care of you. Please come out for a walk with us. And we don't have to change clothes just because the rest of them do. Will you come with us?"

Melina looked out the window and saw it was dark. She didn't want to admit that no one went out after dark at home, and she was a little scared to go out now. She didn't know this place and suppose she got lost? She also didn't want to let Theresa down when she was trying hard to make up for Sonia, so she agreed. Tipping her head back to help dissolve the tears, Melina nodded and agreed to go with them.

Once outside, Melina was no longer afraid. It was exciting, and things were happening everywhere. It felt like a huge celebration with lots of music and laughter coming from groups of students sprawled out as far as she could see. Nothing looked familiar, so she stayed close to Theresa.

"Hey, Theresa and Sonia! Over here!" Melina's oversized boots made it difficult for her to run across the grass to join their friends, but she did her best to keep up. There were blankets spread out, and someone threw one at them so they could join the group.

"When did you get here? Where are you staying? What do you think so far? Are there any parties tonight? Isn't it great to have no parents around?" Hovering at the edge of this crowd of people who all seemed to know each other, Melina's head was undermining her attempt to belong. She wanted to be included, but she wasn't sure how to start. Theresa remembered her promise to take care of her and introduced her to a few of their friends.

"Tracy, this is my roommate, Melina. She lives in the city, not the boring suburbs like us. Pretty exciting, huh?"

"Hey, Melina. It's great to meet you. We're going to have so much fun here! I love those rad boots. Did you find them at the Slightly Used store on Madison? I take the train and sneak down there on weekends when my mom is too busy to notice. I got some great stuff there. I hide it all in the back of my closet when I get home, so she doesn't see it. You'll have to show us around sometime. Oh, this is my friend Pete. Pete, Melina. She lives on the south side of the city. You know it, right?"

"Hi, Melina. Of course, I know it. We go to baseball games there all the time, and it's also a good place to grab a beer; they never check.

But just in case, my friends and I got our fake IDs near there. There's a place, you might know it, right past the ballpark. You park under the overpass and wait for some guy on a bike to come get you. It's probably not too safe; you have to be careful, but you must know that. I'm sure you've been there with your friends."

"Yeah, I've heard of it."

"The best thing about college is that we don't need IDs here. Look around! There are no cops or parents here, but there's lots of beer. Can I get you one? Our cooler is full." Before Melina could answer, Pete was nudging a can in her direction.

"Here, let me open it for you."

Melina nodded and thanked him as he took off to find more friends. She looked around for Theresa and the others, but she was alone on the bright blue blanket. People were swirling around her, but no one she knew. Not wanting to look different, she took a sip and promptly gagged on the bitter taste. She turned away and covered her mouth to stifle the brown liquid coming up from her throat. This was terrible stuff, but everyone else was chugging it down so she figured it was her and tried a few more sips. It only got worse, so Melina crept away from the blanket to find a tree where she could be alone and throw up. In the distance, she heard, "The big party is in town. Free beer. Let's go!"

Immediately, there was a tidal wave of bodies crashing past her. The flashlights were off, so no one saw Melina as she crouched against the tree. She sat still trying to figure out what was happening. She pulled some leaves off the tree to clean her face so no one would see she threw up. Afraid to move, she melted into the ground until she was completely enveloped by stillness. She balanced against the tree as she tried to stand. Her head was fuzzy, and her body felt like jelly. It took three clumsy attempts to get more or less upright. Finally, with the tree as a scratchy prop, she slowly twisted her woozy head to look around for

Theresa and realized she wasn't there. Nobody was there. Maybe not…
suddenly, a flashlight cast a light right in her eyes. Melina looked away
as a deep gravelly voice called out, "Who's there? What are you doing?"

"My name's Melina, and I don't see my friends. I'm not sure how to
get back to my dorm."

"Have you been drinking young lady?" announced the security guard as his searchlight bounced up and down across her body.
Melina looked down at the triangle of light on the ground and realized
she was surrounded by 100s of shiny, aluminum cans reflecting her
shame and confusion. He continued, "I'm supposed to round up any
student I find with a beer can and bring them to the office. You're the
only one here, so come with me."

Melina felt the scratches on her arm as she slowly slid down the
tree and recovered her voice. "I had one can of beer, sir, because I
didn't know what else to do, and it made me sick. My friends are gone,
and I have no idea how to get back to Forbes Hall. I just want to go
to bed. I promise I'll never do it again," whispered Melina who just
wanted to disappear.

He turned off the light and came closer. "My name's Frank, and I
see you're not like the others. Most of them give me the finger and tell
me to fuck off as they run in the opposite direction. Let me show you
how to get back to Forbes. It's not far." He led the way, and five minutes
later Melina saw her new home away from home.

Thankfully, when she pushed open the door, room 503 was
empty. It was also dark, but Melina liked it that way because it made
her feel invisible. She didn't want anyone to see her the way she was,
so she fumbled around as she got ready for bed. As she crept under
her familiar, thin white sheet, she looked over at Theresa's stuffed
animals and fluffed-up yellow bedspread and wondered if she really
belonged there.

Her head felt heavy as it hit the pillow, but she couldn't sleep. She smelled the leftover food on the desk. *Would she always be tagged as the one who loves tacos no matter how bad they are? Why did Theresa's friends assume she didn't like burgers like they did? And her neighborhood? Sonia telling everyone that Villacito and Obregon High School were scary places. That they were simply experiences and that Melina had some magical power to keep them safe if they all went together. These things were her life, not just a curiosity for outsiders to gawk at.*

Trying to erase these thoughts and start over, Melina tossed off her sheet and went to the window. It was dark and quiet out there, but in the distance she saw lights and heard the din of voices. *That must be the town where everyone was headed. Should she have gone? Would that have made her like the others? Did she have to like beer to fit in?*

Finding no answers, Melina dragged herself back to bed and fell asleep.

Margot

4

"No! It still isn't straight," she snarled at the wall. No matter which way she tilted her head, it still wasn't straight. She tried one more time to hang her framed degree on the wall and get it right.

"Owww!" This time as the hammer flattened her thumb, it struck Margot's rapidly decreasing self-confidence along with it. Sitting down to massage her thumb, she squeezed her eyes closed. Maybe the tears she felt welling up would help wash away the pain. That's when the all-too familiar nightmares surfaced in full color inside her eyelids: *Do I really belong here? Will I be accepted by my academic peers? Will my work be respected? Will my parents be proud of me?*

As Margot found herself once again getting tangled inside this sticky web of self-doubt, she heard a weird noise. What could it be? A knock at the door? She didn't know anyone here, but she quickly took a deep breath and mustered a faint, "Come on in," while still pressing against the pain in her thumb.

Seconds later, the door popped open.

"Hi! I'm Harry, and I think we're office mates." Looking at him in utter horror, she wondered if this were another one of her nightmares. *What was this Harry guy talking about, and who was he anyway? He was too old to be a student yet too unkempt to be a colleague. Right?*

Just last week, Shirley had called her with the news. "Margot, your office is 102B. 'B' is for basement. It will be quiet there, and you'll get lots of work done. No one goes down there. The students will rarely find you. You'll have very few interruptions. I think you'll like it."

"Perfect," Margot replied as she smiled on her end of the call. This would make it easy to get on with her research and submit something for publication in the first few months. She trusted Shirley's promise of a quiet space. Remembering names and making small talk could now drop from her bank of worries. Indeed, she would now have her very own hideaway. Maybe she would even drag Biko down there every once in a while to give him a change of pace and a new window for birdwatching. She figured Shirley would show her around to make sure Margot understood the department protocols.

Yes, she thought. *This is the perfect spot.*

"Thanks so much, Shirley. I'll be there tomorrow to move in all my stuff."

Margot hadn't had a chance to check the list she'd hidden in her top desk drawer of names she ought to remember, but she didn't think she had met anyone named Harry. And she certainly hadn't met anyone as disheveled.

She softly stuttered, "Hi, Harry. I think you've made a mistake. I'm just moving into this space and trying to get settled. It's kind of a mess in here right now. I hope you'll come by later, and we can get acquainted."

Trying hard to sound confident, Margot pushed even harder on her thumb to ease that pain while, with her other hand, she furiously twirled a strand of hair to stem the soon-to-arrive headache.

She continued, "This is office 102B. Yours must be somewhere else. Besides, there is only one desk here and, as you can see, not much extra space."

Harry looked a little surprised, but he put down his boxes anyway. "I'm quite sure this is what my letter said, but I can check." At that moment Shirley burst into 102B and immediately felt the tension.

"Oh, I'm so sorry! I meant to introduce you two earlier. Margot, this is Harry. Harry will be here for a few months while Miriam goes on maternity leave. Her doctor recently put her on bed rest until the baby is born. Harry's been one of our best adjunct instructors, and he was available at the last minute to take on her teaching load. There was no office space available because Miriam's graduate assistant is finishing up an important research project in her office, but he didn't mind sharing with you. I think you two will get along simply fine. We'll be bringing a desk down this afternoon, so Harry can get settled."

Suddenly, Margot's framed degree didn't matter. In fact, the hole she had made in the wall was apparently on Harry's side of their private little hideaway. Margot pulled the nail from the wall and looked at Harry with a helpless shrug. Maybe he had a similar degree to hang. She summoned a thin smile while considering how to escape this unexpected moment and make it go away.

She managed to say evenly, "C'mon in, Harry. I was about to go out and grab some lunch. All this unpacking is making me hungry. Do you want to join me? There's a great café right down the street." In her skewed logic, she hoped that by getting them both out of there, Shirley would come to her senses and see that this wasn't going to work. Margot was sure it was Shirley's job to fix things like this.

But even that long shot hope receded when Harry replied, "Oh, thanks, Margot, but I should probably wait here for my desk. I have lots of boxes to unload. Another time. I really appreciate that you're okay sharing space with me." Sensing her lack of enthusiasm, he added, "I promise to stay out of your way. You won't even know I'm here."

Straightening her shoulders and trying to look as if she cared, Margot nodded and threw him another faint smile. She leaned over and nabbed her coat off the chair using her good thumb while leaving Harry alone to create his footprint in their tiny space.

Quickly thrusting herself and her damaged ego up the stairs and outside, she headed down the sidewalk toward Crystal's Café. Margot noticed how the storm clouds overhead had stolen away the earlier sunshine, mirroring her disappointment and adding an overall gloominess to the day. An hour ago, Margot was celebrating her first private office space and professional accomplishment. Even though it was small and in the basement, she had figured out how to make it functional and relatively comfortable. That morning, she and an old friend had loaded an old, empty bookcase and a few boxes into his pickup. Arriving at Anderson, they carefully navigated the uneven stairs down to the basement and reached her office with the bookcase still intact.

"Wow!" said Steve as he looked through the open door. "You've got your very own office, Margot. You even have a small window so you can look up and watch people's feet go by. Where do you want the bookcase to go?"

"Let's put it between my desk and the door, so I can hide when I need to," she said with a laugh. They went back to his truck and retrieved the other two boxes.

"Gotta get to work now, Margot. You okay setting things up in here?" After a quick hug and assurances that she was okay, he left Margot to organize her space. Her books only took up one shelf, so there was plenty of room left for a few personal, comfort items like Biko's photo, her college mug, and a few shells from last year's brief beach vacation to celebrate her graduation. There was also her "thinking" chair. Unsightly as it was, this chair had been with her since freshman year in college. Someone helped her rescue it from a dumpster out behind her dorm, and Margot was convinced that her best ideas had sprung from this dilapidated, mottled gray chair with a hole in the arm. She amused herself by thinking that bad ideas simply melted into that hole. It was also a great hiding place. The springs were long gone, so when she settled into it, she immediately sank to the floor, ensuring that she was practically invisible to anyone behind her.

With these thoughts rumbling through her mind, Margot made it to Crystal's moments before hard pellets of rain began to bounce off the sidewalk. She settled into what had already become her favorite table in a quiet corner at the back of the café and ordered a toasted BLT, along with a sparkling water and slice of lime. Attempting to drown out thoughts of Harry the Disheveled Surprise with her sparkling water, Margot adjusted her focus to how excited she was to have this job. Despite her self-doubts, she couldn't wait to start! As soon as her computer was set up Monday morning, she planned to open her research files and once again dig into some meaningful work. Captivated by these thoughts along with the warmth of the yellow café walls holding up graying photos of long-gone faculty and students, Margot smiled to herself and tried to let go of her frustration.

She glanced around the smallish room where groups of returning faculty chatted amiably. Someday, she would be part of one of those groups, but until then she would be satisfied just to observe them like a good researcher. Still smiling an hour later, she ventured out through the large white French doors of the café into a staggering thunderstorm.

Margot blurted out loud to the sidewalk, "Looks like straddling puddles and mud may be my biggest challenge here! I'd better come up with a solution. Some boots might be in order."

Even as she slogged her way down the wet sidewalk back to the university, there was a lightness in her step, albeit a damp one. She would once again try her luck with the hammer and this time get that degree straight.

As she reached the top of the staircase that led down into the basement hallway, Margot considered taking off her shoes and giving them a good shake to help dry them off. Having convinced herself that

Shirley would have by now taken care of the office snafu, she told herself that no one would notice if she was barefoot. She shook out her first dripping wet shoe when Margot thought she heard voices. Loud voices coming from a hall that until today had been enchantingly quiet.

"Congrats! Here's to Harry! Wow…his own office!"

She soon realized the voices were coming from *her* office. Margot molded her wet shoe back around her foot and slowly squished her way down the hall.

Her door was partially open, and as she squeezed her way inside she heard, "There she is! This is Margot, everybody, my office mate. Margot, meet my friends. They're here to celebrate my new appointment."

She nodded nervously and tried to wrangle her way through the crowd to her desk a few feet away. Finding that impossible, Margot slumped against the nearest wall, noticing that Harry had already hung his degree. It was straight.

She somehow managed to eke out, "Hi everyone. It's so nice to meet you all." One very tall, bearded guy in the crowd called out to her, "We're all adjunct faculty here, Margot. Harry's the first one of us to get appointed to a temporary, full-time position. Harry is president of Balsam's Adjunct Council and has advocated for us to get a shot at these opportunities for nearly two years. It finally happened, so we're here to help him celebrate. My name is Isaac. Hope you'll join us for a glass of champagne."

He handed her a red plastic Solo cup that may have already been used and called out, "Cheers!" Margot accepted the cup and reluctantly raised hers along with the others.

"To Harry!" she added. Oh well, she had no friends here, so she might as well celebrate Harry's good fortune.

Having been an adjunct herself at another university, Margot understood their excitement and was happy for them. *But why did it have to be in her office? Wasn't this a time to celebrate her first real full-time job, not just his temporary one? Why couldn't Shirley find another office for him where Harry and friends could share their excitement? Why was she sharing this ridiculously small space with someone else?* As she peeled herself from the wall, she reflected once again on the small space. She managed to look around through the blurry thicket of Harry's friends.

Somehow, the office looked a little better than it did when she left for lunch. Harry settled in quite nicely: her bookshelf was now filled, and the thinking chair was covered with a bright red blanket that hid the hole for bad ideas. One side of the office now featured posters on the walls, and a smallish desk was appropriately covered with pens, pencils, markers, and pads of paper, all neatly sorted.

Harry noticed Margot looking around and said, "Hope I haven't taken up too much space, but it's great they gave us a bookcase and a chair. I covered the nasty old chair with my lucky blanket. You and I can share it, and maybe it will bring positive vibes to our subterranean space! We've ordered pizza and hope you'll stay and join us."

Margot again managed a thin smile but shook her head and claimed she needed to get home to feed her cat. She wondered if any of her research dreams could be resurrected in this tiny space. What had seemed like a dream hideaway a few hours ago now seemed like an immensely popular space designed for partying. She gave her hair a strong twirl. Tomorrow she would have to do something to liven up her side while ensuring its academic integrity. For now, all she could do was fumble around for her keys, say her goodbyes and make her way back down the long, dark hallway, which was splotchy with puddles from all the squishy shoes. It sounded like Harry and his friends might be there all night.

Little did Margot know that this was an unbelievably significant marker in Harry's life. He had graduated from Balsam ten years ago, just after losing his family in a tragic car accident that happened as they drove home from their last visit to see him. He had been the first in his family to attend college, and they had been incredibly proud of him. It had been a struggle financially for them, but they were looking forward to seeing him walk across the stage and then continue his education. Harry had saved for graduate school and was awarded a fellowship, but he fell into a deep depression after this loss and disappeared for about six months.

As he gradually began to manage his overwhelming grief, Harry returned to the campus to ask a former professor for advice. Dr. Gregory had been Harry's advisor when he first came to the university, and they stayed in touch throughout his four years. Dr. Gregory became like a second father to him, offering to help him get a part-time teaching position while Harry got back on his feet. They both expected this to fill a temporary gap in Harry's career. But instead, he became the most popular teacher around. The students loved him because he was always there for them. He was determined to demonstrate his belief in them, as his parents had done for him. Harry became one of their strongest advocates.

So, this recent full-time, temporary appointment was a real boost for him, and he was determined to make the most of the opportunity and move forward. Being assigned an office where he shared space with a highly touted new faculty member was a dream come true for Harry.

As Margot arrived home, dripping wet and without an umbrella, she was still resentful of what she saw as Harry's intrusion into her coveted space. She opened the door to her dark, sparsely furnished apartment and saw Biko lazily stretched out on their new sofa. Only two weeks ago, they had moved from a three-story walk-up to this newer space closer to the university. She and Biko now shared a one-bedroom apartment on the fifth floor of an elevator building. Her mother was pleased Margot was finally moving up in the world and surprised her with a new white, suede sofa which was clearly the most expensive piece of furniture Margot ever owned. It was nice but already covered with the black hairs of her large, lazy cat. Oh well if her mother didn't visit—and she wouldn't—it really didn't matter.

"Hey, Biko, what do you want for dinner? Tuna okay?" Margot twirled open the can and spooned it out for him as he suddenly summoned enough energy to sprint across the room. As Biko ate, Margot punched the number for Tony's on her speed dial.

"Hi. It's Margot. I'd like to order a small cheese pizza with green olives, extra crispy crust. Twenty minutes? Sounds good. Thanks."

They knew her well at Tony's as this had become her go-to since moving in. While waiting, she uncorked a bottle of her favorite cabernet, pulled a crystal glass (another gift from her mother) down from the cupboard and slumped into the sofa to reflect on her awfully long day.

"Hey, Biko. Guess what? I have an officemate, Harry. Seems like a nice enough guy, but I really wanted my own space. He invited me to stay tonight and share pizza with him and his friends. Why did I come home instead? They all seemed nice enough… I can't quite explain it, but I'm happier being here alone with you."

Her ramblings then turned to work.

"I'm really excited to get to the office tomorrow. I'll need to leave early again, Biko, so don't be mad at me for waking you up. I'll be sure to leave out extra food for you. First, I need to talk to Shirley about getting my computer connected to the university system. I might even get up the nerve to ask her for a different office. Then, I also meet with Dr. Berg and the other faculty at 9:00 to hear about our assignments for the first term. I'll find out which two classes I'll be teaching and what my office hours should look like. As soon as I know that, I can more easily set my research goals because I'll know how much time I have to work on proposals. After that, I should also go out and find a few things to spruce up my desk and maybe hang on the wall. Not sure though. Too much stuff just gets in the way of good thinking. What do you think?"

Biko looked at her and stretched his jaws into a wide yawn. As they watched the sky darken with the threat of even more rain, Margot and Biko patiently waited for the pizza from Tony's and then spent the rest of the evening hours together on their new couch, with Biko once again in the role of an active listener.

Melina

5

Melina woke up with a dizzying headache. Something wasn't right. The familiar crevices of the old mattress that protected the curves of her body were missing. Where was she? Why didn't Mamá wake her up? The sun streamed through a nearby window, creating unusual lines across the ceiling that seemed to be moving ever so slowly in circles. They reminded her of a time when she was little, and her brother tried to scare her by moving a flashlight across the wall by her mattress. That was a long time ago; it had worked then, and it was working now. She was a little startled and for sure alone. Melina's eyes scanned the space around her quietly looking for something familiar. As she shifted her gaze around the room, she saw the bright yellow bedspread and remembered.

"I'm in Forbes 503, my new home," she said aloud to herself. "But shouldn't Theresa be here?"

Tumbling out of bed, dizzy and groggy, Melina thought about her nephews and how she usually cared for them when she first woke up. Back home, she had a schedule and always stuck to it. Things were different here. She remembered her high school advisor, Ms. Ingram, telling her that no one would tell her what to do here; she was on her own. She needed to pull out that planner and start filling it in.

That's when she saw a note on the desk with her name on it:

Melina,

We've got a meeting this morning in the student lounge down the hall. Abby, student advisor for our floor, stopped by to invite us to have breakfast with her at 9:00 and learn about how things work around here. I didn't want to wake you but come on down when you're up.

Terry

Melina was embarrassed that she had been sleeping while others were in her room. *Did they notice her thin sheets? Could they tell she threw up last night?* She quickly looked at the clock with the yellow smiley face that Theresa's father hung on the wall and saw that she might have time to get to the meeting if she hurried.

She wasn't sure where to put her dirty clothes, so for now she threw them in the back of her empty closet. It felt funny to brush her teeth and wash her face by a sink she shared with only one other person. Thankfully, Mamá had given her two of the shared family towels, so she didn't have to use Theresa's, but as she dried her face, she worried that her family might not have enough at home now.

Melina twisted her hair into a loose braid, grabbed one of her new pairs of jeans from the dresser drawer, and threw on the bright green t-shirt from her cousin. Should she make her bed? Probably a good idea since Theresa had tucked in her patterned pink sheets and smoothed out the yellow bedspread. *¡Dios mío!* She had also fluffed her pillows and lined up her stuffed animals. Melina straightened her sheets and tucked them into the firm mattress that hadn't molded to her body yet, and probably never would. Then with flurries in her stomach, she realized she needed to figure out what a student lounge was and how to find it. The closest word to a lounge that she knew was Papá's chair in the corner of the living room, and that didn't make sense here.

Ten minutes later, Melina cautiously opened the door and ventured out into the hallway. The clutter from yesterday was cleared, and it all seemed bigger and a little scarier. There were doors just like hers as far as she could see. *Should she lock the door or simply shut it? Did she have a key?* She didn't remember getting one, but it seemed weird to leave a door unlocked when all their stuff was in there. Since she didn't have much choice, she closed the door tightly and strained to hear voices. She figured they would lead her to the place called a lounge, but she heard nothing.

Oh well, she turned left and let the bright orange carpeting with blue stripes on either side create a path for her. She felt a little less frightened and strangely independent as she began to let her imagination take hold. In her head, Melina was now walking on a stone wall and if she avoided the wide blue stripes, she wouldn't fall off. She dared herself to veer as close as possible to the stripes while always pulling back just in time. For a few minutes, she quite forgot where she was and what she was looking for. She could almost be at home playing with the boys.

As she continued her game in a semi-dreamlike state, she nearly tripped over a small woman scrubbing at a dark spot on the carpet. She reminded Melina of Mamá when she looked up through kind, brown eyes and smiled at her.

"Hello," the woman said in Spanish. "My name is María. ¡Dios mío! This spot is tough to get out. I think it happened yesterday. All the fuss of moving in, someone didn't empty a bottle before they threw it away. But you know, I've seen worse. I haven't seen you before. You must be one of the new girls."

Melina spoke up hesitantly, though she was excited to hear the lilt of Spanish again. "I'm Melina. I just got here yesterday and need to find the student lounge. Can you help me?"

"Of course," answered María, pointing with her head back toward Melina's room. "You need to go back and turn left; you can't miss it. You're looking for the meeting they always have at the beginning of year. It's a good one; they tell you how things work, and they serve food. I'm always here too if you ever need help. A few years ago, the university gave me a small apartment at the back of the first floor. That way I stay and help when no one else is around. I try to keep things clean around here, so you girls can stick to your studies. You remind me of my daughter; she lived on this floor three years ago."

Melina felt an immediate connection with María and felt less lost for a moment. She picked up a wet rag María had dropped while talking and handed it back to her. She thanked her over her shoulder as she hurried in the direction María indicated.

A few minutes later, she heard laughter and music coming from a room up ahead. Forcing herself to move a little faster, she stumbled upon what she was looking for. The double doors were open wide and a huge sign, handwritten on bright blue poster board, was taped to the glass with the message, *WELCOME FRESHMEN!*

Melina had never seen so many unfamiliar faces in one space. *¡Dios mío!* The lounge was a large, sun-filled room with tall windows that overlooked the campus, and a kitchen area way larger than Mamá's. Right now, it pulsated with girls who had rearranged the furniture to cluster together on blue plastic chairs and sagging couches. There was a long vinyl-covered table heaped with food, and empty paper plates were everywhere.

Oddly, Melina felt alone in the middle of so many people. Memories of last night flooded back into her mind. But suddenly someone called out her name.

"Hey, Mel. Over here!" Theresa shouted over the music. Melina looked over to see Theresa and her three friends sprawled out on a couch in the furthest corner. As she started to make her way through the crowded room, another voice called her name.

"You must be Melina! Hi. I'm Abby, student advisor for the fifth floor. Sorry you missed the meeting, but that's okay. You probably partied last night like everyone else. I'll stop by; we can catch up later. There's some leftover food, so please help yourself. The bagels are pretty good, and the coffee's not bad."

Melina had no idea what a bagel was, but she smiled and poured some very dark and cold coffee into a styrofoam cup. It wasn't Mamá's, but like last night's beer it made her feel like she sort of belonged as she held it in her hands without taking a second sip.

Melina carefully stepped around the clusters of chairs and made it over to Theresa's couch without tripping. The girls squeezed together to make a spot for her. Melina felt like everyone was looking at her as she squiggled her way awkwardly between them and somehow managed not to spill her coffee while she explained her late arrival.

"Hey, I didn't know we had a meeting this morning. I should've been here, sorry."

The girls resumed their chatter while Theresa turned to Melina, offering a friendly hug.

"It was really no big deal, more an excuse to have bagels and coffee with our new floormates. You were so sound asleep. I didn't want to bother you when Abby came to the door. I was just so excited last night. With the party in town and all, I hardly slept. Hope you had fun too. You must have been at a different bar. We'll have to compare notes later. I was wide awake by 6:00 this morning. Sometime, you'll have to share your secret for sleeping so well with me."

Before Melina could answer, Theresa turned to her friends, "What we really need to do this morning is register for classes. Remember, Abby told us that all freshmen need to register in person and advised us to get over there early to avoid the lines. We should get going. Have you done it yet, Mel?"

"No, but I have a list of classes my high school advisor recommended. Do you know where to go? Should we do it now?"

The others on the couch grumbled a bit about getting up but agreed it would be a good idea to walk over to Clawson and get in line to register. Other clusters were also headed out, so they made their way past the welcome sign that was now dangling halfway to the floor. They first stopped back in 503 so Melina could grab that list of courses Ms. Ingram had so carefully written out for her on Obregon stationery. She quickly smushed it into her back pocket so Sonia wouldn't see the school's name. At the same time, she could feel the girls searching her side of the room for some signs of decorating. Sonia was the only one brazen enough to speak up.

"Mel...okay if we call you Mel? How about after registering, we come back here and help you put your things out? So far, it looks like Theresa owns the place!"

Melina felt her stomach turn again as she looked down and answered, "I'll do it later, but thanks anyway. And sure, you can call me Mel."

As she said that, Melina wondered if becoming "Mel" would help her fit in and reach her goals. No one had ever called her that before. *Was this how everyone started down a new path, by changing their name?*

On the way over to registration, they all chatted about what they wanted to sign up for and what their backup plans were.

"If Algebra 101 is already filled, I'll put off math this term and go for the Introductory Geology course. I hear it's lots of fun and pretty easy," Sonia shared. "My friend from home did that last year and aced it."

"Well, I don't know," said Theresa. "I've heard that Psychology 101 is really interesting and taught by some great instructors. I'll go for that if my first choices are already filled. Mel, what are you thinking?"

Melina hesitated. All she had was a list of four courses that Ms. Ingram had recommended. No one had warned her that she might need to make her own choices.

She had no idea what she would do, so she simply mimicked the others and responded, "I think Geology and Psychology sound interesting. That's pretty much my plan too."

The registration line spilled out of Clawson Hall onto the green. It was moving ever so slowly as the middle kept ballooning out with friends joining those who saved places for them. Student guides were visibly pumping up the crowd by throwing out balls with the Balsam logo and offering juices and bars. The university's goal of getting students to meet one another was working.

Melina spotted Todd across the green as he tossed a ball into the crowd and called out to him. She wanted to thank him for helping her yesterday. He had disappeared as soon as he deposited her by her room, and she hadn't had a chance to thank him. He remembered her and jogged over.

"How's it going? Melina, right? I see you made it to the line today. Maybe my sightseeing tour helped?" Melina introduced Todd to Theresa and her friends, explaining how they all found their way over together.

"Looks like we might be here all day. Is it always like this?" Melina asked.

"No, this is crazy. Balsam decided to hold registration face-to-face this year for freshmen only so they could get to know each other," said Todd. "I guess it's working. Everyone is talking and competing to catch these balls while they wait. It's not for me. I'd rather get it over and go have some real fun in town. Hey, if you're like me and have a financial aid package, there's a shorter line inside. Do you want to mingle or get this over with?" Todd looked at her and tilted his head to avoid the sun's glare. "Do any of you by any chance have an aid package?" Melina was reluctant to be the only one to answer but she nodded, and he quietly guided her toward a side entrance with a sheepish grin on his face.

"Follow me," he said. "I'll give you another tour."

Melina's face flushed with embarrassment at being singled out, and she looked toward the ground. She was abandoning her new friends and passing up the others who had been waiting in line all morning, but Todd made her feel like she belonged. She was also curious. She followed him inside and up to the second floor. There she discovered a much shorter line where freshmen receiving financial assistance could also register and pick up their food and book vouchers.

Done! Twenty minutes later, Melina was registered and had her vouchers. She was feeling more confident by the hour and felt like she might belong here after all. Todd had gone to help some other people, so she walked out of Clawson alone. She now allowed herself to look directly at others and muster a shy smile when they looked back. She didn't see Theresa or Sonia. They were probably inside by now, but Melina still had to find Anderson Hall where the Psychology Department was. That's where her part-time job would be. The letter she received said she should report to a Ms. Shirley Munson today before 5:00 to sign the paperwork and create a schedule around her classes.

As she looked for a sign to help her through the maze of crosswalks and buildings, Melina's insecurities started to creep back. She'd never had a job before; Papá always said no when she suggested it. *Suppose she couldn't do it? What if they didn't like her? Would that mean she would lose her financial aid and need to return home?* Her head began to spin, and she felt a little dizzy. Just then, she saw a sign with an arrow pointing the way to Anderson Hall. She took a deep breath and gingerly put one foot in front of the other. She would succeed. She could do this. After all, *wasn't she living her dream? Isn't this what she thought about every night when she stared up at the posters taped to her wall at home? No one said it would be easy.*

"You must be Melina," said a friendly voice from behind the front desk. "I'm Ms. Munson, but please call me Shirley, like everyone else. Did you register for classes yet?" Melina looked around to find a face that went with the voice. She saw a smallish, dark-skinned older woman with hair neatly pulled back into a bun, beaming at her with a generous smile. Melina felt her worries start to melt away.

"Yes. I'm Melina, and I'm happy to meet you Ms. Munson."

"No! Remember I'm Shirley, and my smile disappears when anyone calls me Ms. Munson. Makes me feel old," said the woman with a twinkle in her eye.

"Okay. I'll remember, Shirley, and yes, I did register for classes today."

"Good. Now we can sit down and figure out your work schedule," said Shirley. "C'mon over here, and let's take a look."

They sat down together and planned the hours Melina would work for the department. Wrinkling her nose and peering over her glasses, Shirley looked at Melina's class schedule. "You want to be careful, especially as a freshman, not to overload yourself. We all want you to succeed. If you have two morning classes, we won't schedule you until late afternoons on those days. You'll report to me, but most of your work will be for the faculty. You will help them with making copies, running errands, and keeping track of their student appointments. If you have time, I can walk you around now so you can meet some of them, okay?"

"Sure. I'd like that. Thank you," responded Melina.

Shirley led her down the hallway. They made the rounds on the first floor, and the faculty who were around seemed friendly enough, but were busy preparing for the start of classes the following week. Several asked if she was taking a Psychology course, and when she told them she was, they seemed interested. They asked her what section she was in, but she had no idea what that meant so she simply smiled. She wondered which one would be her teacher. As they went down the stairs to the basement level, Melina noticed it was different from the first floor, so quiet and empty. Shirley commented that there were only two faculty down there and that it was usually peaceful. She added, with a wink, that if Melina ever needed a break from all the busyness upstairs, this was a perfect place to come and just sit. Her voice turned to a whisper when she added, "I sometimes come to this bottom stair just to gather my thoughts."

As they approached office 102B, Melina heard voices seemingly agitated about something: "I think the expanded student support services will make a huge difference for our students and just imagine the first stand-alone Latinx Center!"

A female voice responded, "But what about the software I need to apply for grants and do my research? How will I reach the goals I set with Dr. Berg?" The voices stopped abruptly when they heard Shirley's perfunctory knock on the open door informally warning them to settle down.

"Hi, Dr. Pearson and Dr. Sanders. I'd like you to meet the department's new student assistant. This is Melina García. She's a freshman and will be helping around the office. If you have anything she can help you with, just let me know and I'll assign it to her."

Dr. Sanders immediately jumped up with a huge smile and came around from behind his desk to shake her hand.

"Hi, Melina. I'm so happy to meet you. Welcome! I'm new here too, sort of, so we'll have to stick together and figure things out. Please call me Harry." Melina took his hand and smiled back but was quite sure she could never call him Harry.

The other person in the room, Dr. Pearson, seemed flustered and was suddenly too busy at her computer to get up or look Melina's way. With barely a glance, she distractedly waved her hand toward Melina. The only memory Melina had of Dr. Pearson from that first day was the huge leather briefcase perched on the ledge behind her.

She must be especially important, thought Melina. *No wonder she wasn't very friendly. I'm just a student helper.* She made a mental note to be especially respectful toward her, and to remember to call her Dr. Pearson.

Melina left Anderson Hall with Shirley's warm hug settling on her shoulders like a soft, wool cape in the coolish late afternoon. She would report to the Psychology Department on Monday afternoon at 1:00, ready to start her first job. How exciting was that? Melina felt lighter and less confused than she had at the start of the day when she woke up late and missed her first meeting. That wouldn't happen again! She was beginning to see how the pieces fit together in this new world of hers, like she was starting to live inside her dream rather than simply peering at it from the outside. She had her first job! She had a real bed and a bathroom that she shared with only one other person, and she didn't have to trip over toys to get there!

These thoughts carried her back home to where Mamá was probably standing in their little kitchen right now, starting the griddle for Papá's tortillas. Papá was slumped in his recliner, most likely, with his eyes half closed after working two shifts. *Were they living their dream of finding a better life in America, or were they still waiting for it?* Melina could never be sure about Mamá and Papá. They didn't talk much. They worked hard and worried about so many things. Suddenly she wanted to be with them and make sure they were okay. *Did she really deserve this when Mamá and Papá had been waiting more than 20 years for their own dream to come true?* She brushed away a few tears. Maybe she didn't really belong here. She looked up and realized that Forbes was straight ahead. Could she honestly call this home? The front doors felt just a little heavier than they had this morning.

She took the stairs up to the fifth floor, instead of the elevator; it felt more like home that way. Melina kept her head down as she slowly approached her room and worried about how she would tell Theresa she had nothing to add to the room, not even a bedspread. What would Theresa say? Would she move down the hall to be with her high school friends? Thankfully, Melina walked into an empty room, so she could put it off a little longer. Theresa had left a note saying she had gone into town with her friends. They would be at the Antler Bar and hoped Melina would join them when she got back to grab something to eat. Melina had no money for food, only vouchers, and she guessed the bar wouldn't accept them.

As she went over to sit on her colorless bed and think about what to do, she noticed a plain, brown package neatly tied with string. *What was this?* There was a small white envelope taped to the front. She opened it and read a short note in Spanish:

> *I hope this will help you. It gets cold here at night. My daughter, Dulce, left it in my room when she graduated two years ago. Welcome to college, and good luck.*
>
> *María*

Inside was a beautiful, blue quilted bedspread with small yellow flowers, a perfect match for Theresa's brightly colored yellow one a few feet away. Melina smiled and hugged it tightly to her chest before smoothing it out across her plain white sheets.

6
Margot

Gulping down a quick breakfast of key lime yogurt and peanut butter toast as she sat on the couch, Margot mentally went over the schedule for the day ahead of her. After her early morning department meeting, she would quietly whisk herself away to the basement and her desk where she would finally get back to the work she dreamed of doing. She had so many proposals to get out and manuscripts to put the finishing touches on. Brushing crumbs off the couch and piling the dishes in the sink, she gave Biko a cursory pat as she dashed out the door. Heady with excitement, she pressed the elevator button.

An elevator, no more walk-ups! A real job! These were definitely new experiences for her and as the elevator landed on her floor, she almost floated through the doors; she was so anxious for the day to start. *Damn, something was missing!* She noticed the very profession-al-looking man who joined her a few floors down and knew she had to go back upstairs. Margot got off at two and ran up the three flights to start the day all over again. Out of breath, she reached her door and sifted through her purse, feeling for the keys that she knew lay at the bottom. Margot yanked them out and shoved them into the lock. She hurried past Biko, who had already finished his tuna and was settled into a long morning nap, to grab the brand-new brown leather brief-case she had left leaning against the wall behind the couch. Margot flinched a bit when she noticed again how professionally scratched up it was to appear older, (and more important?) than it was.

Feeling a little sheepish about carrying an empty briefcase, she slung it over her shoulder and ran back out to wait for the next elevator. This briefcase was another gift from her parents to congratulate her on her first real job. Her initials engraved in gold on the front ensured that everyone would know who this expensive accessory belonged to and be duly impressed. Margot simply hoped it would help her fit in and carry her work to and from home. Once again, her mother's words floated through her mind: *Remember, Margot. It is all about first impressions and how you present yourself.* With a deep sigh and forced smile, Margot stepped outside and pulled her shoulders back as she glided along the sidewalk toward campus.

The brilliant azure sky promised a day filled with endless opportunities and a bright new beginning. Stepping onto campus, however, there was a different feeling today. Where there had recently been an air of peacefulness and tranquility, now there was a boisterous exuberance all around her.

Of course, the students have arrived, she reminded herself. In her fantasy world, Margot envisioned a quiet, pristine campus where serious work took place. She had quite forgotten that a university campus was rarely like that outside the library. When she was a student, the library was her sanctuary, a cocoon where she escaped from the other students, who didn't seem to share her academic goals, and she didn't try to understand theirs. When she needed a break, Margot rode her motorcycle into the countryside by herself and let the fresh air rejuvenate her as it blew through her hair. That bike had been her rebellious secret. She bought it with the money her grandmother left her. Margot knew her mother would consider it inappropriate, so she never told her about it. She also didn't wear a helmet. It was the one time she bypassed her parents' tight boundaries and felt independent. Except for her ringtone, those days were behind her, as she pursued the future that was expected of her.

Today, students were sprawled out across the benches and littered the green space all over campus. Some laughed loudly; some threw frisbees; others clustered in small groups getting to know each other through quiet conversation and cups of coffee. Margot wondered if any of them had registered yet or bought their books. And why were they here so early? Maybe they stayed up all night?

But, she thought, *they did have their coffee.* Something she had totally forgotten about. She hurried toward Anderson Hall and what she hoped would be a pot of Shirley's freshly brewed coffee. Margot crossed the threshold to the maze of hallways that would lead her to Shirley's office. As she entered the department's office, she was greeted with a loud and newly familiar, "Hi there! Ready for our first department meeting of the year?"

There stood Harry, with his jumbo smile and a steaming mug of coffee conspicuously emblazoned with the Balsam University seal firmly in his hand.

How is he always here? thought Margot. *Maybe he sleeps in our office? So much for settling in by myself.*

Shirley was close behind and welcomed Margot with a fresh cup of coffee. "I'll loan you this cup today, but tomorrow you should bring your own. Mugs are sold in the university store, and the Dean loves to see them on everyone's desk. Meanwhile, the meeting's been moved up this morning to accommodate Dr. Berg's terribly busy schedule," said Shirley. "We'll convene in the conference room down the hall in 15 minutes; Dr. Berg begins on time, no matter what. Once last term, he formally started a department meeting with only me in the room. He asked me to note in the minutes that he and I were the only two there on time. There are still some faculty convinced their budget requests won't be approved this year due to their tardiness that day."

Margot made a mental note to set a timer alerting her at least ten minutes before every meeting. She and Harry tried to look nonchalant in front of Shirley as they waltzed out of her office and then sprinted down the hall. Margot's coffee spilled over the sides of her loaner mug, down her hand, and onto the freshly polished floor. So much for starting the term with a clean, dry slate. First it was her muddy leg; today her coffee-splattered hand.

Dr. Berg was just approaching the conference room when they arrived. Margot recognized some of the others from her interview. Suzanne, Edie, and Rene were already seated but stood when they saw Harry and Margot, to offer hugs and warm handshakes.

Everything will be okay, thought Margot. *This isn't so scary after all.*

After all, they had beaten Dr. Berg to the table, and the faculty seemed genuinely happy to see them. Remembering how much she liked Rene from her post-interview dinner, Margot found a chair next to him and sat down. Remembering her mother's advice, she immediately found the lever under her chair and inched it a bit higher. That way, no one could overlook her, and her voice would be heard.

A few others raced through the door just as Dr. Berg started the meeting with Shirley by his side.

"Thank you all for coming in early today. As this is the first day of the term, there are many, many meetings and I thought it would help to start ours first thing. My apologies for cancelling the individual appointments I had with some of you. Let me begin by introducing our newest faculty members, Margot Pearson and Harry Sanders. They will be sharing an office, 102B. I hope you'll stop by to welcome them personally and answer any questions they may have."

The faculty offered an appropriate round of applause and then turned their attention back to Dr. Berg, who referred them to the agendas that were neatly stacked and placed at intervals around the table.

"Since classes begin next week, we have important business to cover today. There are committee assignments, budget requests, personal goals, and teaching loads to discuss. Please refer to the documents at your place for all the details, but first let's start with committee assignments. We are fortunate to have two new faculty members this year to help shoulder the committee load. I hope that Margot will agree to represent us on the Curriculum and Program Evaluation Committees. Margot?"

Margot quickly nodded, twirled a strand of hair, and made a note.

"Harry, you will replace Miriam on the Commencement and Professional Development Committees, and it would be helpful if you could also serve on the Adjunct Hiring Committee. Okay?"

Harry immediately agreed and flashed his unique smile around the table. Margot wondered if he slept wearing a smile.

Dr. Berg continued, "You all may have heard that we have a rather large freshman class this year. That is generally good news, but it also means larger classes and more introductory sections. I am assigning Margot to help us out by teaching three General Psychology 101 sections, and one research class. Harry, according to the faculty handbook you are only allowed to teach Miriam's previously assigned load while she is on leave. Rene here can bring you up to speed on the syllabi and assignments for her classes. Margot, since 101 is basic, I don't think you will need much assistance. Suzanne, however, will share the departmental syllabus with you. You can be creative with the research class and use your own work as a guide."

Taking an extra deep breath, Margot nodded and wondered what happened to the minimal teaching load she had been promised. After all, the contract read that in her first-year faculty role, she would serve the needs of the department. *I guess the needs can change quickly*, she thought.

"We won't dive in too deeply on the budget today, but I might as well prepare you for what is bound to come our way soon. Many of you requested additional resources in June, and I submitted most of them. Until last week, I thought there was a good chance our department would be granted additional funding, especially with the increase in enrollment. Unfortunately, the Board has directed the university to invest more of its revenue to ramp up student support services rather than add resources to the academic side of things. That includes upgrades to the student activities center, creation of a new Latinx Center, expansion of the Learning Assistance Center and the hiring of more student counselors."

Rolling his eyes, he continued, "The Board, in all its wisdom, believes it's important to assist the new students who may not be traditionally prepared so they will persist and be successful. They don't trust that we as faculty have the skills necessary to retain students without additional support. I don't agree, but for now that's how it is. Questions?"

Suzanne's hand shot into the air. "How are we supposed to teach and conduct our research without the funds we requested?" Before he could answer, arms popped up around the table like a wave of firecrackers.

"It will be difficult for me to teach the research course without the software package I asked for," Rene added. As other faculty took turns vexing how their requests were especially urgent and necessary for their work, the friction around the table was palpable. The earlier smiles came unglued as sidebars took over and squabbles intensified the rivalry. Margot regretted raising her chair and wished she could disappear under the table. It was her first meeting, and she certainly couldn't show her disappointment. It was clear that the research funds she had been promised would not be forthcoming. She kept her eyes averted and pretended to study her notes about committee assignments.

Dr. Berg allowed this to play out for about five minutes and then called the meeting to order again. "I know how disappointed you all are, but this department will play ball and accept things as they are."

With much fanfare, two senior faculty members forcefully pushed their chairs back leaving black marks on the newly polished floor and stridently left the room murmuring something about how much their work was not valued. Dr. Berg sighed, asked Shirley to add this exit to the minutes and then continued.

"The last item on our agenda is related to personal goals. We have a new form this year. I need you to complete it by the end of the week and give it to Shirley by 4:00 on Friday. Please note, you must include your goals for teaching, professional development, institutional service, and publication. I will meet with you individually before the end of the month to review them and make any necessary revisions. Questions?"

After the budget announcement, it seemed that all the air had been sucked out of the room and there was no space left for further questions. Dr. Berg declared the meeting adjourned, gathered his papers, and without looking up, abruptly left the room.

The faculty left the room in groups of twos and threes, feverishly discussing the bombshell announcements. Margot headed for the basement alone. Her head was spinning. *Does this happen at all the faculty meetings? What should I do now? Will my position survive?*

Harry was already there, waving his arms around and talking in his naturally spirited way to Isaac and another adjunct friend. Margot assumed that they were as upset by the budget denials as the other faculty, but she couldn't have been more wrong.

"Can you believe the administration is spending money on student services? It's finally emerging as a significant university endeavor,"

Harry exclaimed as he sketched out Dr. Berg's earlier announcements to his two friends.

"We really made a difference, Harry! All the meetings we held with students, and the letters we wrote to Board members telling the personal stories about students being admitted but not supported. It worked! The sad part is that it wasn't the stories that impacted them; it was the data we collected on how tuition revenues dropped off when they left. Whatever, apparently, it all paid off."

Harry looked up and realized that Margot was in the doorway.

"What'd you think of the announcements this morning, Margot?"

"Well…," she began as she tried to organize her thoughts into a coherent response.

Before she could finish, he continued, "On the Adjunct Faculty Council, we've been requesting this kind of student support for over two years. Every fall, the university eagerly accepts kudos from the community when it announces that its freshman class is increasingly diverse and then simply assumes the new students will succeed with little assistance beyond their financial aid packages. When they have problems or fail, the university points a finger at the high schools' failure to prepare them, and the faculty complains that these students never should have been accepted in the first place."

Margot rolled her eyes and nodded. Harry took that as a cue to continue.

"Now it looks like the students will get more resources with additional counselors and an expanded learning center, amazing! They will even have a brand-new Latinx Center. This is a major acknowledgment that a growing number of our students are Latinx and represent the first generation in their families to go away to college. They have financial aid packages but not the hidden resources their roommates have, like study strategies, understanding a syllabus, the confidence to sit in the front row, going to a faculty office to ask for help, or reaching out to family members who understand the college experience. They need a secure place where they can ask sensitive questions and relax in a welcoming space with others in similar situations. This is a big campus, and it can be tough to connect with other students outside of class when you don't understand how to navigate university expectations and opportunities. It's also tough when you're faced with very traditional faculty who continue to teach the way they were taught, behind a lectern reading from prepared notes or showing a PowerPoint with no eye contact and little attempt to know them outside of class."

Suspending her disbelief over this unexpected litany spewing from Harry, on top of Dr. Berg's grim announcements, Margot slumped behind her desk to sort things out. Harry and his friends were pleased their work had finally been acknowledged, and they forgot she never responded to his question. Instead, they rushed out the door to spread the word. Margot's head was once again throbbing as the vibrations of their "victory" echoed down the hallway.

She looked up to see Suzanne at the door. "Is it okay if I come in? I need a quiet place to unravel the events from today's meeting, and you seem like the rational person I need right now. By the way, who was that rowdy crowd? Friends of yours? They seem ready to celebrate something."

Margot again rolled her eyes and nodded. She motioned Suzanne to the chair with the red blanket, suddenly happy that the gaping hole in the arm was covered. "That was my office mate, Harry Sanders. Remember? You met him at the meeting earlier today. He's only here for a few months, but he gets overly excited."

"Oh yeah. I know Harry; we all know Harry. Be careful with him, Margot. He's often on the wrong side of things around here. You don't want to stir up trouble your first year, and Dr. Berg can hold a grudge."

Suzanne then let out a deep sigh with no attempt to muffle it and closed her eyes for a few minutes. While Margot wondered if Suzanne had fallen asleep, she took two aspirins from her top drawer chewing them quietly.

Suzanne was, in fact, watching her and said, "It looks like you're as sick about this as the rest of us. I don't know how they expect us to do our work and meet our goals without the resources we requested. The students will be fine. The ones who belong here will succeed, and the others…well, they'll probably leave. That's just how it works."

"That's how it should work, right?" Margot echoed. "I mean if they can't do the work and meet our standards, why should we work hard to prepare lectures and grade their papers? I never had any extra help."

"None of us did! We all worked hard, and now we have publication goals," added Suzanne. "That software package I requested is crucial for my research goals. I may start looking around for another job if this isn't resolved soon. There are universities who still respect their faculty and put their needs ahead of students."

"Maybe if we just go to Dr. Berg and let him know how we feel…?"

Suzanne laughed and interrupted Margot, "I think Dr. Berg is biding his time as department chair while he positions himself to move up the ladder to a deanship here. He always supports the administration, no matter what. Last year, none of our budget requests were approved, but he brought in a huge grant that went directly to his graduate assistants so they could assist with his research. He received a presidential award at commencement for his outstanding ability to attract money to the university and support students. Hah!"

Margot flushed at her naivete and apparently foolish suggestion.

Sensing her embarrassment, Suzanne softened her tone. "I didn't mean to come in here and make your day worse. I hope you aren't sorry you accepted this position. We all agreed that you were a great fit for this department, and we really need you to help us with those introductory sections. They take time with the grading and all, but they're easy enough to teach. I just hope your classes aren't too big. Last year I had a hundred students in one, and I pretty much gave them all A's if they showed up. What else could I do? Funny thing was that nobody cared. The students all gave me great evaluations, and Dr. Berg was more than satisfied."

Suzanne seemed to calm down as she wandered through her meandering list of complaints, so Margot didn't feel the need to form any coherent reactions. That was good because she was in a complete fog. Eventually, Suzanne left with a promise to drop off the 101 syllabus in the morning along with her notes from last year. Margot murmured in appreciation and decided she should probably head home and get started on those professional goals. It was clear she would get nothing done if she stayed here. She felt let down. Her teaching load was overwhelming. Her research and publication goals were nearly impossible without the software she expected. This office and this job, a dream seemingly fulfilled a few weeks ago, no longer offered excitement and opportunity. The dream was built on lofty promises that were on the verge of being broken one at a time.

What had she walked into? Margot looked around. Her framed degree would have to sit on the floor and wait until tomorrow for its official hanging. Instead of trying to upgrade her side of this suddenly oppressive and small space, she hoisted her expensive but empty briefcase to her shoulder and headed for the door. She wouldn't tell her mother that no one had noticed the briefcase. No, she would tell her that everything was just fine.

7
Melina

Melina peeled herself from the chair she loved most in the library. The way its soft gray leather engulfed her body reminded her of the mattress she left at home. It was a good fit. Placed in front of an old wooden table, it sat in a windowless corner behind a floor-to-ceiling shelf that held more books than she had ever seen. Her high school locked its library, so unless you made an appointment, you couldn't go in. Too many books had been stolen or had pages ripped out when students thought it was easier to take the pages with them than it was to sit down and read. Being here in Balsam's library made her feel like a real student. It also made her invisible. Here she didn't need to make excuses for not going into town or smoking pot in Sonia's room. The books didn't care that she wore the same thing every day. When she walked in, the librarian smiled and nodded in the direction of Melina's chair as if to say, "It's empty. Just waiting for you."

Sometimes, Melina got so lost in her books that a student worker would have to remind her it was closing time. "Melina, it's time to go." They all knew her name and tried to save her chair by piling books on it until she arrived after work. Sometimes she was so tired that she took a short nap there before diving into her homework. She also figured out how to sneak in food, so there was little need to eat by herself in the dining hall. Just yesterday, Shirley handed her a treat at the end of her shift.

"Melina, I know you're headed to the library, so I wrapped these brownies in a folder to look like homework. Hope it works!"

"Thanks, Shirley. I'll try not to make a mess." She loved her work in the Psychology Department. The faculty always needed something, so she was too busy to think about the rest of her life at Balsam. She ran around three hours a day Monday through Friday making copies, running errands or calling students to remind them of their appointments. Last week, she had her review, and Shirley shared how pleased the department was with her work. Melina felt proud but surprised because the faculty rarely looked in her direction or offered any type of compliment. Another place where she felt comfortably invisible.

She hated Sundays because the library closed at noon and she didn't work.

"Hey, Mel! C'mon over," yelled Sonia from the far side of the fifth-floor lounge. "We're sharing our favorite music so we can stream it back in our rooms. Do you have any faves on your phone?"

Melina shook her head nervously as she made her way across the carpeted floor to join them. It was another endless Sunday afternoon, and most of the girls on her floor were hanging out in the lounge after studying all weekend for their upcoming exams. Melina was still trying to fit in, but it was hard. She had, with great difficulty, hidden the fact that she didn't have a cell phone, and that the music she listened to and loved came from Mamá's kitchen radio back home.

Mamá always listened to mariachi and ranchera music. As she cooked, she sang along and often moved her hips to remembered dance moves. Melina pictured the grayish dent in the linoleum where Mamá's feet felt the music. *Did Papá once dance with Mamá?* She would love to see them sharing the music together. Melina doubted that the girls in this lounge would know that music, so she sat down silently and pretended to appreciate theirs. She felt awkward as her floormates let out a collective scream every time they discovered how much music they had in common. They shrieked names like Travis Scott, Migos and Lizzo, when they shared their playlists. Amid all of this, Melina felt lonely as she sat by quietly outside their cloud of excitement.

No one noticed. No one, that is, except Theresa. Although Theresa didn't totally understand her roommate and was too polite to ask any personal questions, she did care about her and tried to find ways to include her. Amid all the noisy lounge talk, Theresa came over and settled herself next to Melina.

"These are really awesome, Mel. Want to share one? It's a nutrition bar. My mother sent a package of snacks for us that I stashed away in the fridge under my bed. I'm starving, and these will hold me over for a while until we go into town and have lunch. Wanna come with us this time?"

Melina, who had never had a nutrition bar, thanked Theresa, took a bite, and immediately tasted sawdust. *Why would anyone eat this as a snack?* she wondered to herself, while outwardly smiling at Theresa. She washed it down with a glass of water and secretly wished she had another one of Shirley's brownies.

She was still avoiding the conversation she needed to have with her roommate. Theresa deserved to know why Mamá would never send snacks for Melina to share, nor anything to help brighten up her side of the room. Melina should tell her about her family and where she came from, but she didn't know how to start. *Maybe tonight if they were alone?*

She was curious about the town, though she knew it would cost money that she didn't have. Melina had quickly realized that not everyone ate all their meals in the campus dining room. Yesterday, in fact, she had been there almost alone, with just a few others who sat shyly by themselves in different corners of the room. *Maybe I could walk to town with Theresa, pretend I'm not hungry and then just come back to campus?*

She was getting tired of making excuses for everything: no cell phone, no music, no posters on her side of the room, no closet full of clothes. She agreed to walk into town with Theresa and her friends. The walk was short and simple. Just ten minutes from campus, it was a one-street town lined with bars, smallish restaurants, and a 7-Eleven. There wasn't even a stoplight.

Today, the main street was jammed with students, all relieved to take a break from studying for exams. Melina was overwhelmed by the town's simplicity and apparent safety. All the doors were propped wide open, and the college-aged staff leaned against each opening, warmly greeting everyone and inviting them in for free food and drinks to celebrate the weekend before exams. There was noise everywhere, establishments were full, and dancing bodies crammed into the bars and restaurants. Melina wondered if it was always like this. No one seemed worried about anything.

Melina dropped her defenses and went into the Antler Bar with Theresa and her friends. They met up with some girls they knew from Forbes and squeezed into their booth.

"Let's request some Lizzo and then order something beyond the free stuff," suggested Sonia.

"Yeah, the burgers and Crispy Sweet Potato Fries are the best," added Theresa. "Everyone in?" Heads nodded around the table, and Melina went along with it, losing herself in the lightheaded feeling of possibly belonging.

She laughed along with the others as they told stories about their families and pointed out cute guys at the bar. At one point, Sonia and a few others left the table and began to dance. "C'mon, Mel. Join us. I'll bet you're an awesome dancer!" Theresa pulled her up, and Melina reluctantly followed. She had never danced publicly, only at family fiestas. She felt self-conscious dancing in a college bar when everyone was screaming and showing off. She tried her best to fit in, but she kept picturing Papá and how much he would disapprove. He worried about her all the time. Sometimes it felt suffocating, but right now she realized how much she missed him. For what seemed like an eternity, she tried to follow along with Theresa, but it wasn't her music and she felt awkward and completely out of place.

When she finally sat down, she realized the others were going over the bill and dividing up what they each owed for the food.

Sonia announced, "Looks like we each owe about $15 plus tip. I'll collect it, okay?" Melina's thoughts of belonging quickly vanished. Her head started to pound, and she felt small trickles of sweat drip down her face. She realized how stupid she had been to imagine she could be like these people. *Sure, she was sort of having fun, but had she forgotten that she could not afford this kind of fun? Had she forgotten why she came to college?* It wasn't to eat and dance. It was to work hard, earn a degree and make her family proud. She anxiously looked around to see if anyone noticed her discomfort.

At that moment, Theresa leaned over and seemed to read her mind. "Mel, if you forgot to bring your money, I'll loan it to you. Okay?"

"Thanks, Theresa. I really appreciate it." Melina would need to explain to her later how it might be a while before she could pay her back. So far, she hadn't had the courage to explain anything to her roommate. *How much longer could that last?* she wondered.

As the girls continued to laugh and have fun in the cramped booth, Melina silently slid away from the end seat she had intentionally grabbed earlier and headed back to campus alone. She needed to think about all the parts of going to college that Ms. Ingram hadn't warned her about, the small things that everyone else seemed to take for granted. She also thought about Mamá and Papá and what they had sacrificed to let her leave home. She wasn't contributing to the monthly rent or caring for her nephews. She wasn't working a real job like Mamá and Papá who held down several jobs between them. The more Melina thought about this, the more embarrassed she felt about how she behaved today. She had no right to go into town and eat food she couldn't afford or dance publicly just for fun. *Was her dream worth it? Was she being selfish?* She wiped the tears from her face and started to walk quickly. Maybe if she got back to the safety of her room and the blue quilt, she would feel more confident that she was doing the right thing. Maybe she could even Skype home.

As these thoughts tumbled around in her mind, she pulled open the heavy front doors to Forbes and noticed a familiar figure sitting in the foyer on a small plastic chair.

"Melina, I'm so glad it's you," called out María, in Spanish. "Please come back to my room. There is something I need tell you."

Melina was so grateful to see a friendly face that she neglected to notice the worried look on María's face.

As Melina walked into María's room, she immediately felt at ease. Something was cooking that smelled like home. Maybe it was chiles, or was it fresh cilantro? She wasn't sure. The radio played Mamá's favorite mariachi music. A statue of the Virgen de Guadalupe, Mexico's patron saint, looked down on them comfortingly, and the warmth of María's simple furnishings made Melina long for home.

"Melina, come here and sit down. I have something I want to tell you, but first tell me how things going for you? I haven't seen you around lately. Have you made some friends?"

As she sank into the red and yellow pillows on María's plastic-covered sofa, Melina let out a deep sigh and she couldn't stop the flood of words that spilled out in Spanish. It felt like a dam had broken, and her insides emptied at a dangerously high speed. She shared with María all the secrets she had been keeping from the other students.

"María, they all go into town to eat, and they always ask me to come. How do I tell them I have no money, that I eat in the dining hall or the library alone? My family struggles just to feed everyone and pay the rent at home. The other students, they all think I keep losing my cell phone, but I've never had one. Even if I did, how would I pay for the service? My side of the room is plain and doesn't fit in with all the others on the floor. I don't have extra pillows or posters or stuffed animals. And I'm always wearing the same clothes because I don't have anything else. I wash them in the sink when Theresa is away and hang them in the back of my closet to dry. I can't afford the machines in the laundry room."

An hour later, the words suddenly dried up, and Melina fell back into the pillows as she finished telling her story. She wiped the tears from her face, but they weren't from sadness. She felt relieved that she had finally let go of the secrets that kept her from really belonging. María looked at her with a deep understanding and reached over to give her a hug.

"Oh, I'm so sorry, Melina. I know it's hard. My daughter told me the same stories. You know, as hard as her classes were, she said that was the easiest part for her. But everything else was difficult because she was so different from the others. I'm here for you if you need someone to talk to, Melina. My daughter is coming to visit next weekend. I want you meet her. Maybe you can come over for dinner, what do you think?"

Melina was afraid she would really cry now. To have someone listen and understand her story was what she craved.

"Thank you, María. I would love that. You're so kind."

"Of course! Now listen, Melina, your papá called here this afternoon. He wants you to Skype him tonight; he'll see you at 7:00." Melina nodded and blinked back her tears. It was bad enough that she had made the mistake of going to town, but she had missed a call from home. She was so ashamed. What must María think? As if María sensed her thoughts, she said, "Melina, it's okay that you missed the call. I spoke to him in Spanish, and I told him you were fine and studying for exams. You'll Skype tonight at 7:00 and listen to what he needs to say. Don't feel bad that you weren't here; they want you to live your life here at college, or they wouldn't have let you leave. They are scared, just like you. You'll see them online at 7:00, okay?"

It was already 6:30, so Melina thanked María and rushed to her room hoping that Theresa wasn't back yet. She needed to talk to Theresa and explain herself, but she was embarrassed about so many things and wasn't sure Theresa would understand. She kept avoiding it even though it couldn't last forever. Melina grabbed the laptop from her desk and went to her favorite hiding place at the end of the hall. Across from the lounge, there was a smallish, closet-like room with no windows and bare walls. Inside were a small marked-up table and a plastic chair. The other students never went in here because they thought it was a housekeeping closet, but this was Melina's hideaway, where she went when she needed to be alone. Her family always cried when they Skyped, so Melina was too embarrassed to call them from her room, where her roommate and others might overhear. But this time, she was worried too, because no one ever called her by surprise. As she nervously entered her password, she couldn't stop thinking about all the things that could be wrong at home. *Was Mamá sick? Did Papá lose his job? Were the boys okay?*

She waited for the computer to connect…it was taking so long… then, suddenly, there they were, her family with Mamá in front.

"Hi, Mamá," she said a bit too hurriedly. "Is everything okay? What's going on?"

"Papá received a Notice to Appear in court next week for a removal proceeding, and he faces two charges. We are so afraid. He wants you to go with him, Melina. We contacted Mr. Salgado who will present his case, but he wants a family member there too in case he needs to get a personal message to us. You speak English better than any of us."

"How did this happen, Mamá?"

"There was a raid at his work a month ago. Papá was in the back room on his break when the ICE agents arrived. He got the signal and slipped out the back with a few others before the agents got to the factory floor. Honorio's car is always parked a few blocks away in case of raids like this, and Papá was lucky enough to make it to his car. Honorio dropped them at a bus stop several miles away, and two hours later Papá got home. We didn't know what happened to him. We were so worried when he missed dinner. Since that day he's afraid to go back to work, and he stays inside every day. He won't even turn the television on. The factory, it's worried about more fines, must have reported him because yesterday, we received a notice telling him to come to court. He works so hard, and he's been there more than 20 years. There should be some way... Mr. Salgado will help us plead for asylum, but Papá really wants you to go with them."

Melina took a deep breath and tried to hold back her tears. She forced herself to be strong for Mamá. This is something they all worried about for years. Mamá and Papá had been here for over 30 years but still didn't have their papers.

"Amá, when is his court date? I have exams, and I have to take them or I will fail my classes and maybe lose my scholarship."

"Melina! Since when are your classes more important than your family? Your father needs you. We all need you. You're going to have to come home next week. His hearing is at 9:00 a.m. Thursday morning, and we need you there."

Melina could see the worried faces of Tía Rosa and her brothers behind Mamá. They were all nodding. How could she say no? It might be bad for her schoolwork, maybe even her future at college, but she would have to figure out a way to be there for Papá.

"All right, Mamá. I'll come. I will be there for Papá."

After assurances of what a good daughter she was, they ended the call as Mamá started to cry. Melina gently closed the laptop and sobbed quietly in the little closet. No one here on campus would understand what she must do. Family comes first; it wasn't even a question, but she didn't think her teachers would understand. To them, classes and exams came first, and if students didn't show up...well, that was their choice, but it would certainly be marked down in their record and added up at the end of the year. She also had a job, her first one ever! Other people relied on her too. She didn't know what to do, and there was no one to talk to. María would understand, but she couldn't bother her again. María had been so kind to her, but she had her own family to think about. Calling Ms. Ingram was out of the question. She didn't want her to think she couldn't solve her own problems after she worked so hard to help her get into college. Theresa seemed nice enough, but her family was perfect, and Melina was ashamed to let her know that hers wasn't.

She made it back to her room where, thankfully, it was dark and empty as usual. With Theresa out, there was no need to explain anything, only another secret to bury. She put her computer back on the desk and slipped into her pink pajamas for bed. Tossing and turning, Melina spent a sleepless night tangled up in her blue bedspread. She couldn't get Papá out of her mind. Apá was a good man and had always seemed so strong. He was a quiet presence in their house, but when he spoke everyone paid attention. What he said mattered, and his words guided their lives. When Amá wanted to move to a safer neighborhood, Apá said no. He reminded her that Villacito was part of their family, and they had a responsibility to stay and help make it safe for everyone. Welcomed here many years ago when they first arrived, moving out was not an option. She never asked about it again. No one argued with Apá. His words were final and highly respected by family and neighbors.

It didn't make sense to Melina that after 30 years he still didn't have his green card. She knew the law, but it just didn't seem fair. By all reasonable measures, Papá had earned it. He had worked at the same factory for 20 years and only missed two days of work: once when Melina was in trouble at school, and then again to see her off the day she went to college. He was always there for everyone else even when it might have caused trouble for him. A few years ago, when a cousin had a court hearing, he asked Apá to be a witness for him. Apá went with him for a special Saturday session and stood by his side, even though it could have brought attention to Apá's undocumented status. When it came to family or friends, you could always count on her Apá.

He had never learned much English; he was able to speak Spanish with his co-workers, and when he came home, he entered a neighborhood of fellow Mexicans, few of whom had the time to learn English. Her mother's jobs took her into the homes of English-speaking families, so she had learned some over the years but not enough to help him in court. Besides, she was too nervous to even try. There were many cousins who spoke some English, but they all worked hourly jobs and could not afford to lose their wages. Her brothers each worked two shifts at the factory. Their wives were twin sisters who had returned to Mexico a year ago to help their own mother, who was sick and dying. No, they were right, Melina was the only one who could do this with no immediate consequences that they understood. She must go back home no matter how much it affected her success at school. School was less important than keeping the family together, a roof over their heads, and food on the table. And this time, it might mean losing Papá.

Melina didn't sleep more than 15 minutes, so the next morning, she was exhausted but up and out early, before Theresa even stirred. She reached the dining hall long before anyone else and as she sat by herself, she tried to figure out a plan. She checked her schedule as she peeled a banana and tried to swallow some cereal. Her exams began on Tuesday and ended on Friday. Melina didn't know what would happen if she missed her exams, but it probably wasn't good. She needed to find the courage to tell each teacher she had an emergency at home and could not be there this week.

What would they say? Would they fail her?

She had never asked so much as a question in class. Ms. Ingram had told her to sit in the front of the class where the teachers would get to know her. But the students who sat down there seemed so confident always nodding their heads and raising their hands. They all seemed to know each other as they casually slid into those seats with their perfect clothes and bookbags carefully tucked under the chairs. Melina had no bookbag. Her books often toppled to the floor as she slipped into the back row while trying to pull her homework from the right folder. She could feel the graduate assistant behind her tapping her foot waiting to collect the work so she could sit down. The others back there had little to turn in and just wanted to doze or play games on their phones. Melina just wanted to be invisible. She was the only one taking notes and paying attention. When class was over, she carefully re-balanced her books and notebooks between her arms before heading to the next class. She aced all her quizzes and turned in all her homework, but only the teaching assistants knew who she was.

¡Dios, mío! Her worries took over her thoughts, and she pushed aside her barely touched cereal bowl. The banana peel had fallen to the floor, causing her to slip as she got up. She wiped away her tears,

pushed it all down and headed to her morning classes, but hardly heard a word that was said.

"Hi, Melina! How are you today? This is a big week with exams and all. The faculty need our help more than usual getting ready. Hope you're prepared for a pretty crazy week," Shirley called out as Melina arrived for work that afternoon. Melina smiled and pretended to be full of energy and excitement, but she was so tired of pretending all the time, to everyone. She started work by delivering mail to the faculty. She became nervous when she took Dr. Pearson's mail to her office because Dr. Pearson was one of her teachers; Melina knew she needed to talk to her about missing the exam, but she didn't know how. She said a silent prayer that she wouldn't be around, and as it turned out, none of the faculty were. It was a relief.

After helping Shirley for about an hour and pretending once again that everything was okay, she took a break and went down the stairs to the basement level where she knew it would be quiet and she could think. As soon as she reached the stairway and was out of sight of the office, the storm that was building inside her came thundering out. Melina couldn't control herself any longer; all her emotions surfaced, and giant tears flowed down her cheeks. She barely made it to the bottom step. Unable to move any further, she collapsed there in a heap and put her head in her hands.

Between her sobs, she heard someone approaching. *Could today get any worse?* Oh, sure it could because it was Dr. Pearson, the teacher she feared the most. She tried to get up and hurry away, but instead, her legs buckled. Dr. Pearson seemed surprised, yet kind, as she approached and hesitantly joined Melina on the bottom step. Melina was horrified. She didn't want anyone, especially someone like Dr. Pearson, to discover her secrets. Trying to stanch another awkward stream of tears, Melina took a deep breath and rested her head on her knees. She didn't want to talk to Dr. Pearson, even though she knew she should.

8
Margot

Margot trudged listlessly down the stairs to her office, thinking how once again she had wasted two precious hours. Another program evaluation committee meeting that went nowhere, despite having a clear agenda. After grading student papers until midnight last night, Margot had stayed up until 2:00 a.m. to review the huge file of documents scheduled for discussion today. As usual, that discussion never happened. Instead, the last several meetings had been hijacked by several senior faculty members who took issue with the wording of the overall committee charge. They went on endlessly about how this was simply another administrative ploy to eliminate programs.

With the meeting agenda laid out neatly in front of them on the conference table, the less senior committee members pretended to listen to these useless diatribes while sending out texts and wishing they could be somewhere else—anywhere else! At the end of their scheduled time, the chair called for a motion to adjourn. At least three faculty members promptly raised their hands along with a loud "aye," and the room cleared out with a shouted reminder from the chair that the next meeting was important and not to be missed. Margot was junior faculty and had no choice, so she would of course prepare, attend, and get even more frustrated and further behind with her own work.

Just before Margot reached her office, the stack of yet-to-be discussed reports from the meeting precariously balanced on her arms went flying in a million directions.

"Damn!" she exclaimed as she bent to gather them, though for what purpose, she didn't know.

As she chased the runaway paperwork, she passed by Melina, who had dropped off the mail a few minutes earlier. They nodded to each other as Margot scrambled to retrieve the crumpled and defiant papers. She wearily dropped into her chair, placing the now useless committee folders on a far corner of her desk. She sighed again, for the millionth time today, and mindlessly shuffled through the mail. She noticed a familiar return address and perked up: *Maybe this time!*

Margot scrunched up her face and took a deep breath. She tore open the envelope and read,

> *After careful peer review, we have determined that your manuscript is not a good fit for our journal. Perhaps if you work on the revisions suggested by the reviewers, we can reconsider it later.*

"Damn, damn, damn!"

This was her third rejection, and she was running out of publication options. She knew, however, the reviewers were right. Margot was embarrassed and knew she could do better, but she simply didn't have the time while attending useless meetings every week and teaching three intro classes, plus a research class that was generating little excitement. There was no way she could meet the goals she turned in to Dr. Berg at the start of the term. Those goals included the publication of two journal articles, submission of a research proposal to the IRB, and the acceptance of at least one grant application— all by the end of the year. Dr. Berg had heartily approved them and pledged his support, stating what an excellent addition Margot had been to the faculty, and that he had the utmost confidence in her to meet her goals.

How, then, had everything gone so terribly wrong? Had she been too ambitious? What happened if she didn't meet her goals?

She blamed her publication failures on the heavy teaching load she had been assigned. She hadn't expected to teach four classes, and she wasn't enjoying them. Margot was prepared, probably over-prepared, to cover the content outlined on the department's syllabus, but the students seemed totally uninterested. Were they learning? She had no idea. No one asked questions or even looked up at her; her students were buried deep inside their phones and laptops during class and in a hurry to leave when the time was up. No one came to her office hours, and the assignments the students turned in were terrible. From Margot's perspective, the only positive thing to happen during the first few weeks was that several students from each class transferred to other sections, which gave her fewer assignments to grade. Even with that streak of luck, she didn't have the time she needed to revise her articles, work on her research, or submit proposals. Nothing was going as planned; even the research class was unsatisfying. Those students, who were supposedly more advanced, seemed to be taking the course simply to satisfy a graduation requirement. They had no interest whatsoever in her research, or any research for that matter, which depressed Margot even more.

What were they doing here?

As she slumped behind her desk, she allowed the dark clouds of depression to completely envelop her. She closed her eyes and thought about the life she had imagined for herself when she took this job: a vibrant researcher and recognized author, deeply engaged in writing and speaking engagements, surrounded by aspiring, young scholars who sought her advice and mentorship. This was the life her father enjoyed; he was an internationally known researcher who frequently spoke at global events and had been recruited to teach at several prestigious universities. She started to fear that this life wouldn't happen here at Balsam State.

How long could she continue to stand behind a lectern and talk to herself while students busied themselves with video games on their laptops?

It was from this agitated and dreamlike state that Margot heard voices in the distance.

"Hey there, Margot. How's it going? Do you mind if a few of my students come into the office to discuss the upcoming exams with me?" It was Harry, of course, and as usual he was surrounded by several exuberant students. She barely looked up as she wondered why he didn't seem to mind having this gaggle of noise always by his side.

"Come on in," she murmured with little energy.

Several students carried folding chairs in from the hallway and followed Harry to his desk. As they arranged the chairs to create a tight circle around him, they nervously nodded at Margot. She thought she recognized one or two of them as refugees from her classes, but she couldn't be sure. Just in case, she avoided eye contact.

Margot tried to get back to correcting papers, but she couldn't help overhearing what was happening on Harry's side of the office.

"Can you explain the basics of Freud's theory and how it's different from Adler's?" asked one student.

Another asked, "What exactly is 'cultural suicide,' and can you give me an example?"

Harry patiently answered every question and made sure the students understood before moving on. He never chided the student for not doing the reading or not paying attention in class. Margot was quite sure that this content had been covered because it was on her syllabus too. Why was he letting them off the hook this way? Wasn't it a form of cheating? These students clearly were not being responsible; they were getting help from an instructor just before their exams.

Margot tried, but she couldn't concentrate. She shuffled the student papers on her desk, trying to motivate herself to somehow get through them. Glancing at the first few pages of each one, to see if any looked promising, she thought what she saw looked suspiciously as though it were hastily copied from Wikipedia. She considered stashing the papers in the garbage and telling her students to start over. *Did the manuscripts she sent to publishers affect their editors the same way? Was it possible the students also didn't have time to put more effort into their work? No, impossible! These papers were the reason they were here. Their only job was to spend time on their assignments. That was what college was all about, wasn't it?*

She leaned back stretching her hands over her head and decided she needed a break, a change of scenery. Margot gingerly stepped around Harry's students, who didn't seem to notice her at all. Her basement office, which once seemed like a warm and stimulating cocoon, had turned into a cold dungeon, where she was held prisoner by lousy student papers and depressing rejection notices. She thought she might escape to Crystal's Café where she could at least nourish her soul with comfort food.

As she made her way toward the staircase, she found a young woman quietly sobbing on the bottom step. The stranger's distress resonated with her uncomfortably. The young woman wiped her eyes and tried to stand but stumbled and nearly fell.

Margot reached out to steady her and quickly realized this was the office assistant. What was her name? Melina?

"Melina, are you okay?" she asked quietly.

"I'm so sorry," sniffled Melina. "I didn't know anyone was down here. I'll get back to work right away." Melina turned to get up, but

Margot gently guided her back down with a soft touch and quietly sat next to her.

"Melina, it's okay; stay right here. It looks like we're having the same kind of day. I get so frustrated on days like this. Right now, I feel like doing just what you are doing, sitting on a step by myself, so let's just sit here together, okay?"

Melina nodded slowly and looked up at her cautiously. *Was this really the same Dr. Pearson, who was so smart and so busy that she never had time for students? Who lectured her class and never even looked up?*

Dr. Pearson seemed to have it all together and was certainly not someone who had any problems. Melina was so surprised by this that she momentarily forgot her tears.

"Dr. Pearson—" she began.

"Please. Call me Margot."

"Okay…Margot. I guess I should have come to you before now. I need to talk to you, but I don't really know where to start."

A heavy silence encompassed them like a shroud as they self-consciously huddled together on that bottom step. Grasping for ideas on how to rescue Melina from the ledge she seemed to be teetering on, Margot chided herself for not knowing what to say or do. *She was a psychologist, for Christ's sake! Hadn't she been trained to help people when they needed it? Why was she so stymied by a student whose frustrations were easy to understand, right? Shouldn't she simply put her arm around Melina and tell her everything would be okay? Or would it be better to tell her that all first-year students get frustrated and not to worry? Exams would be over soon, and if she studied, she would be fine. Maybe she should show empathy and let Melina know that she, too, was frustrated?*

None of these ideas seemed right, so Margot simply sat on the bottom step with Melina and waited for a better idea to occur to her, or for Melina to say something. The peace and quiet was soothing, and Margot was able to let go of some of her own fears and frustrations. Sensing that Melina didn't want to talk, she discreetly squinted over her shoulder and noted that the tears had been wiped away, but the puffiness of Melina's face and the feverish blinking of her eyes told Margot she was not yet out of the woods.

This quiet turmoil was abruptly interrupted by Harry's posse who exuberantly rounded the corner.

"Hey, Melina and Dr. Pearson! We're headed out to the Antler with Harry for a burger. He's agreed to keep answering our questions about the psychology midterm. And guess what? He's paying! Wanna come?"

Harry caught up with them and repeated the invitation. "We'd love to have you both come." Winking at Margot, he added, "Dr. Pearson here can probably answer some of those really hard questions that I can't!"

Margot looked up at him incredulously. *Couldn't he see how inappropriate this was?* Melina with her dried-up tears and puffy face certainly didn't want to go out for burgers with this boisterous group.

To her surprise, Margot heard, "Thanks! I'd like that. I'm starving and could use some extra help with the psychology class." Melina gingerly picked herself up from the bottom stair, wiped at the puffiness around her eyes and headed out with them, without looking back. How was it that Melina had been sobbing and unable to talk a few minutes ago but now seemed eager to join the group?

"What are you waiting for?" asked Harry. "Aren't you coming too? I'm paying. You don't want to miss that once-in-a-lifetime opportunity, do you?" As if in a trance, Margot simply shook her head and told them to have fun.

Well, guess I was right, thought Margot. Melina was simply jittery about her exams, nothing a burger couldn't solve. Thinking about burgers made Margot hungry, and she thought she'd better spend some more time on her own exams.

A little while later, with Biko curled around her ankles and her empty glass demanding one more refill of the cheap cabernet she had come to crave in the evenings, Margot put the final touches on her exam. She wanted it to be rigorous and send a message to those students who hadn't been doing the readings or attending class. She also planned to use it as a springboard to advise probably a third of her students to drop the course before they failed. They could still withdraw without a penalty, and Margot figured they would probably be relieved to have one less course to worry about.

There! One short essay question at the end. This was the one that would help her separate the wheat from the chaff, a favorite expression of her mother's used to describe how they weeded out poor performers at her firm.

Positioning herself squarely behind the lectern the next morning, Margot explained the rules for her exams: no late arrivals, no working past the time allowed, no make-up exams, and no exceptions. Margot repeated these warnings to each class. Scrutinizing each class for signs of confusion, she noticed many empty seats and no eyes lifted toward her. Everyone had their heads buried in their laptops. Hopefully, they were writing down her cautionary words. Announcing at the start of each session that it was too late for questions about content, she reassured them that if they had been studying and attending class regularly, they would be fine.

"Any questions?"

With not one hand raised in any class, she promptly dismissed the students, exhorting them to head to the library and study. She felt generous giving up this final class session so the students could study a bit more. Even though she worried that she was lowering standards and sacrificing rigor, she convinced herself this was fair, and rationalized that her colleagues must be doing it too.

But at this stage of the semester, Margot had to admit that something felt off. She'd hoped for more interaction with her students, waiting for them to ask her about the content she knew so well, or to come to her office hours. After all, Harry's side of the room was always crowded. *Where were the questions; could she be doing more to encourage them? Her professors hadn't done anything more. She was teaching the same way she was taught, but why wasn't it working?*

Pushing these thoughts aside, Margot satisfied herself believing the students understood her exam rules and were now headed for the library. She hurried to her office, realizing she had also just bought herself extra time to get some real work done. Maybe she could finish that manuscript she had been working on or start researching for the grant she was co-authoring with Rene. With her graduate assistant, Heidi, doing the actual administration and grading of the exams, Margot now had five days all to herself.

Focused on puzzling out how she would prioritize the next five days, Margot was in a cloud when she passed Shirley in the hall.

"Margot! Glad I caught you. Wanted you to know that Melina is leaving campus for a few days. That means that you'll need to do more of your own copying and printing over break. I'll try to borrow another student helper from Sociology to help us out. She's had a family emergency and won't be back until next week. Okay?"

Stunned, Margot replied, "What about her exams? She can't just leave, can she? Did she ask if that was okay?"

"Family has to come first, Margot. I told her to take whatever time she needed. We'll figure out how to handle it when she gets back."

This must somehow be related to the girl's crying on the stairs yesterday, thought Margot. *But how bad could it be if Melina raced off with the others to share burgers with Harry? I guess she just doesn't understand the high standard she has to meet to succeed here. Surely, her family emergency could wait until exams were over.* Realizing that Melina would fail her exams if she didn't take them and as a result could lose her job in the department, Margot felt a twinge of regret. She wondered if she could she have said anything that might have helped Melina understand the importance of this week? Maybe she could have helped her set priorities and put her family's emergency on hold for a few days?

Thinking about Melina brought back memories of Margot's own freshman year. She'd practically slept in her cubicle by the social science reference section of the library. Her hair was greasy and tangled, and she wore the same torn jeans and t-shirt to every exam. They became her good luck clothes, as she aced every one of them. Greeting her parents who picked her up at the end of the week, she was eager to tell them how well she had done! Her mother eyed her disheveled attire, smiled gratuitously, and listened, but something seemed to be holding her back from her usual ebullient praise.

Only when they got into the car, did Margot ask if everything was okay. That's when her mother shared that Margot's grandmother had died a few days earlier. Margot was crushed. She was named after her grandmother and was looking forward to telling her stories from college.

"What happened? Why didn't you call me?" she asked.

"It was very sudden," Margot's mother replied with her eyes focused on her lap where her hands trembled ever so slightly. "She had a heart attack and died on her way to the hospital. We knew you were taking exams and didn't want to distract you. The funeral was Tuesday. I'm sorry you weren't here, but there was nothing you could have done. And your exams were SO important. This weekend we will go together to the cemetery so that you have some time to take it all in. All right, Margot?"

It was not all right, but under the rivulets of tears flowing down her cheeks, Margot understood why they had not called her.

Although this memory brought Margot close to tears again, she understood that her parents had done the right thing. She couldn't miss the exams, and there was nothing she could have done at home. Acing those exams gave her the strong academic foundation necessary for her to graduate magna cum laude. *How was it that her freshmen students didn't see that? Why didn't they take it seriously? Didn't their families expect more of them?*

With these thoughts continuing to swirl through her head, Margot unlocked the door to her office. She let out a deep sigh of relief to find it empty. It was a rare treat to pretend the space was hers and hers alone.

Margot slowly circled her desk, allowing her fingertips to appreciate the feel of the polished wood and take in the significance of it all. She felt nourished by the all-encompassing peace and quiet of this compact hideaway she might inhabit for the next five days. Yes, this break from teaching classes was exactly what she needed. Her phone rang, and in her dreamlike state, Margot answered without checking the incoming number.

"Hello, dear." *Oh no, it was her mother!* "We heard this was the university's exam week with no classes, and we thought you might want to come home for a few days. It would be nice to see you and hear all about your work."

"Hello, mother. How nice to hear from you. How is work? How is Dad?"

"We are simply fine, dear. Thank you for asking. We are free toward the end of this week, Thursday and Friday. We have plans for the weekend, but perhaps just a few days away from work would do you a world of good. What do you think?"

"Thanks, Mother, but with no teaching this week I have so much work to catch up on. It might be—"

Her mother interrupted, "We won't take no for an answer, dear. How about if you come up Thursday afternoon and stay until Saturday morning? That still gives you time to catch up and spend a few days with us. I can try to leave work early on Thursday, so why don't you plan to get here around 4:00? Is that all right?"

Briefly muting her phone, Margot exhaled deeply, unmuted her phone and reluctantly accepted her mother's invitation. What choice did she have?

"Thanks, Mother. I look forward to it."

"See you Thursday, dear, and bring something nice to wear. We'll have a few friends over to congratulate you on your new position. They can't wait to see you."

Margot hung up and threw the phone onto her lucky chair. Maybe the phone call was just a dream, and her mother's invitation would disappear into the covered-up hole on the arm. Next, she reached into her top drawer for the bottle of Advil. Her head was already throbbing, and it was only Tuesday. Being showcased by her parents was not how she planned to spend her break!

9
Melina

"Wait up, Melina! Let me walk with you," called out Harry. He watched her trying to smile through her puffy, tear-stained face and figured she was nervous about the exams like everyone else. Maybe he could offer some reassuring words. He caught up to her as she wiped away one last tear and forced a smile in his direction.

"Melina, we haven't had much time to get to know each other. How're things? Do you like working in the department? You're a freshman, right? I've noticed how conscientious you are around the office. I love that my copies are always ready and stacked so neatly on my desk when I need them. You know, when I was a freshman here at Balsam, I was also a student worker. I worked in the math department, and some of those faculty were difficult. I don't think—I know—I was not as responsible as you are. There were days when I called in sick rather than delivering their mail or making more copies."

Melina was startled. No teacher had ever talked to her like this, like a friend. This made her nervous because she didn't know what to say. She stumbled a bit but cleared her throat and tried to sound calm.

"Things are okay, I guess," she stammered. And then, out of nowhere, she blurted, "I…I have a problem. I don't know what to do. I need to go home."

Embarrassed by her outburst and feeling flushed and a little faint, Melina looked down at her boots that seemed uglier than ever. After a silence that seemed like forever, she dared to look up. Harry's face was also looking down, and he seemed to be in another world. She started to turn around and head back to her dorm. She really didn't belong here. She would leave in the morning for home, where she really fit in. But Harry looked at her with a genuine warmth in his eyes.

"Melina, you're not the first to have a problem that doesn't seem to have a solution. I've often wanted to go home also. It would be so much easier than staying here and fighting every day to be respected. You know, I'm what they call an adjunct, or part-time, faculty member, and the other faculty really don't want me to have an office or come to their meetings. My best friends here are the students like you who I can really talk to, and sometimes help."

Harry motioned to a nearby bench, indicating that Melina should sit down. At the same time, he called out to the others, "Go ahead. We'll meet you there."

"Tell me, Melina. Why do you need to go home?"

Melina was embarrassed and knew there were splotchy red patches from her neck oozing toward her face, but something in his voice, or maybe his eyes, told her she could trust Dr. Sanders—or Harry, as he preferred. Maybe he could help her. She had nothing to lose, so while fingering Mamá's cross, she choked back her shame as her story tumbled out.

"My parents came here from Mexico 30 years ago, and we live on the south side of the city in Villacito. Mamá and Papá work so hard and have so many jobs just to take care of us, but they don't have their legal papers. My brothers and I were born here and do our best to help, but there are so many problems. Papá's work was raided about a month ago by ICE. He lost his job, and now he must go to court for a hearing. He doesn't speak much English, and he needs me to go with him. We have always been afraid that he or Mamá, or both, would be deported back to Mexico, and we'd never see them again. It keeps us all awake most nights. I need to be there for my family. They live three hours away, and my parents don't understand about exams. They're proud of me but are worried and don't really know what it means for me to come home and miss exams."

Melina thought she should probably stop, but Harry nodded and with what seemed like a genuine interest encouraged her to continue.

"I don't have money for the bus to get home, and I don't know how to tell my teachers I won't be here. They won't understand, and if I fail their classes I may lose my scholarship and I'll have to go back home for good. I've studied hard, and I think I'm ready, but I just can't be here. I'm so ashamed."

By the time she stopped, Melina's stomach was churning and she knew she wouldn't be able to stand up without crumbling onto the sidewalk.

Harry was quiet at first and then slowly began, "Melina, you sound like a wonderful daughter, and your parents sound like loving, responsible people. You should feel proud and not ashamed. Family should come first and definitely ahead of exams. Everybody may not agree with that, but I do. We'll think about this together. I hear a couple of parts to your problem. Let's break it down and come up with a solution. First, you need to get home tomorrow, and you can't afford the bus or the time it takes to get there. I have a car and will be headed toward the city. Is that where your family lives?"

Melina quietly nodded.

"If you can wait 'til afternoon, I'll take you. It won't take three hours by car. What do you think?" Melina brushed away a tear and nodded again.

"Second, you need to tell each one of your teachers before we leave, and schedule make-up exams with them. Have you told anyone yet?"

Melina was beginning to feel some hope, but she shook her head. "No. I'm too afraid. I don't know what to say."

"Some will be easier than others, but the most important thing is to tell them the truth. Be honest and explain it's an emergency, and emergencies don't schedule themselves around exams. Let them know how hard you've studied and that you're considering majoring in their subject. Also tell them you love their class and what a great teacher they are! Just kidding about that last part, but it never hurts to throw out a compliment or two."

Melina listened carefully but still wasn't convinced.

"What about Dr. Pearson? She said there are no make-ups—if we miss her exam, we'll probably fail her class. I can't do that, but I'm too scared to talk to her."

"Well, Melina, Dr. Pearson isn't really as scary as you think. She's also having a tough time fitting in around here and might be more flexible than she appears. Don't ever forget that no matter how confident someone might seem, we're all dealing with something. It's not just you, Melina. But now you have a ride home, so you also have extra time tomorrow morning to make the rounds and talk to your teachers. Begin to map out in your head how you'll do it. Start with the ones you think will be easiest for you, and work your way up to Dr. Pearson. That will give you the confidence you need. I'll be in my office if you get stuck, but I'm confident you can do this yourself. Okay? Make sense?"

Melina wanted to hug him but didn't think that was right, so she simply nodded and this time threw him a genuine smile.

As much as Harry wanted to talk to the teachers for her, he knew she needed to do it herself. He would check discreetly to find out who her teachers were. If there were any especially difficult ones, he could put in a good word for her. For sure, he would try to talk to Margot when she came to the office. He also knew it was against university policy to drive a student off campus, but he was willing to face the consequences if anyone reported it. He would never forget how Hank Gregory had driven him to the hospital after his family's car accident. It was against policy then too, but Hank hadn't thought twice about it. It was time for Harry to help someone without worrying about consequences.

Harry jumped off the bench as if lightening had struck. "Let's go get a burger! I think you'll like the students who are with me today. They're all worried about the exams. Maybe together we can help them break down their fears too."

When they reached the Antler, they found the students had ordered burgers for them. They were a little cold, but it was a nice gesture and at least they didn't order tacos for her. As Melina squeezed into the booth with the others, they jokingly, but willingly, made room for her. She felt as if she might belong after all. Harry's students talked about exams, how tired they were, and how they couldn't wait for exams to be over. Harry was at ease with everyone and made it seem like they were the only ones in the bar at that moment. Melina felt so comfortable and was thrilled when they invited her to join their study group. She felt herself letting go and genuinely laughing for the first time since she arrived on campus.

Everyone shared strategies on how to stay calm before exams. Harry shared a few meditation techniques to help them relax; they all laughed as they closed their eyes and tried to picture something that made them happy while taking a deep breath, counting to five and letting it out. Harry swore it always worked for him when he was stressed. Melina closed her eyes and pictured the kitchen at home, and Mamá dancing to the music on the radio. She could feel the muscles in her neck already feeling less tight.

On their walk back to campus, one of the girls, Luna, looped her arm through Melina's, and they strolled along together. They talked about their teachers and what it was like to fit into this new, hugely different place. Luna invited her to an Exam Yoga session the next day at the old Student Center. Melina had never heard of yoga, but she trusted her new friend and agreed to meet her there at 11:00. She was still worried about Papá, but things seemed a little more manageable as she broke away from Luna with a warm hug and headed into Forbes. Armed with Harry's advice about talking to her teachers and Luna's invite to the Center, she was hopeful that tonight she could get some sleep. Tomorrow might not be so bleak after all.

The next morning, Melina woke up with real purpose. She knew she had a tough day ahead, but thanks to Harry, she now had a plan. Going to her closet, she reached for her one nice dress and pair of shoes. If she was going to make the case to her teachers, she might as well look presentable, as Mamá would say. As she headed out the door, she saw the note on her desk from Theresa.

Mel,

My study group pulled an all-nighter, and we crashed in Sonia's room. I came back around midnight to let you know, but you were dead to the world. See you later and good luck with your exams!

As Melina read the note, she felt a cloud of guilt closing in on her. Theresa was nice enough, but they didn't have anything in common. She always felt like an outsider with her and her friends. She felt bad that she hadn't told her why she didn't help decorate their room; didn't accept her invitations to go out to eat; or why her parents never sent a care package for her to share. Theresa's mother sent curtains for their windows and snacky food for them almost every week. She wanted to open up to Theresa about her family, but she didn't know how to do it. Maybe after exams, she'd figure it out.

As Melina sat in her usual corner of the dining room by herself eating her banana and Rice Krispies with chocolate milk, she made a list of the teachers she needed to find this morning. She also made some notes about what to say. Writing it down made it real. First, she would go to Dr. Gregory. He always seemed to be in a good mood and smiled at the students when they walked into class. Maybe he would understand. He would, at least, listen to her.

Then there was Dr. Silverman. She let students choose their own projects and didn't complain too much when they were a little late. She always encouraged them to set their own goals and use their personal experiences to make sure an assignment was relevant. It made sense that she would understand Melina's situation.

The next two she wasn't sure about. Dr. Stakes had a reputation for being tough about late assignments. He had also stressed the importance of the exam, which would be an essay written during a strictly timed and supervised session.

Then there was Dr. Pearson, the toughest of all. She never, ever looked at her students and always talked about how important it was to meet what she called "rigorous" standards. So many students had left her class, maybe because of this. But Melina remembered yesterday afternoon on the basement stair when she sat with her. It was confusing, almost like she was another person. Dr. Pearson, for sure, was the hardest one to understand. Well, Harry had given her the courage to try, so try she would.

As Melina headed for the door, she suddenly froze as if struck by a thunderbolt. She suddenly realized she had NO idea where her teachers were when they weren't in class. Well, they must have offices just like

Harry and Dr. Pearson, right? Yikes! Why didn't she know this? Who could help? Her head was spinning so fast she thought she might faint. She sat on the closest chair to steady herself and think. She felt so out of it and once again embarrassed by her ignorance. She fingered Abuela's cross which brought her small comfort but no answers. There was only one person she could think of; it was worth a try. She turned toward Anderson and Shirley's office.

"Hi, Melina! I thought you left this morning to go home," said Shirley with a confused look as Melina approached the Psychology office.

"I'm leaving this afternoon instead. Harry, er...Dr. Sanders, is giving me a ride. I need some help this morning."

"Whatever you need, Melina. I'll try to help."

"Well, I need to let my teachers know I won't be here for exams, but I don't know how to find them. Can you tell me where their offices are?"

"Of course. I have a faculty directory in my desk drawer. Follow me, and we'll find out where they hide!"

Melina was so thankful, she almost squealed with delight. Instead, she silently crossed herself and followed Shirley into an office that felt warm and friendly. She had decorated her space with pillows on comfy chairs, and lots of family photos. She even had a plant in the corner. Melina felt at home as soon as she sat down. Relaxed, she proceeded to give Shirley the list of her teachers. Moments later, she had their office locations added to her list. After thanking Shirley and receiving a hug in return, Melina virtually floated out of Anderson Hall with her fragile sense of courage rebounding. Maybe this was going to work after all.

As she was figuring out which way to turn to find Dr. Gregory, she glanced at the clocktower. *Wow, was it already 10:45? Wasn't she supposed to meet Luna at 11:00 for something called Exam Yoga?* She thought about setting priorities, just like Harry and Ms. Ingram advised. She reasoned that her college future might depend on talking to her teachers today. In Harry and Ms. Ingram's eyes, that would for sure be the number one priority. But they also taught her that she needed to manage her time and set her own priorities.

It only took a few minutes for Melina to decide that Luna was priority number one. Luna did what friends do: She linked arms with Melina, invited her into a study group, and then asked her to join her for an activity separate from the others. This all made Melina feel special. Melina decided she would talk to her teachers later, after spending time with Luna, so she headed in the direction of the old Student Center. She felt stupid that she had never been there until now. She spent most of her time studying, going to class and working in the Psychology Department. Walking into the Center opened a whole new world for her. There was so much going on! She couldn't take her eyes off the bulletin boards filled with free things to do and crashed into Luna.

"Melina, look at you, *chica!* You look awesome, all dressed up. But come with me. We only have a few minutes before the session begins, and I'll need to loan you some comfortable clothes. You'll be lying on a floor mat, and these clothes are way too nice for that." With that, Luna led Melina into a smallish room with lockers along the wall where several other girls were changing for yoga. She opened a locker and threw a scraggly pair of gray sweatpants and t-shirt toward Melina. "C'mon, *chica*, we don't have much time." Melina quickly changed and followed Luna and the others into a large room with long blue mats spread out all over the floor. Standing at the front of the room was a young, brown woman with dark hair drawn into a long braid that trailed down her back. "*Hola!*" she called out as their small group entered. "Pick a mat and *empecemos*—let's get started!"

With one leg in the air and the other "threading the needle," Melina closed her eyes and prayed that one more deep breath would help her relax. *¡Dios mío! I can't hold my breath that long.* She let it out on the count of 10. *Was everyone else getting this right? Am I the only one who can't do it? Are they all watching me?* An hour later, with sweat beading up and down her arms, Melina had a general idea of what yoga was but wasn't sure she liked it. She listened to the drum that signaled the end and tried to get off the mat without falling. Once again, she just wanted to be invisible, but Luna sensed her tension and gave her a wet hug. A few others smiled and welcomed her to the group. Melina was achy, but maybe she would come back.

In the locker room, Melina quickly wriggled out of the borrowed sweats and confided to Luna about where she was headed. Luna listened with warmth and compassion; she understood. As Melina prepared to dash out the door to find Dr. Gregory, Luna hugged her again. "*Chica*, I hope this will go well. Your teachers will understand, and your family needs you. You're doing the right thing. I'll see you when you get back. *Buena suerte*, my friend. Here's my number; call me if you need anything." With a quick squeeze, Melina hurried off to find her teachers.

10
Margot

Fumbling around her cluttered closet to find the clothes her mother might like, Margot once again wondered why this still mattered at all to her. *Why did she care if her mother approved of her clothes? Wasn't she an adult with advanced degrees, a profession, and a full-time job? Didn't her mother understand that at a university, people cared more about what was in their heads than what was on their bodies?* Margot's colleagues usually looked intentionally careless about their wardrobes. They wanted to be respected for their minds and not how they looked.

In her mother's world, both appearance and intellect mattered, but it seemed to Margot that appearance always came first. Her mother was meticulous about her wardrobe and always found time for a weekly hair appointment. At home, her look was casual but in a carefully tailored way. She wouldn't know a comfy, loose-fitting sweat suit if it walked up and clawed at her slim-fitting khakis! With that thought, Margot threw hers into the "no-go" pile that would stay right here with Biko. He would surely appreciate this once-in-a-lifetime opportunity to nestle down into the middle of Margot's comfort clothes for a few days. That pile was definitely bigger than the one she was taking, and she tripped over it as she backed out of her closet.

Her mother wouldn't be direct about Margot's look, but her feelings would be clear. Once, Margot was headed out the door for her first day at a summer internship back in college. Her mother called after her,

"Honey, I hope they like that cute little skirt you picked out for your first day! Be sure to keep your legs together and ankles crossed when you sit down. And keep your hair out of your eyes. Maybe we should trim those bangs when you get home."

Another time, she attended a reception at her mother's firm, and a senior partner commented on how nice Margot looked. She thought that would please her mother, but as he walked away, she commented under her breath, "He's the worst dresser in the firm. I wish someone would talk to him about it. It really affects our clientele."

Happily, this visit was only for two days. She would survive. She always did. Margot wanted to get on the road early, so she could avoid rush hour around the city. She left her office early without saying goodbye to anyone. They knew she was leaving, so it really didn't matter, did it? Her graduate assistant would administer her exams and email her if there were any problems. She was looking forward to being in the car alone for the three-hour trip and getting away from all the departmental angst that was swirling around. She would let the NPR radio commentary push away her current anxieties as she listened to its more global concerns. They were much easier to deal with.

Margot finished packing her suitcase and gently ousted Biko for the last time. He protested with a howl and arched his back before slipping under the bed. She knew he hated it when she left, so she loaded his favorite tuna into the blue dish with his name on it and called out to him. Then she lined up a few bowls of that dry food he hated, but it would keep him from starving until she got back. The tuna lured him out more than her leaving, but she gave him a farewell nuzzle anyway. She wished he could come with her, but her mother was allergic and besides, his black hair would cling to her immaculately clean chintz coverings.

Three hours later, caught up on all the global crises thanks to NPR, Margot felt the familiar crunch of gravel as she pulled into her parents' driveway. She was early, so there would be no one home yet. She wasn't sure her father was even in town, and her mother worked extraordinary hours. She found the key hidden in its usual place under a thorny rosebush by the back door and let herself in. Once inside, she staked out her place in the bedroom she used to call home. She hadn't stayed here in years, and it truly felt like a foreign territory with a different dress code and different norms from those she and Biko lived by. After hanging up her clothes and shutting the closet door, she sat down on the carefully made bed to take a look around her old room. Clearly, her mother had hired a decorator to come in and make more than a few changes.

The once sky-blue room was now painted white and filled with artwork Margot didn't recognize. From a recent trip? From the decorator's playbook? All Margot knew was that her posters and memorabilia from school were gone. Where? Maybe her mother had created a nice, neat pile somewhere in the house labeled, "Margot's Things."

As she feverishly twirled her hair, she made a mental note to ask. In the meantime, she walked over to the vintage dresser, the one from her grandmother, and fingered the polished surface. She sought some warmth, something to bring back happy memories, especially those of her grandmother. But none of her small trinkets were there. *Where was the little carved pony she loved as a child? Or the china dolls with the cracked faces and coarse hair? Where were the framed pictures of her grandparents, the ones in the crackly wooden frames?* Everything she once cherished seemed to be missing. Apparently, her things didn't fit the decorator's theme.

Giving up all hope of feeling at home, she left this room and searched the house for a comfortable place to sit. When nothing called out to her, Margot stumbled into a sunny corner filled with chintz pillows that looked somewhat cozy. She plopped herself down, missing Biko on her lap, and let her mind wander back to the days she lived here. She was often alone, just like now. Sometimes she invited friends over after school, but she always worried they would make a mess. They all commented on how pretty her house was, but they never knew where to hang out. There was no place for kids to put their feet up, and the only food in the fridge was grownup dinner food...no snacks, and certainly no soda. Margot had spent many hours by herself in front of the computer in her room either doing homework or gossiping with the few friends she had. That all seemed so natural at the time. It was only now that Margot realized it might have been a little unusual for a teenager to spend so much time alone. Of course, it probably helped her become the valedictorian and be admitted to her first-choice college. Those things mattered, right? Margot found herself second-guessing some of her earlier assumptions.

The sound of tires on the gravel driveway abruptly shattered Margot's reverie, and she jumped up. Without thinking, she hastily fluffed the pillows and stopped to take a quick look in the hallway mirror and smooth out her shirt as she made her way to the back door. As she opened the door, her mother stepped from the car, phone to her ear. Margot couldn't remember a time when her mother didn't have that silvery badge of success by her cheek. She had been one of the first in the neighborhood to have a cell phone, and everyone noticed. Despite everything, she was excited to see her mother. It had been a long time, and she felt a familiar tingle that reminded her this was home and this was her mother. Her mother was tough, but it was her toughness and high standards that had landed Margot where she was today.

Broadcasting a smile in her mother's direction, Margot knew not to interrupt the call. She waited as her mother wrapped up some presumably important business transaction.

"Margot my dear, how wonderful to see you! We are so thrilled you found time to spend with us. I can't wait to show you off to our friends. Your father is out of town for an honorary induction ceremony of some kind, but he'll be back tomorrow. In the meantime, let's you and I go out for dinner tonight and catch up. How about our favorite little café?"

Margot struggled to remember any favorite café they shared, but part of her routine was to always express enthusiasm and go along with it.

"Love to, Mother. Great idea!"

"Wonderful, Margot. Just give me a few minutes to change. You might want to put on a skirt. You know The Harbor is casual, but around here nothing is too casual. I could loan you one if you forgot to bring a skirt." Eying her up and down she added, "I think I can find something that might fit."

"No. I'm fine, Mother. Be ready in a few." Margot retreated to the room they still called hers and found the appropriate skirt. It was a little short, but since it had a matching sweater set Margot knew it would meet her mother's general guidelines. Quickly shedding her current outfit, which Margot already thought looked quite nice, she took a deep breath and swept her hair back. She crossed the colorful Turkish carpet that defined the large living room to meet her mother in the imposing foyer. A few minutes later, she heard the clicking of her mother's signature heels on the polished wood floor. How long had it been since Margot heard anyone clicking down a hallway? None of her colleagues at school wore heels. She wondered if they even owned any. She certainly didn't herself.

Settling in at The Harbor Café, Margot finally relaxed a bit. They shared a cozy table by a corner window, overlooking a large expanse of colorful gardens leading down to the lakefront pathway. She was thankful they had the corner table, and she made sure her mother's chair faced the window, so she wouldn't constantly scan the dining room for acquaintances. Margot might have a shot at her full attention this way. It was a lovely setting —fresh flowers and a basket of warm bread seemed to invite a genuine and uninterrupted conversation. Margot treasured these rare moments when she could feel her mother drop her guard and honestly engage with her.

Her mother reached over and affectionately patted Margot's arm.

"Margot, let's order a bottle of really good wine and have a girls' night out! It's been so long since the two of us spent time together. I've missed hearing about everything you've been up to. Or what about champagne to celebrate?"

Margot nodded and motioned to the attentive waiter, who clearly knew her mother. He quickly returned with two crystal flutes and a bottle of bubbly in a silver bucket that crackled with ice. They toasted to being together and settled in for a nice, long evening.

"Margot, tell me about your job, and especially your new apartment. I want to hear all about it."

Taking a deep breath to calm her nerves and steady her voice, Margot began.

"Everything is great, Mother. My office is perfectly located to let me get work done. I'm working on several articles and doing research for a grant that I'll be submitting soon. The Chair, Dr. Berg, really liked the goals I set and congratulated me on my ambitious agenda. The students are interested in my lectures, and the people I work with are supportive. We're all busy, so we don't see each other often but that's okay."

Margot ticked off this ridiculously false snapshot of her life without taking a breath and was relieved when it was done. Over the years, she had developed an automatic response syndrome to her mother's questions. She simply reported a list of expected achievements, knowing there would be little specific follow-up.

"I'm delighted to hear about your goals, dear. After listening to your father for all these years, I know how important it is to please your department chair. If you keep publishing those articles and submitting grant proposals, you'll soon be ready to move on. Once you've established your reputation, I'm sure your father can help you find a position at a more prestigious institution. You know he has connections around the world and would love to help you move up when it's time."

"Thanks, Mother," replied Margot as she nervously twirled her hair. She was on autopilot now. "I'll be good here for a while. I love my new apartment. Biko and I are settling in nicely. The beautiful, white couch you and Dad sent is the centerpiece of the living room and makes it all look so elegant."

Elegant was a word Margot knew her mother would want to hear, so even though the space around the couch was festooned with Biko's toys, as well as her own books and papers, it didn't really matter. She knew her parents would never find the time to visit. What mattered most to them right now was the illusion of Margot's early success, so they could more easily paint a picture of it to their friends. Even though she was not at a prestigious institution, their friends would picture their daughter living in an elegant apartment, as a forerunner to future accomplishments.

Struggling to distance herself from the fantasy life she vividly depicted, Margot asked, "How's everything at the firm, Mother? Still the same old politics and difficult clients?"

"Not much has changed, dear, but I was recently named managing partner. Less client contact, but more respect. All those dinners and networking finally paid off. You'll see some day how important they are. Tell me about your network at school, Margot. Any promising contacts yet?"

Oh, here we go! thought Margot. This was always the inevitable question from her mother.

"Well, the person I see the most, Harry, is very respected around campus. He was elected president of a faculty group that really admires him, and the students give him the highest evaluations. Our offices are close by, and we give each other advice all the time."

"That's nice, dear. I assume he's older and well published. Keep it up, but make sure to expand beyond the school. You know, attend conferences, seek out presentation opportunities; you know how it goes."

Margot nodded and took a huge gulp of the bubbly in front of her; it was disappearing fast.

After what seemed like hours, their conversation veered into a more gossipy mode, and Margot's fanciful shield melted away. It was always easier to listen to her mother go on about the neighbors' inadequacies than to hide her own. She listened to her mother gloat about their next-door neighbors' recent divorce. She had predicted it for years and wondered why it took them so long to figure out they weren't right for each other. Then there were the Bensons across the street, who had recently taken another vacation; how would they ever be successful if they continued to travel so much? The Hanleys down the street just had their fourth child!

"Can you imagine?"

By the time they finished their second bottle of champagne and started for home, Margot's head was spinning, and not just from the champagne. Through the fog brought on by the sparkling bubbles, Margot wondered if she would remember the details of the fantasy she had just laid out at dinner, so she could repeat them when she saw her father the next day. At least her mother was happy for now and had something, fabled as it was, to brag about to her friends.

She carefully laid her head on a starchy, white pillowcase and was asleep in minutes.

"Morning, Dad!" Margot exclaimed in her cheeriest voice when she arrived at the breakfast table the next day. "How was your induction last night? We missed you at dinner."

"Darlin', it was just another ceremony. I've had enough of 'em, but I hear your life is going swimmingly well. Tell me about your research. I know how important it is to you. What are you working on?"

As Margot searched for answers in the recesses of her mind, her mother came through the arched doorway. For once, Margot was grateful for the interruption.

"We've all been invited to have lunch with the Shermans today. They would love to see Margot and hear all about her first job. I think their daughter, Judith, is also home. Won't it be fun to catch up with our old friends?"

Margot hoped her anguish didn't show; the Shermans were among her parents' most unappealing friends. Judith, in particular, was impossible. She would regale them all with her brilliant accomplishments as a second-year associate at the city's largest law firm.

At least I won't have to talk, Margot thought. She could once again practice her active listening skills.

"Sure, Mother. That sounds great!" She thought her father rolled his eyes before he also agreed, but she couldn't be sure.

That night, after suffering through the never-ending lunch with the Shermans and then enduring an evening get-together at her parents' club, Margot fell into bed utterly exhausted. She was completely worn out and depressed from wearing that pasted smile all day, as well as clothes she didn't like, and shoes that killed her feet. At least the pillow wasn't so starchy tonight. She wondered how early she could leave in the morning to get back to her anything-but-elegant apartment and comfy clothes. Biko certainly didn't require fake smiles and uncomfortable clothes. As always, he would simply let her vent about the weekend and patiently wait for her to finish. He had no high expectations of her; his only ask was for food twice a day and a cozy place to nuzzle. What simple pleasures. Margot's were veering more in that direction also.

Rrrrr…rrr! Was she dreaming or was that her phone? Who would call her here? Margot felt the warmth of the sunlight streaming through the perfectly hung white lace curtains at her window as she tried to shake off her sleepiness. Stretching her arm toward the nightstand where she left her cell, she could see the call was from a university number.

"Hello?" she said cautiously, but with curiosity.

"Hi," answered her graduate assistant, Heidi. "I'm sorry to interrupt your weekend, Dr. Pearson, but I wanted you to know that one of your students didn't show up for the exam. I just found a note she left on your desk. With grades due tomorrow, I thought you'd want to know. Usually if someone misses an exam, we notify them before grades are submitted so they can drop the class with no failure on their record. What do you want me to do?"

"Did you read the note, Heidi?"

"No. It was taped shut and had your name on it. I didn't think I should open it."

Margot didn't know many of her students by name, so she didn't think to ask who it was from. She was curious, though, about the excuse.

"Heidi, do you have the note with you now?"

"Yes. If you want me to read it to you, I'll open it."

"Yes, thanks."

"It's from Melina García, Dr. Pearson. Here's what she says," and she recited the contents of the letter:

Dr. Pearson,

*I will not be able to take the psychology exam this week.
I must go home and help my family. I tried to find you
but you were gone. I can make it up when I return.*

Sincerely, Melina

"Heidi, how well do you know Melina?"

"Not very well, Dr. Pearson. I just know that she always comes to class on time, takes a lot of notes and sits in the back row. She seems pretty shy. When she hands in assignments, she smiles but never says anything. I think she works hard because she aces her weekly quizzes. When class is over though she keeps her head down and leaves quickly. And, as you know, she's the department assistant, so I also see her around the office sometimes."

Embarrassed that she hadn't recognized the name, Margot was now wide awake and confused by what Heidi was telling her. *Why would a student miss an exam to help their family? Couldn't that wait until after the exam? Was there a death in her family? That could explain why Melina was crying on the basement stairs at Anderson, but why didn't Melina tell Margot instead of running off with Harry to the Antler Bar?* Margot didn't know what to think; students were often inexplicable to her. Whatever the reason, there was no excuse for missing an important exam and there had to be consequences.

Of course, she would advise Melina to drop the class. Rules were rules, and she had explained them clearly in her last class. However, since Melina was the department assistant, she felt obligated to tell her directly, to avoid any repercussions. Margot knew Shirley would understand, but she also wanted to tell her first, in case they needed to hire a new student assistant.

"Heidi, I'm headed back now. I should be there by lunchtime. Please leave the exams and Melina's note on my desk. Oh, and if you have contact information for her, please leave that too. I'll try to reach her today."

"Sure thing, Dr. Pearson!"

Margot quickly threw her clothes into her suitcase and left a note for her parents, who were still sleeping. She thanked them for their hospitality and carefully tucked the key under the rosebush on her way out. She was grateful for a reason to skip the awkward goodbye that always included false promises to visit and call more often. Margot assured herself that her parents would also appreciate her early getaway, so they could get on with their day.

Swinging onto the highway, Margot uneasily tried to wrap her mind around what could possibly cause a college freshman to put her education in jeopardy by missing their first important exam. After an hour of complete bafflement, she turned on NPR, to listen to something she could understand.

11
Melina

A little before 2:00, Melina schlepped up the stairs of Anderson Hall, where Harry waited to give her a ride home. Hugging Rosa tight against her chest, she felt the weight of everything crashing down on her. The well-worn suitcase was a concrete reminder of where she came from and why she was going home, instead of taking exams. With her shoulders hunched and her stomach twisted in knots, Melina worried that Harry might change his mind and be disappointed in her. After all, he was a teacher and expected his students to take exams, didn't he? Distracted by her worries, she didn't notice Shirley coming toward her on the stairs. Melina bumped into her so hard that Rosa landed with a thud on the top stair.

"Melina, are you okay?" asked Shirley in her gentle voice that always comforted Melina. "You don't look so good. Can I help with anything?"

"No, thank you. I need to find Dr. Pearson though. Is she around?"

"I haven't seen her, Melina. She said something yesterday about going home this week, so she may have left already. I'm sorry."

Melina thanked Shirley and wondered if this was good news. She was scared to talk to Dr. Pearson, but she had to, didn't she? Continuing down the hall to Harry's office, she realized that Dr. Pearson might also be there. She took a deep breath and held on to Rosa even tighter with all her strength.

Knocking softly, Melina wondered why the door was closed. Had Harry left without her? Then she heard his friendly, "Hi! C'mon in, whoever you are." Relief encompassed her like a warm blanket, and she managed a smile as she opened the door. Harry was alone and surrounded by mounds of paper, making it seem like he was locked behind an impenetrable fortress.

"Melina, so glad it's you. I'll be done in a few minutes. Hope you don't mind waiting. I've almost finished my grading. You can sit at Dr. Pearson's desk if you like. I think she left earlier, not sure."

Not wanting to bother him, Melina sat down quietly to wait.

Brushing the hair out of his eyes, Harry looked up, "By the way, did you get to see your instructors this morning, Melina?"

"Well, yes, but I didn't see Dr. Pearson."

"Why don't you write her a note and explain that you need to go home? You can leave it on her desk. That way she'll see it first thing when she gets back. Sound good?"

Harry tossed a pad of paper across the room toward Melina. Startled, she jumped up to grab it. She wasn't sure this was such a good idea, but it was easier than trying to explain it in person. She picked up a pen and carefully wrote out what she hoped was a respectful note to Dr. Pearson. Wanting it to be confidential, she carefully folded it and taped it shut before writing Dr. Pearson's name across the back.

An hour later, Harry wrapped up his "few minutes," and they headed out to the parking lot. As Melinda clutched Rosa and Harry slouched under a bulky backpack with more student papers inside, they crammed into his smallish, well-used car and started out for the city.

Melina was about to put her head back and close her eyes when Harry asked, "How did your meetings go this morning, Melina? Did you find everyone but Dr. Pearson?"

"I had a plan just like you suggested, so right after Exam Yoga—"

"Whoa, wait a minute," laughed Harry. "Exam Yoga? What is that, and why wasn't I invited?"

"Oh, it was a relaxation class that Luna goes to. We all lay on mats and twisted ourselves into weird shapes. My body still hurts, but I've never been to the Student Center so it was kind of fun; there's so much going on there. The yoga teacher reminded me of one of my cousins, and she even spoke some Spanish. If they let me come back to school, I might go back there."

"Melina, nobody ever told you about the Center? I'm really sorry; that should have been in your welcoming packet. It's an excellent resource on campus and has lots of activities going on all the time. The university is planning to expand it, and I'm on the advisory committee. We'll have to talk more about it later. But I interrupted you. Please go ahead."

"Okay. My strategy was to talk to the teacher I thought would be the easiest one first, Dr. Gregory. You know, he always comes to class with a smile and laughs a lot. I thought he might understand. I went to his office and explained that my father needed my help this week, and I had to go home. He listened to me and nodded but didn't say much. I couldn't tell what he was thinking, and my legs started to feel all tingly. Just when I thought I might fall down, he asked me to sit. I sort of fell into the closest chair and didn't dare look up. He came around his desk and sat down next to me. I was scared to look up but when I did, I could tell he cared.

He said, 'Melina, I hope your father will be okay. I'm so sorry for your family. Of course, you must go home. This is important, and we'll schedule a make-up exam. Come see me when you return, and we'll go from there. Okay? I can see how upset you are and how difficult it was for you to come here. I respect you for that and wish you well.' He was so nice, but I was afraid he might change his mind so I said thank you and left quickly."

"I knew Hank Gregory would do the right thing," said Harry. "You were smart to go to him first. Good strategy, Melina. What happened next?"

"I tried to find Dr. Silverman, but she wasn't in her office. I didn't have much time, so I decided to look for Dr. Stakes and try her again later. After Dr. Gregory, I felt a little better about going to their offices, but it still made me nervous. I never knew students could go to teachers' offices. They're so busy, and we're just students they see in their classrooms a few times a week."

"Melina, students are the reason we're all here. Haven't you noticed on your class syllabus that all instructors include where their offices are and what their office hours are? They should be telling you in class also, but it's required to be on their syllabus. When you get back, pull out all your syllabi and see where they're listed and what their office hours are. Did you find Dr. Stakes?"

"Well, I never paid much attention to the syllabus and didn't know that, but yes, I found him. His door was closed. I knocked, but no one answered. The light was on, so I thought someone must be in there. I figured he was busy and I shouldn't bother him, but I knew I didn't have a choice. My knees began to feel weak, but I knocked a little louder. This time a gruff voice barked out, 'Who's there? I'm busy and don't have time for small talk!' I don't really know what small talk is, so I just told him I was a student who needed to talk to him for a minute. He yelled again, 'Well then, don't just stand there trying to break down my door; come in!'

"I thought I was going to cry, so I blinked really fast. I almost ran away, but instead I forced myself to slowly jiggle the knob and try to push the door open. It was locked. I decided to leave, but suddenly the door snapped open, pulling me with it, as Dr. Stakes stood there glaring at me and blocking the entrance. 'Who are you? I don't recognize you.

What class are you in?' I told him I was in his freshman English writing class and that I couldn't take the exam. He didn't move, but as I recovered my balance, he took his glasses off and leaned toward me.

"'Do you understand how important this exam is, young lady? Do you know that if you don't take it tomorrow morning, you will probably fail my class, and I will have to report you for violating the Code of Student Conduct? That will go on your record. Have you no respect for our policies? What is your excuse anyway?'

"I could hardly talk I was so scared, and I had no idea what he was talking about. His face was really close to mine. I kept backing up while I tried to tell him that I had to go home because my father needed help, but he interrupted me. 'You are now at a university, and your family needs to understand that you cannot go home every time they need someone to sweep the floor. I'm sure that whatever their personal problem is, it can wait until exams are over. I'll see you tomorrow at 10:00. And don't be late! This exam is timed.'

"He slammed the door in my face, and I was by myself in the hallway. I held onto the wall and saw a bench that was close by. I didn't know what to do, but I was shaking all over and couldn't stop crying. I just about fell onto the hard, wooden bench and squeezed Abuela's cross, hoping no one would come by. Suddenly, I felt a hand on my arm. 'What's the matter, sweetie? Did you just see Dr. Stakes? You're not the first one to sit on this bench and cry. We should put up a plaque that says *Stakes' Crying Bench.*'

"Turns out it was the office manager for the English department. I told her what happened and that I would be missing his exam tomorrow. She seemed to understand and asked for my name, which he never did. She told me her name, Anne, and asked me to come see her when I returned to school. Anne handed me some Kleenex and wished me luck at home. I got out of there as fast as I could just in case Dr. Stakes came out of his office. I sure didn't want to see him again, ever!"

Harry took a deep breath and shook his head. While he didn't want to criticize another faculty member, this disdain for a student's dilemma was totally unacceptable. He made a mental note to schedule some time to meet with the English Department Chair when he got back. Meanwhile, he assured Melina that Anne sounded like a good person who would probably help her.

Continuing with her day's narrative Melina said, "I took a little break after that, to calm down and think about what I was doing. I walked to my favorite place on campus, a hidden garden out past the football field that's surrounded by dark green bushes and beautiful flowers that stretch toward the sun. There's never anyone there, so I go to stretch out on the grass when I feel confused. It's always peaceful and gives me a private space to think about things. I was so upset and scared. A million questions popped up inside my head: Did I really belong here? Was my dream a selfish one? My family is important to me, and they already sacrificed so much. Maybe I should stay home and help out? I could get a job in the city and help them with the rent and the babysitting. Mamá and Papá could work fewer hours. They've worked so hard, and they're getting older. Maybe it's my turn to look out for them? It would be easier than trying to fit in here! And the Student Code of Conduct; what is that, anyway?

"Then I did what I always do when I'm in the garden: I looked up at the blue sky with the marshmallow-like clouds floating by, so beautiful yet untouchable. I believe my dreams are like those clouds, beautiful but impossible to reach. For sure, they are not standing still and as they move across to the horizon, they change shape. I love watching them. They look like a unicorn one minute, and a jaguar the next. There's no predicting. The interesting thing is that they don't stay still, and they don't stay the same. That always reminds me why I'm here. I want to keep moving and be a good person who makes a difference, but just like the clouds, I don't know exactly what that looks like. I also believe that's what Mamá and Papá want for me, but it scares them just like it scares me."

Melina looked over at Harry who nodded his head as he drove.

"You know, Melina, you're so right about dreams being beautiful, yet often hard to reach. We all have dreams. You may think that because we faculty have jobs and are older, we have fulfilled ours, but that's not always true. We're also watching those clouds! Sometimes, we get frustrated and confused just like you. When we think our dreams are impossible, it can sometimes make us cranky and not so nice to others. For instance, take Dr. Stakes. Maybe he has dreams that he will someday have a prestigious position with fewer papers to correct and more respect. He hasn't reached that dream, so he may take it out on students like you and act grumpy. I'm not saying that's the case for him, but it's something to think about. Maybe he needs to find a quiet garden like you did!"

That made Melina laugh. She couldn't picture Dr. Stakes lying on the ground, and she certainly hoped he never discovered her garden. But it also provided food for thought. She assumed her teachers had reached their ultimate goals and were no longer striving to be something more. Maybe she was wrong. She thought back to when she shared a bottom stair with Dr. Pearson who talked about having problems. Maybe she wasn't so alone after all.

"So, did you ever get back to Dr. Silverman?"

"Yes, I did. She was in a hurry to get to a meeting, but she sat down with me and listened to my story. When I told her why I couldn't take her exam on Thursday, she thought about it for a minute and then said, 'Melina, let's come up with an alternate assignment for you. Come in to see me when you get back, and we'll create a project that will combine your experience at home with our subject matter. It won't be easy and you'll have a tight deadline, but at least it won't pressure you into taking an exam at the same time your family really needs you. Does that sound reasonable?' I nodded, and she gave me a little hug and hurried off to her meeting. She even knew my name!"

"I'm proud of you, Melina. I know that wasn't easy, but you did it. Now, focus on how to help your father and stick all of this into one of those clouds you just described. Let it go for the next few days. It will be there when you get back. Do you think you can do that?"

Melina nodded and suddenly felt the boulder that had been threatening to crush her for the last several days fall away from her shoulders. Just telling Harry how she handled things made her feel more like she could do this. She had planned and carried it out. Everything didn't go as she hoped, but Melina could begin to let it go for now. She put her head back and took a few deep breaths, just like the yoga instructor had shown her. She was soon fast asleep.

Melina and Papá were just about to walk into his hearing when she felt a gentle tug on her arm... "Melina, we're coming into the city. I need you to give me directions." Emerging from a deep fog and forcing her eyelids open, Melina was embarrassed to realize where she was and that Harry was trying to wake her up. She looked out the window and was comforted by the grittiness and noise surrounding them. This was home, and she realized just how much she missed it.

"Oh, I'm really sorry. Take the 18th Street exit. Our house is just a few blocks from there. I'll show you where to turn."

The sight of the familiar street carts selling elote and fruit by the curbs brought a broad smile to Melina's face. Despite the cold, she rolled down her window to make sure she didn't miss the smells of Juan grilling his well-known chorizo at the corner of 18th and Ridge, or the roasted chiles coming from Lupita's stand.

Harry noticed the abrupt change in Melina and said, "Wish my neighborhood smelled like this one! I'd have all my meals on the sidewalk." Melina straightened a bit as she suddenly felt proud of where she was from. Maybe she should bring Sonia here to show her what it was really like.

A few blocks further, Melina told him to take a left. Her family lived in the small brick bungalow on the right. The postage stamp yard was tidy, and the sidewalk swept clean despite the leaves that were falling everywhere. An American flag was set into the garden by the front door to assure ICE that this was a loyal American family. The garden looked well-kept as always, with its guardian St. Joseph planted squarely in the center. Melina always helped Mamá plant new bushes in the spring after the cold, windy winters took some away. In the fall, together they covered the bushes to protect them. She worried that no one helped Mamá this year.

Harry slowed the car, as the street and sidewalk were filled with children playing soccer and jumping rope. One skateboarder seemed to head straight for the car when he suddenly recognized Melina inside and jumped off, shouting excitedly in Spanish.

"Hey everyone, Melina's here!"

Suddenly, the car was surrounded by children of all sizes jumping up and down, giggling and tapping on the windows. Harry spotted a tear fall down Melina's cheek, and wondered why she seemed stuck to her seat.

"What are we waiting for, Melina? I think there're some people here excited to see you," he said as he jumped out of the car.

Melina brushed away the tear and was quick to follow. She was in the middle of a million hugs from cousins and neighbors when she looked up toward the front door and instantly froze.

"Amá!" A tiny woman with white hair carefully pulled back on her neck was wiping her hands on a brightly colored floral apron. Her smile literally stretched from one ear to the other and through it, a flood of tears stained her face. Melina broke through the sidewalk hugs and raced up the stairs to throw her arms around her. They quickly disappeared inside as they leaned heavily into each other for support.

"Amá, I've missed you so much! How are you doing?"

They sat on the familiar plastic-covered couch in the living room and hugged each other tightly.

"Amá, I'm here now; I'm home. I'm here to help with everything. Where's Papá?"

"Oh, Melina, let's talk about all that later. Right now, let's just celebrate that you're home."

As Melina nodded, two little boys chased each other out from the back room.

"Lina! Lina!" they both shouted as they jumped onto the couch. They had grown so much in the months she had been gone, and oh, how she missed the noisy chaos they brought to this house. Dumping three red trucks in her lap, they dashed away as fast as they had arrived. But where was Papá? Pulling herself together, Melina stood and realized that she had forgotten all about Harry.

Oh, Santo Dios, where was he?

She pulled her mother's frayed, but perfectly ironed, bright yellow curtains aside to look outside, and through the bars she saw Harry bouncing a soccer ball on his head. He was in the middle of a group of boys who were laughing and teasing him. She was so embarrassed. He was her teacher, and her cousins were playing with him! She ran to the door and down the stairs.

"Harry, I'm sorry. I was so excited to see my mother that I forgot! I don't want to keep you any longer. I know you want to get home too. Thanks so much for giving me a ride. My family is really happy I'm here for them."

As the soccer ball came back at him, Harry yelped, "Melina, I haven't had this much fun since I was a kid playing on my street. I'm not a bad player, but your cousins are killin' me. Guess I'm losing my touch. Thanks for giving me the time to have some fun."

Grabbing her suitcase from Harry's battered back seat, Melina turned to walk toward the house while Harry waved goodbye to his new soccer friends. Just then, Melina's mother scolded her from the top step.

"Melina, this nice young man brought you home and you're not going to invite him inside?"

Melina's face stung with shame from Mamá's unpredicted outburst. Of course, Harry didn't want to come inside. He might have fun playing soccer in the street, but her house was small and well, so simple.

She clutched Rosa and started to invent an excuse for him, "He has to…" when Harry threw his huge smile up the stairs toward Mamá and accepted her invitation. Melina rushed up the stairs ahead of him, hoping her nephews wouldn't come back with their trucks, and spoke to her mother in English.

"Mamá, this is Dr. Sanders. He teaches in the Psychology Department, and he gave me a ride home today."

"Señora García, please call me Harry. It's such a pleasure to meet you. I'm so glad I could help by bringing Melina home today. Family is so important, and it's good she's here."

Mamá summoned a friendly, yet dignified, tone, and returned the greeting in careful English.

"Dr. Sanders, are you thirsty? It's a long ride. I made horchata today, with extra cinnamon. It's one of Melina's favorites."

Melina's stomach was in knots as she knew how awful this must be for Harry. She sank onto the couch and looked up at the Virgin for help; she was sure Harry had no idea what horchata was and probably wouldn't like it even if he did take it just to be polite. Before she could speak up, her nephews came crashing around the corner and practically knocked Harry over. Their trucks flew in all directions, and Harry pretended to fall on the floor with them. They giggled and jumped all over him. He was laughing so hard; he could hardly talk.

He managed to say, "I would love some horchata, Señora García. I know Melina won't believe this, but I've had it many times. Vendors are always selling it in the street outside the ballpark, and the more cinnamon the better. My dad and I used to love sharing it when we went to a game. Now, let's take a look at these nifty little trucks." Harry and the boys started tumbling around on the floor, completely ignoring Melina.

As Melina's stomach calmed down and Harry seemed okay, she gave in to the temptation to take in being back home. Everything was untouched from when she left a few months ago. Jesus still commanded the center stage of respect over the couch, and the Virgen de Guadalupe was hung with great care right inside the front door, and by the entry to the kitchen. Ever vigilant, that Virgin! Most of the furniture was covered to keep it clean, but not Papá's brown recliner with the two flowered pillows squished into the corners to fit around his body. It sat in the corner by his small TV, with the pile of Mexican dailies neatly piled beside it. Melina felt safe. Most of all, she let her guard down and allowed herself to smile at the familiar smells from the kitchen that now wafted into the living room.

Oooh, Mamá made pozole! Melina closed her eyes and could already taste it, with its rich broth and red chiles burning the top of her mouth.

Melina heard Mamá's familiar plastic-soled, pink slippers tap across the cracked linoleum floor as she came back into the room.

"Here you go, Dr. Sanders. I hope you like it." She watched for his reaction to her horchata as he sipped and continued.

"We are honored to invite you to eat with us. I cook the pozole since last night. Some of the family, Melina's cousins and aunts and uncles, are going to come over to say hi. I know they would love to meet you."

It was a done deal. When Mamá invited you to dinner, there was no arguing, and there was no need to either; Harry was fine with it. In fact, he was still rolling around on the floor with the boys.

Before Melina knew it, there was standing room only; everyone showed up to welcome her back. Tía Rosa arrived first with her five kids. Tio Federico followed with his brothers and mother, Melina's great-aunt. When her brother, Carlos, arrived from work, one of the boys scrambled right up his leg and tried to stuff the blue truck into his mouth. Carlos twirled him around before reaching for Melina to give her a big hug.

She started to break away but instead of letting her go, Carlos whispered, "Melina, we need to talk. Come back here so I can explain." They quietly left the living room that was now pulsing with the comforting vibes of friendly support and closed the door to the boys' bedroom.

"What's wrong, Carlos?"

"I'm really sorry they dragged you out of school to go to court with Papá. I know how hard that must have been for you, but Papá and I had problems. Roberto too. We talked him into contacting Mr. Salgado who has helped others in the neighborhood, and he will be there tomorrow. But you are the one he trusts, and he is so scared. Tomorrow, Papá will plead guilty to two charges, and Mr. Salgado will ask the judge to schedule a trial date for asylum relief. That is such a long shot for Mexicans, but he will try. The only good news is that the court date won't be for three years, so Papá will have time to get ready and save some more."

"Is there any way Papá can avoid deportation?"

"There is another kind of relief that Roberto and I asked Mr. Salgado about, a U-visa."

"What's that?"

"Remember last year when cousin Diego's jacket was stolen, and he was threatened with a gun?

"Yes. I went over there and tried to talk to him, but he wouldn't listen to anyone."

"That's right. But after you left for the university, Papá had a long visit with Diego. He wouldn't talk to anyone, and he wouldn't leave his room because he was so scared. Papá told Tia Lupita that he would come over and try to help. Diego reluctantly let him into his room where he still had the curtains taped shut and the lights out. Papá got him to name who it was in the Kings that took his jacket and pulled the gun on him. Diego was afraid they would come back and hurt him, but Papá explained how our neighborhood would never be safe if we kept being afraid of the gangs. Diego was ashamed and couldn't look him in the eye, but he was still too scared to do anything himself. He did understand about keeping the neighborhood safe, so he described the gang member and gave his name to Papá. After that, Papá went to the police station and filed a report. From that information, they were able to track him down and charge him with a felony. He's in jail now, but his brother followed Papá home after he testified and knocked him down while threatening to take care of his whole family later."

Melina leaned over and dropped her head to her knees. *How could she let this happen? If she had just been home, maybe Diego would have opened up to her.* She squeezed her arms hard to stop the trembling as she looked up at Carlos, "Is Apá okay? Diego shouldn't have let him do that."

"Papá thinks it was the right thing to do, Melina, but he still has headaches that make it hard for him to work. Mr. Salgado thinks this might qualify Papá for a U-visa, so he will also file for relief with USCIS. I guess it's a tough case to make and requires lots of documents, but it does give us another option. Again, the court date would be three to four years off."

Silence filled the room as they stared at the walls with unspoken fears about what could happen next. There was nothing more to say. Papá was a good man; they just had to prove that he deserved to stay here with his family.

Beyond the bedroom walls, the Virgin continued to welcome a parade of neighbors and relatives through the front door, all of them offering hugs and tears of happiness to have Melina back home. They all knew why she was home, but like Melina and Carlos they buried their fears that night.

Harry stayed throughout the evening, mostly playing hide-and-seek with her nephews, who loved his boundless energy. For his part, Harry was having fun and didn't have a better place to go. With no family left, his old house felt lonely and he avoided going there as much as possible. It belonged to him now but only in name. It was no longer a home. If it hadn't been for Melina, Harry probably would have stayed at school, grading papers and hitting the Antler with his friends. Now he was back in the city, he really should check on it, but he was in no hurry to get there. So, he stayed at Melina's until the last uncle left. He gave Melina's mother a warm hug and thanked her in his rusty Spanish before heading down the stairs with a plastic tubful of pozole to take home. He turned toward Melina and with a quick nod wished her luck as he promised to be back in two days for the return trip to school.

Mamá smiled and sank into the plastic couch, her tiny body tilted toward Melina. It was close to midnight, and she had been on her feet all day long. Her ankles were swollen, but that was so normal she hardly noticed. Melina dragged over a small wooden stool and lifted Mamá's feet to relieve some of the pain. Right after work that morning, she had rushed home to finish getting ready for Melina's welcome-home party.

Melina noticed how tired and frail she looked. Her hands were knotted together, and her head drooped toward them. Now that their English-speaking guest was gone, they slid easily back into chatting in Spanish.

"Mamá, let's sit for a while. I didn't see you dancing or laughing like usual tonight. Are you okay?"

Just then, the tears Mamá had been pushing away all day came pouring out like a tropical storm. Mamá crumbled, shaking, into Melina's arms and Melina held her tightly. "Melina, I'm sorry, but we're so scared about what will happen tomorrow. What if your father gets deported? He's been working any job he can find. He's afraid to come home, and he's also afraid every day when he leaves to look for work. He goes out the back door and comes home through the alley. When he's home, he doesn't talk; he sits in his chair and stares at the TV with the volume off in case someone comes to the door. We don't know what's going to happen, but we need you. Thank you for coming home."

School seemed so far away, and those exams…who cared? Mamá and Papá, her whole family, were more important to her. Melina pulled her mother close and wrapped her arms around her tightly, trying to take on some of the pain. That's when she allowed her own eyes to close and give in to total exhaustion. They slumped together as one, Mamá and Melina. Sleep crept in like a cloud, to protect them from their fears about what the next day might bring.

In what felt like only an instant later, bright light poked at her eyes, trying to pry them open. In the distance, Melina heard the familiar sounds of tortillas sizzling, and her nostrils filled with the smell of strong cinnamon-flavored coffee. Sunlight streamed through the yellow curtains, and she realized it must be morning. Where was she? As she shook herself from a very sound sleep, she felt the dull, but real, aches acquired from spending the night on the couch spread out across her body. As her eyes began to focus, she saw Mamá in the kitchen, getting breakfast ready. She didn't tap her feet to music on the radio, as usual. In fact, while standing guard over the stove, Mamá ran her fingers over her rosary and sometimes moved her lips in prayer.

Oh yes. Today was THAT day. Where was Papá?

"Amá, let me help you. Where is Papá? What time do you leave for work?"

"I won't go to work today, mija. I'll go to court with you and Papá and Mr. Salgado, but I won't say anything. I'll just sit there. He'll come home from work in a few minutes. We'll have breakfast and catch the bus by 9:00."

Just then, Melina heard the back door creaking slowly, and Papá walked in, eyes half-closed, dragging his tired feet after working two different jobs without any sleep. Melina ran to him and drew him into her entire being as if to say, *I will keep you safe. You can count on me.*

She didn't want to let go, but she could see he needed to sit down. He collapsed into the pillows lining the recliner while Mamá brought over his familiar chipped red mug from Mexico, filled with strong, fresh coffee. Melina smiled as she remembered how special that mug had always been to him; his mother had given it to him when he left Puebla.

With a deep sigh, her father rested the mug on the little table next to him, rubbed his forehead and closed his eyes. His lips moved as he fingered the rosary around his neck. Just when Melina thought he might fall asleep, he opened his eyes and looked toward her. "*Mija*, we need to meet Mr. Salgado in front of the courthouse at 10:00. I have some personal papers, and he will bring any legal papers we might need. He will present my case, but maybe they need more details from you, mi hija. There might not be a translator at the hearing today, so I want you to tell me what is going on while Mr. Salgado is arguing. This is important to me, okay?"

"Of course, Apá. That's why I'm here."

Twenty minutes later, leaving the boys under Josie's watchful eyes, Melina and her parents hustled down the steps, past the American flag planted by their front door. There was no wind today, so it dangled limply from its pole. They kept close to one another as they made their way to the bus stop, nodding to neighbors who were just coming home from the late shift. No one spoke, but the silence acted like a steel cord connecting them and daring anyone to separate them.

Two buses later, they saw Mr. Salgado waiting for them on the front steps of the courthouse. Papá nodded, and they followed him inside through the metal detector where they emptied their pockets as if they could unload their fears. Sensing Papá's fear, the guards called him to the side for an extra pat down causing him to drop all his papers. Melina tried to help, but she was told to stand back by Mamá who was shivering with fear.

Mr. Salgado signed in and led them to three rickety wooden chairs lining the corridor outside the hearing room assigned to removal proceedings. They joined at least 100 others waiting to be called while Mr. Salgado assured them he would come back when it was their turn. Melina could feel the fear up and down the otherwise dark, deserted hallway as families fidgeted with documents they brought with them or twisted their rosaries. Some of them held stacks of paper nearly a foot high, while others held slim envelopes. Papers occasionally slipped to the floor, and someone scrambled to put them back in order on their lap. At the end of the day, some of these families would be smiling while others would be in tears. Finally, Mr. Salgado came into the hallway with the judge's clerk and called out Papá's name, "Carlos García!" Hearing it in this context sent a chill up Melina's spine. She and Papá quietly got up and held on to each other as they followed them into the hearing room. Mamá stayed in her chair, silently moving her lips and working her rosary like never before.

Melina felt the weight of Papá's body against hers as they entered the tiny courtroom. "Apa, it's going to be okay." She tried to support Papá as they started to follow Mr. Salgado to the front desk, but the clerk stopped her.

"Sorry, miss, but you must stay back here. The front is reserved for lawyers and their clients."

"But he's my father, and he needs me." Papá struggled to move forward with Mr. Salgado as the clerk steered Melina to the back of the room with other families. She didn't know who would cry first.

What was that contraption? What was happening to Papá? As Melina strained forward to figure out what was happening up front, she felt a gentle pat on her knee.

"They're just putting headphones on him, so he can hear a translation of what's going on."

"But they're so big! Do they hurt?"

The white-haired woman next to her smiled and shook her head as Melina continued to worry about Papá. He seemed to shrink under their weight.

"Mr. Salgado, your client has been called to this removal hearing to answer to two charges. Is he prepared to plead?"

"Yes, your honor. Mr. Garcia pleads guilty to the two charges presented today. He admits that he illegally entered this country 30 years ago, and he also admits that he has been working illegally."

Melina leaned forward and whispered to the equally frightened faces around her. "My father is a hard worker, sir, and hasn't had time to study English. His job doesn't require it, so his family helps him out. He is a good citizen and responsible father. He has been here for 30 years, never missed a day of work, and committed no crimes."

No one in the back row paid any attention to her. They were all practicing their own scripts.

"Mr. Salgado, is your client seeking any relief?"

"Yes, sir. We request a trial date for an asylum hearing."

"Trial set for April 24, 2025. You will file your application in the next two months before April 24, 2021. Dismissed. Next."

With his chin buried in his chest, Papá came back up the aisle toward Melina. He was trying his best to be invisible. If he didn't look up, maybe no one would see him. Maybe they would forget that he just pleaded guilty to two charges. Charges that could lead to his removal from his family and home. He was scared and ashamed.

As they made their way back down the hallway to Mamá, Mr. Salgado leaned in and said, "Mr. García, we'll meet next week to start the application for your asylum relief. Once that is done, I'll begin the U-visa application. We need to collect a lot of paperwork, and I'll be asking your family for help. For now, you should stay home. If anyone comes to your house, you don't have to talk to them unless they have a warrant. Do you understand?"

A uniformed guard escorted them out, and that was it. No answers. No employment. Just more shame. More fear and sleepless nights!

For several hours after Papá's hearing, their home resounded with silence, but food filled the hushed space as Mamá fired up the tiny grill in the kitchen and made tortillas. Papá sat silently in his chair, his face staring blankly at the quiet TV, where an old soccer game was being replayed. They sat down together to share tortillas and roasted chiles, but no one spoke. When they finished, Papá gathered his things and headed out the back door to look for work, any kind of work. He still hadn't slept, but that didn't matter. He probably couldn't sleep anyway.

Before leaving, he looked at Melina with his sad, tear-filled eyes and said, "Thank you mija. I'm sorry." Then he hugged her with all the strength he could muster and made his way out past the Virgin's protective eyes. Melina could tell he felt ashamed and scared. She wanted to run after him and tell him to be careful, that it would be okay; she would always be there for him. But she didn't. All she could do was cry.

The next morning was like the old days, but without school. With both Mamá and Papá at work, Melina took care of the boys. She conjured up one of those clouds that Harry had suggested, and carefully tucked yesterday's hearing and the asylum trial into their billowy folds. They remained hidden as long as she rolled around on the floor with Berto and Hugo. They squealed with laughter as they played hide-and-seek, and she laughed right along with them. It all felt so natural. Just as she was about to heat up their lunch, there was a light tapping on the front door. Berto scrambled over the toys as he tried to beat Hugo to see who it was.

"Shh, boys," Melina cautioned. They were too little to understand that no one opened that door unless they knew who was on the other side. She lifted them both so they could all look through the peephole that Papá had installed. Melina was stunned to see a familiar face, and she opened the door.

"Ms. Ingram! Please, come in."

"Melina! Gabriela told me you were home, and I wanted to stop by and say hi. I hope that's all right."

"Of course it is," said Melina, as she wrangled the kids and kicked some of the toys to the side. "I came home to be with Papá in court yesterday, and I need to get back to school tomorrow." Ms. Ingram had never been to her house, but Melina was so happy to see a friendly face that she forgot to worry about the mess all over the floor.

"Yes…I can't stay long; this is my lunch break, but I wanted to ask about your father and also hear about your experiences at Balsam."

The boys loved having a new playmate, so they put all their trucks in Ms. Ingram's lap as she and Melina sat down.

"Berto and Hugo, go wash up for lunch while we talk, please." They raced each other down the hallway as Melina carefully sifted through her experiences before deciding which ones to share.

"Well, we went to court yesterday, and Papá pleaded guilty to two charges and his lawyer asked for what's called asylum relief. The judge scheduled a trial date to hear his case in four years! Four years! Mr. Salgado, Papá's lawyer, is also applying for a U-visa. We have lots of papers to pull together and don't know what will happen next. We're scared. My parents are working so many hours, to make sure there's enough money if he is deported. I came home this week to help them, and I feel like I should stay, in case anything happens. They need me here, but I should also be at school. I just missed my exams, and I'm afraid I'll be in trouble when I go back. I'm really confused right now."

She hadn't meant to share all of this and immediately wanted to swallow her words and pretend they never came out. Could she trust Ms. Ingram? Did she have to report conversations like this one? Papá was supposed to be home, not out looking for work. Melina kept her head down, afraid to look up.

"Melina, you did the right thing to come back. Your family needed you, and you were there for them. I can also see how much you enjoy being with your nephews, and in your home." Leaning over to give Melina a hug, Ms. Ingram continued, "I will pray for your family and do whatever I can to help. And, Melina, you can trust me. Now, tell me about Balsam."

Melina took a deep breath and shared details with Ms. Ingram that she hadn't told anyone else: how hard it was to make friends, how she couldn't be honest with her roommate, how embarrassed she was that she couldn't afford to go out to eat or fix up her side of the dorm room.

She didn't even have a bookbag like everyone else on campus. How out of place she felt all the time.

Ms. Ingram's shoulders slumped.

"I should have prepared you better than I did, Melina. The first year in college is a tough time for everyone. You're away from home, living with people from different backgrounds, and it takes time. My first roommate in college was horrible! We didn't get along at all. She had parties in our room all the time, and she smoked, even when I asked her not to. I finally moved out, but it wasn't easy because she was pretty popular and no one understood my side."

"Eww!" cried Melina. "Mine isn't like that. She's never in the room. She and her friends spend every night in town at the Antler or studying in someone's room, where they sneak in beer and smoke pot. They always invite me, but I don't think they mean it and I really don't want to go."

Just as Ms. Ingram started to respond, Melina looked up and started to giggle. Sure enough, Berto had flown his paper airplane toward the couch, and somehow it had landed in all its sparkly red glory on top of Ms. Ingram's head. Everyone ended up in a heap on the couch, the boys screaming and the two women holding their sides from genuine laughter.

Five minutes later, Ms. Ingram stood to leave, after a promise from Melina that she would open up to her roommate and start writing in her journal so that all these thoughts didn't get buried too deep. Melina thanked her for coming and thought once again that things might be okay.

That was yesterday. Today, she was headed back to school to face the consequences. It was time to chase down that cloud where she had stashed her worries and face them in real time. It helped a little that she found a new blue bookbag on the front stoop under a note that read, *Hang in there, Melina!*

12
Margot

If Margot expected Biko to come skittering to the door when she turned the key and jiggled the lock open, she was sadly mistaken. He was peacefully buried deep down in the pile of clothes she had left on the floor two days ago. As she plopped her suitcase on the bed to unpack, he arched his back and stretched out his front paws. This was as grand a welcome as she could expect, and it was sweet. After a brief snuggle, they headed to the kitchen together where she refilled his bowls with some more favorites and then turned her attention to the reason she had come back early—Melina.

Margot wasn't entirely sure about the protocol surrounding a missed exam. She knew it needed to be reported to the Dean of Students. *Was it a violation of the Student Code of Conduct? Would it require a hearing or was it simply a matter of counseling the student?* She had not read the multiple files of electronic documents Shirley sent her when she accepted this position, so she didn't know anything about student rules and regulations but she needed to find out. First, she wanted to read the note that Melina left for her. *Maybe she should also contact her and find out why she had left for home early? What could be so important that it couldn't wait a few days?* She didn't understand why a first-year student would go home and miss an important exam unless she was planning to leave school anyway. It was all a mystery to Margot, so she left her suitcase on the bed and threw on some comfortable clothes as she headed out the door toward her office to figure it out.

The first thing she noticed when she unlocked the office door was the red light blinking on her university phone.

Oh good. Melina must have called and left a message explaining what happened. Maybe there was a good reason for missing the exam. If someone in her family died, she probably wouldn't need to report this to the Dean.

Margot rushed around her desk, careful not to knock over the teeming piles of exams and list of student grades to get to her phone. The message was from the Dean's Office and Margot was disturbed to hear the words coming through the receiver:

> *Dr. Pearson, we're following up on all first-year students who missed more than two exams. It's been reported that one of your students, Melina García, missed several of hers. We need to know if she missed yours. Under our new, early intervention procedures, if she did, she will need to meet with a counselor this week to explain what happened so we can review options with her on how to successfully complete the term. If you excused her, this will not be necessary. We will need to hear from you by 9:00 Monday morning. Please leave a message at this number. Thank you.*

Margot hung up and sat back to consider what she should do. She wanted to talk to Melina before returning this call, but Heidi didn't leave any contact information for her. Margot had no idea how to reach her. She reached for the note from Melina and scanned it again looking for clues. If only Melina had given a reason, that would make it easier for Margot to excuse her and let it go. But Melina had done nothing to help her out—no reason for leaving, and no phone number. After their brief time together on the staircase last week, Margot felt an unspoken bond, but she needed more than that to flout university policy, especially as a new faculty member.

It occurred to her that maybe Shirley was in the office today even though it was the weekend. Since Melina worked for the department, Shirley would certainly know how to reach her. Margot locked up the office and went upstairs to check. The office was open, but Shirley wasn't there. On the counter, however, was a list of all staff, including student workers. Margot skimmed it until she found Melina's information; there was no phone number, but she found out that she lived on campus, in Forbes Hall.

Not sure where Forbes was located, Margot realized she had never bothered to explore the campus beyond the faculty-frequented areas: classrooms, conference rooms, research labs, the auditorium. She stepped out into the sunlight and searched for a sign, a map, a campus directory. With an unexpected sense of accomplishment, she easily found Forbes on the map and headed toward the other side of campus to try and find Melina. It was a beautiful day, and Margot was thankful she had returned early. The campus was quiet and seemed so idyllic, especially with a light chill in the air and the leaves beginning to carpet the ground.

As she entered Forbes, she barely noticed the woman balanced on a ladder, holding a blue plastic bottle, and stretching to reach the top of the glass on the front doors. Margot tried to scoot around the cleaning project but felt the dampness from the Windex spray in her direction as it caught the gust of wind from the door. She ignored it and went in search of a directory listing the students and their room numbers. Finding nothing, she returned to the front door.

"Excuse me," she said to the woman washing the windows. "I'm looking for a student, Melina García, who lives here. Do you know where I can find her?"

"Ah, yes, I know Melina. She went home to help her father a few days ago. She has not come back."

"Do you know what happened to her father?" asked Margot. "I'm one of her professors, and she missed my exam last week. I need to talk to her."

The woman gingerly stepped down a few rungs and answered, "I don't know, but I think maybe it's serious. Melina left in a hurry."

"Thank you. If you see her, please tell her that Dr. Pearson needs to talk to her as soon as possible?" Margot quickly pulled a card from her pocket with her office number on it and handed it to the cleaning woman.

"Yes, Doctor, I let her know."

With that brief exchange and no clear direction to take, Margot left Forbes. Instead of heading back to the office, she veered off toward Crystal's. Maybe if she sat in her familiar corner with some comfort food, she could puzzle out what to do. As she ordered her usual, she felt someone come up behind her.

An unfamiliar voice asked, "Dr. Pearson? I'm Jack Stakes, and I'd like to talk to you, if you don't mind my interruption."

Puzzled and irritated by the unexpected disruption of her time alone, Margot had no choice but to invite him to sit down.

"Jack, I don't believe we've met. Have we?"

"No, we haven't, but we do have something in common. We both have a student, Melina García, who decided her family was more important than our exams. She came to see me last week to tell me she had to go home because her family needed her. I told her that wasn't possible and that I expected to see her for my exam the next day.

Still, she didn't show up. I reported her to the Dean of Students, and I checked to see what other exams she may have missed. Yours was one of them. Did she come to you also?"

"Actually, I left a little early, but she wrote me a note. But I did receive a message from the Dean's Office, asking me to confirm that she missed my exam. I tried to find her today, but she hasn't returned yet. Do you have any idea what was so important?"

"No, and it's not my concern. She's a university student, and Ms. García and her family need to understand that her work here comes first. I didn't excuse her from the exam. Did you? This place is getting too soft. Instead of seeing a counselor for advising, students like her need to pay a price for not taking our work seriously. I'm here to ask you to join me by going to the Dean and requesting a penalty that she will remember."

Margot felt stuck. On the one hand, here she was, a first-year faculty member who should probably not argue about something she really didn't understand. Also, who was she to question a curmudgeonly, but probably tenured, senior faculty member? She was inclined to agree that Melina should have taken her exams and waited to go home, but she remembered sharing that moment on the staircase and felt an inexplicable connection with her. As she twirled her hair, deep in thought, she could sense Jack Stakes staring at her. She also felt his impatience, and an arrogance that bordered on an extreme dislike for anyone who disagreed with him.

"Dr. Pearson, there really is nothing to think about. This student has unexcused absences from at least two exams, maybe more. If she missed yours and you didn't excuse her, she needs explain herself. We can schedule a meeting with the Dean and Ms. García to decide how to proceed. She will need to present us with a written statement and a promise that it won't happen again. Maybe this will scare her enough that she will start taking the university and our classes seriously. She's not the only one, but she's the one who had the temerity to interrupt me and then not listen to what I said. Do I have your confirmation that you will join me in this meeting?"

Lost in a tangle of emotions, Margot could not summon a rational reason to turn him down, so she simply replied, "I'll be there. Just let me know when and where."

Barely satisfied, Jack Stakes rolled his eyes as he abruptly stood to take his leave. With a deep sigh and shake of his head, he once again excused himself from interrupting her. No further conversation was needed, so with a pompous stride he returned directly to his table across the usually cheerful room where he sat alone, buried behind a stack of books. He looked neither right nor left but kept his eyes focused on his books, oblivious to everyone else.

Margot watched him for a few minutes and wondered how many people saw the world as he did, with his rigid certitude, and such stark terms. She thought that it certainly would make things easier if there were a right or wrong answer for everything and realized that probably, too often, she also behaved according to some kind of one-size-fits-all policy book and followed formal procedures to a T. It worked in the past, so why did this time feel different?

No longer hungry, Margot pushed back from the table, canceled her order and left the café. Having no specific plan other than getting away from Jack Stakes, she decided to head back to the office.

Maybe Melina's left a message by now. Oh, how much easier it would be if someone had died in her family! She was still looking for a concrete hook on which she could hang her thoughts and examine them in a rational way. Margot was mad at herself for giving in so readily to Jack Stakes, and for not asking more questions. *She probably did the right thing by confirming that Melina had missed her exam without* being excused, but what if she was wrong? What if Melina had a good reason for going home, and all Margot needed to do was excuse her? Margot herself had been such a different kind of student. She never would have missed an exam for her family, and her family never would have asked her to. It was challenging to put herself in Melina's shoes, yet...

By the time she reached Anderson Hall, Margot was convinced she had done the right thing. She didn't have to like Jack Stakes' abrupt demeanor or rude demand, but she did need to listen to a senior professor who might be in a position to decide her fate in the future. She felt a bit calmer until she realized she was about to step onto the bottom stair of her basement hallway, the very spot where she and Melina had experienced that brief but meaningful connection a week ago. She couldn't put it into words, and she felt odd thinking she could figure it out simply by sitting there, but just in case she took a seat on the cold, hard step.

Margot sat in total silence for a few minutes, until she noticed a bright light coming from her office. Surely, she couldn't have forgotten to lock it, not with all those exams inside! She abruptly stood up, while admonishing herself not to keep getting lost in her thoughts.

As she came closer, she was unnerved to see that someone was clearly inside. Perplexed by this unexpected interruption of the quiet time that she was desperately seeking, Margot quickly pushed open the door. *Oh no, Harry was back early!* So much for puzzling out her dilemma alone.

"Hey there, Margot. How was your break?" Harry asked, without his usual welcoming grin. He seemed to be in some kind of funk, which was unusual for him.

"It was okay. I went to spend some time with my parents, so I can't say it was fun. But it was good to get away for a few days."

Margot intentionally didn't ask Harry about his break. She didn't want to prolong the conversation, but Harry was in a mood to talk.

"Margot, did you find a note on your desk when you came in today? A note from one of your students, Melina?"

His question got her attention. Harry got along so well with the students; maybe he could be helpful in this instance, and he did seem to know about Melina's absence.

"Yes, there was a note. She didn't give an excuse, just said she had to go home for her family. That really isn't enough for me to formally excuse her, but I hope she's okay. Do you know what was so serious at home?"

"Yes. I took Melina home myself and urged her to leave you a note. She tried to find you, but I think you left early. Melina really wanted to talk to you in person, but I have to tell you…she was pretty afraid of what you might say."

"Well. I'm sorry to hear she's afraid of me. I tried to find her today so I could understand what was going on, but she wasn't in her dorm. Some of the faculty, one in particular, are pretty upset that she missed exams. Jack Stakes is scheduling a meeting where she'll be asked to explain why she left. He's requested that I attend, to confirm that she missed my exam."

The more she talked, the more Margot could see Harry's face redden, and his entire body turn to a state of agitation. She'd never seen him like this. Margot had clearly triggered something as he pounded his desk, sending papers flying all over the room. He stood up with such force she was afraid he might explode.

Harry literally bellowed, "Margot, I took Melina home because her family really needed her. It was something that couldn't wait. We exist because of the students, yet we never put them first! Melina had a responsibility to her family—who doesn't know at all how a university works. Her parents didn't go to college! They're so proud of her, but to them, family will always come first."

Harry took a deep breath and sat down.

"Hey, I'm sorry, Margot, but this has become personal for me. I lost my family a few years ago, so I understand Melina, and I want to help her. I am also sick and tired of the traditional faculty here like Jack Stakes who see punishment as a more effective strategy than intervening when a student needs help."

Stunned by Harry's outburst, along with his personal confession, Margot was speechless. Her mind went back to her own family visit this weekend, and she recalled that no one was even home when she arrived. *How can families be so different?*

She gathered her thoughts and reminded herself to ask Harry about his own family later. For now, all she could muster was, "Harry, please tell me what was so important. If I just knew, I could think about formally excusing Melina. But with no idea, I can't really go up against Jack Stakes."

"It's not my story to tell, Margot. All I can say is that it was exceedingly difficult for her, and in the end, she really had no choice."

Surprising herself, Margot responded, "Harry, what should I do? How does this work? Is there a chance that Melina might be asked to leave school?"

Harry's anger returned.

"With Jack Stakes in the mix, anything can happen. He is an angry man with no empathy for students. His work is his life, and he expects the same from his students. When his wife was alive, he showed a little more empathy but when she died, he threw himself into his work and cut himself off from all personal relationships. He also has a son who has been in a state institution for most of his life. On most weekends, Jack visits him and always comes back grumpier and more difficult to deal with. I pity students who take any of his courses on a Monday morning. There's a part of me that feels sorry for him. He's had a rough time, but I can't rationalize how he treats our students. Trouble is, he's a senior, tenured professor who brings in lots of money to this university. He will be here until the day he dies. No one likes him, but everyone is afraid of him, so they just leave him alone to frighten our students."

"That's quite a story, Harry. How do you know so much about him?"

"Everyone at Balsam knows about Dr. Stakes. He took a sabbatical to care for his wife when she was too sick to keep working. There was a memorial service in the chapel when she died. She was well liked here, and we always hoped she would soften him up."

"I can see that didn't work. Keep going. What will happen at this meeting?"

"At this meeting, Melina will be asked to explain why she missed her exams, and Stakes will probably want some written proof for her excuse. Her other professors may also be asked to offer their thoughts on Melina's overall attitude and performance, and to share their perspectives. After that, Melina may be put on a temporary leave where she cannot attend classes or access university services. She will also give up her job in the department."

"I don't see how putting a student on leave helps this kind of situation."

"It's an antiquated process that marginalizes students and makes them feel ashamed. She needs the job to pay her university bills, and she needs support to figure out how to succeed here at Balsam, without giving up her family responsibilities. Last year when I chaired the Adjunct Council, we wrote a proposal that would require counseling for any student during the first term who missed any major markers, like poor attendance, missing assignments, and important exams. It was accepted by the Dean's Office but not by some of the more traditional faculty who insist that early, supportive intervention is too soft. Jack Stakes led that group, and this is his way of showing us that our proposals don't matter."

Margot nervously twirled her hair, and she felt a dull throb starting at the back of her head. To think that she was contributing to this process disturbed her.

"Is there anything I can do to help Melina?"

"Why don't you go back over to her dorm and try to find her? I'm sure she'll tell her story, although it might be difficult for her. Once you understand, maybe you can coach her on what to say at the meeting and talk to the other faculty who might attend due to Stakes' bullying."

Harry's words swirled around in Margot's throbbing head, as he stepped out to grab lunch. She closed her eyes and tried to untangle her thoughts. She had never taken Harry seriously; after all, he was an adjunct who would only be here for a few months until Miriam returned. He never seemed profoundly serious, always hanging out with students. His impact on her now was surprising. *Why was this so different? She'd never been the kind of student to miss an exam for any reason. But she'd also never been the kind to sit on a staircase and fold into herself with sadness. Who was Melina? What was it about her family that had torn her apart so much?* In the end, Margot decided that she had to try and find out.

Margot rose from her chair with such a flurry that her neatly piled exams flew across the room. She hesitated, and almost stopped to tidy everything, but no; there wasn't time for that now. Walking with a blind intensity across campus, Margot was oblivious to her surroundings and stumbled over a small garbage can that a group of students was using as a goal for some game they were playing. The can inflicted minor damage on her knee and elbow, but she didn't have time for that either, or for the giggling she heard from the group of quad athletes.

She reached Forbes quickly, but she realized she still had no idea how to find Melina.

This dorm was a mini high-rise, and there was no directory. She wondered who created such unfriendly, sterile environments for students and vowed to get on some faculty committee that might do something about it. As she wandered around the lobby area, she heard voices, and possibly crying, coming from the end of the hall. Seeing no one else in the lobby, Margot headed in that direction. She would just peek in to see if anyone could help her.

What Margot saw surprised her. A young person, a student, she thought, sat there, next to the small woman who had earlier been cleaning the front door. The student's head was buried in her hands and was concealed behind a screen of long, dark hair. She was crying. Margot cautiously knocked on the open door.

"Hi...Remember me? I'm sorry to bother you, but I was here earlier looking for a student who lives here. Her name is Melina García. I don't know where to find her."

With that, the student raised her head, and Margot saw that it was Melina. The older woman stood and walked over to Margot.

"I remember you. Dr. Pearson, right? I am María. Melina is right here."

"Melina, I'm so sorry to intrude, but I found your note and want to hear why it was so important for you to go home. Should I come back? We really need to talk tonight or tomorrow, but it doesn't have to be now."

Melina desperately tried to stop crying; she shook and gulped air in an effort to pull herself together. María offered her some Kleenex and spoke to her, kindly and softly, in Spanish.

With her hand partially covering her mouth, Melina said, "Thank you for finding me, Dr. Pearson. I feel really bad, and I would like to explain what happened in my family. I had to go home. I had no choice, but I know I'm in trouble here."

María motioned Margot to the small couch, indicated that she should sit down, and then quietly left, giving Melina the space she needed to tell her story.

An hour later, it was Margot's turn to brush back tears. She told Melina about the meeting in the Dean's Office and assured her that they would go together. She wanted to sound as though it were no big deal, but since she wasn't sure herself, she may not have been too convincing. She hugged Melina and thanked María before rushing across the lobby toward the front door.

As she left Forbes, Margot was at first surprised by how dark it was; was it really that late? Luckily, a full moon lit up the sidewalk. She now knew what she must do, and all she wanted to do was go home and confide in Biko before making the phone call.

13
Melina

The silence of the house still blanketed Melina as she slid into the car beside Harry. Mamá waved to him from the front step and blew him a kiss for taking care of her daughter. Harry once again sent a huge smile floating up the stairs toward her as he pulled away from the curb. It was a gray morning, and the street wasn't filled with the joyful chaos of children like it had been when they arrived. No. There was a silence, a deathly silence, that was wrapped in fear and anxiety. Doors were closed up and down the street, but the common element was that nearly every house had hung out their American flag to prominently display the loyalty and trustworthiness of the families inside.

The comfort of yesterday's interlude with Ms. Ingram had also disappeared, and Melina felt sick to her stomach. She wrapped her arms around herself tightly to stop from shaking. She kept replaying the courtroom scene with Papá and was overwhelmed with fear and anger. *He had always tried to do the right thing. He was a responsible man working overtime to take care of his family. What they were doing to him just didn't make sense. He had tried to get his papers a long time ago and was denied due to legal issues he didn't understand. He figured that if he kept out of trouble and had a job, everything would work out. And what had she done to help? Nothing! She just sat in the back row when they dismissed him and criticized his lack of English. Why didn't she do more? Did Mr. Salgado do enough? Could she have helped him? And setting a date four years away for another hearing? How does a family prepare for that? Would Papá ever be the same?*

She closed her eyes but couldn't sleep. There were too many thoughts in her head, all competing for attention. Melina knew the feelings she'd kept folded up in the clouds for the last few days needed to be released. What could she do? She could probably talk to Harry, but she was afraid to hear what he might say. She stole a peek at him as he steered them away from her family and back to school. He quietly hummed along with the music on the radio, and she understood that he was respecting her need for silence. But…she needed his help.

"Dr. Sanders, I mean, Harry, what happens now? I think I'm in big trouble."

Harry turned off the radio and glanced in Melina's direction. He had been preparing for this moment.

"Let's take it step-by-step, Melina. The first thing you need to do is go back to your professors and let them know you've returned. Tell them you want to make up your exams as soon as possible. Hopefully, that will be the end of it. You'll take the exams and start going to classes just like before. There's also another possibility; you may be asked to meet with a counselor who will be assigned to support you. The Counseling Center is a place where you can feel safe to ask questions and tell your story. You can let them know about your family, and trust that everything you tell them is confidential. They will advise you about student policies and point you toward university resources that no one else has probably told you about."

"Does a counselor cost money? Will they take away my scholarship and job? Does everyone have to know?" asked Melina.

"Melina, it's not a punishment. A counselor is there to help you, and it doesn't cost anything. You don't need to tell anyone if you don't want to."

Melina sank even further down in the front seat to think about what Harry just said. She would find her teachers first thing in the morning and ask about taking the missed exams. *She knew Dr. Gregory and Dr. Silverman would be okay, but what about Dr. Stakes and Dr. Pearson? Dr. Stakes had been so mean, and she never even saw Dr. Pearson. Suppose they were angry with her and didn't understand about her responsibility to her family? What if they wouldn't let her make up their exams? In high school, seeing a counselor meant a student was in trouble; the next step was suspension. Everyone laughed and gossiped when someone had to see a counselor, and she was sure the counselors talked to each other about the kids they saw.* Now she had a headache and her stomach hurt. She closed her eyes and tried her best to hold onto the tears that threatened to overflow.

Melina remained like that for the rest of the ride back to school. She knew she should thank Harry for explaining things to her, but she was too afraid to talk. If she opened her mouth, she knew she would start to cry. Harry returned to his rock 'n' roll radio station and left Melina to meander through her own private world of anxieties and confusion as her head pounded.

After what seemed like several hours, but was less than three, they pulled up in front of Forbes Hall. Melina took her time getting out of the car as she struggled to stop her legs from giving out beneath her. They barely supported her as she reached around the back of her seat for Rosa and her new bookbag. With her stomach rumbling and her head pounding, she barely managed to thank Harry for his kindness. She tried to sling the new bookbag over her shoulder the way the other students did and headed toward the large glass doors that ominously beckoned to her. Melina knew she would never really fit into that world even with a blue bookbag. How different it was from her real home, where Mamá waited on the top step to offer her a warm hug. She watched Harry drive away and considered fleeing in the other direction, toward the bus station. *Wouldn't it be easier to just sneak on a bus with Rosa and head back home? Her family needed her, and this dream of hers, to go to college, wasn't what she thought it would be.* Indeed, it was becoming complicated with as many confusing parts to navigate as Papá's enduring struggles with the immigration authorities.

Melina dragged herself through a dizzying fog, toward Forbes, unsure of what her next steps should be. *What if Theresa had come back early?* Even though Melina had promised Ms. Ingram she would talk to her, it seemed way too difficult right now. As she became more and more depressed, she saw someone waving wildly waving at her through the glass door. María! Melina almost screamed out loud with relief. María would understand. She found a renewed strength in her wobbly legs.

Once inside, María's hug warmed Melina and reminded her of Mamá's.

"Oh, I'm so happy to see you, Melina! I was worried when you didn't come back! Are you okay? How's your family?"

As soon as Melina heard the word *family*, she could no longer hold onto her mask. Wet tears gushed down her face washing away the mask and soaking into her scarf, while her whole body shook, as if lightning had struck.

María steadied her and said, "Come with me, Melina. I have something that will make you feel better. Let's sit and talk, okay?"

"Thanks, María," sniffled Melina. "I'd like that very much."

Together, with their arms around each other, they headed down the hallway and into María's room.

"Sit here, Melina. I'm going to make us some herbal tea and cinnamon eggs."

After lighting a little yellow candle that smelled like lilies, María disappeared into the kitchen to prepare her antidotes to Melina's sadness. Surrounded by some of the comforts of home, Melina started to feel as if there was hope. She felt comforted by the Virgen de Guadalupe; in fact, there were several here who kept watch over them, just like at home. The familiar plastic coverings, flowers, the smell of cinnamon cooking in the kitchen, even the yellow candle was the same one Mamá lit when she was feeling stressed. The pounding in Melina's head lessened a bit, and her stomach began to settle down.

"Here we are! I hope this will make you feel better." María popped back into the room carrying a colorful plastic tray filled with tea and cinnamon-covered eggs, surrounded by sprigs of mint. These were familiar remedies to Melina, and she smiled for the first time since returning home a few days ago.

María sat beside her and once again asked about her family. This time, Melina was ready to talk. She shared everything from the past two days and felt her burden lessen because she was describing it to someone who understood. María gently prodded her along as she laid out the pieces and helped her fill in details when she occasionally faltered.

María waited until she was sure Melina was done. She then took a deep breath.

"Melina, I'm so sorry to hear all this. I'm going to share with you something that I never talk about. When my daughter, Dulce, was enrolled here at Balsam, we had the exact same problem, believe it or not. My husband, her dad—he also didn't have his green card and he was summoned to court for a removal proceeding. My English wasn't too good, and Dulce came home to support him at his hearing, just like you did. We did not have a lawyer like Mr. Salgado, so she pulled together all the documents she could find. She missed so many classes.

When she came back to school, she had to meet with faculty here and work hard to prove herself and get back on track. I didn't work here then. Anyway, my husband got deported back to Mexico, and we haven't seen him since. Somehow, Dulce got it into her head that it was her fault her father was deported, as if she could have done anything more, or differently. She's still too sad to talk about it."

Melina felt her tears start up again as she listened to María. "I'm so sorry about your husband, María. Do you know where he is?"

"He's back in Reynosa with his mother and six brothers. He has a good job and sends money to us when he can, but we miss him. He's a big help to his mother. It's okay. It is what it is. We know he is safe, and we don't have to worry any more about someone coming to our house in the middle of the night."

"Why do you and Dulce stay here? Don't you want to be with him in Mexico?" asked Melina.

"Well, Dulce graduated from the university and has a good job in the city. She was born here; she's a citizen, you know. Me, I can't leave her here alone; she is my daughter. This is where our life is. And the university hired me after what happened to her."

"What happened when Dulce returned and talked to the faculty? Did they understand?"

"Not really, no. They didn't understand; they told her she missed too many classes. She lost her scholarship and came home."

"But I thought she graduated. What happened?"

"Well, there was one person who helped us, a nice professor. She helped Dulce write a letter of appeal, so she was able to get another scholarship and come back the next year. She also helped me get this job. With my job, plus a part-time one here for Dulce, we were able to pay for school and she graduated in six years. We got special permission to live in this room together. She didn't have many friends, but she studied hard. Now she has a good job, and she visits with me sometimes on the weekend."

Melina's body sank deeper into María's couch. She tipped her head back and took a few deep breaths. As she drew in the air, it hit her again that she may be facing some serious trouble. She didn't regret her decision, but she worried that Mamá and Papá would blame themselves if she came home for good. She would also be another burden for them. "What will happen to me now? My teachers don't understand why I left, and they'll ask me to leave the university, right? If I get sent home, I don't think I'll be able to come back. I won't be lucky like Dulce because I don't have a teacher here who cares about me. Dr. Sanders is a nice person, but he's not one of my teachers. Maybe he can help, but I'm not sure I can ask him."

"Melina, sometimes people surprise you. You never know. Do you know Dr. Pearson? She was here tonight looking for you. Isn't she one of your teachers?"

Melina sat up straight and reached for more tea as her stomach started to churn again.

"What did she want?" she stammered. "Why was she looking for me? Dr. Pearson seems kind of mean and not very friendly to students. I couldn't even find her to tell her I was leaving. I know she's probably mad."

Melina put her head in her hands, crying uncontrollably. María held onto her as if she were her own daughter and silently vowed to comfort Melina for as long as it took her to calm down. Without warning, their closeness was interrupted by a soft knock at the half-opened door. María looked up to see Dr. Pearson.

"I remember you. Dr. Pearson, right?" asked María. At this, Melina looked up through her tear-stained face and tried to stop trembling. That was impossible, so she covered her mouth and worked at steadying her voice.

"Thank you for finding me, Dr. Pearson. I'm embarrassed, but I would like to explain what happened in my family."

María hesitated for a moment and lifted herself from the couch. She motioned to Margot to take her place. "Can I get you some tea, Dr. Pearson?" Margot, who was nervous herself, accepted it readily and settled in at a respectful distance from Melina, leaning toward the girl with undivided attention. She didn't know what to expect, but she was ready to listen.

Melina took a deep breath and told her family's story. Instead of starting with the details from last week, she zigzagged across her background, talking about her family and their home, their neighborhood...the smallness of it all, the chaos, the love. She talked about Mamá and Papá and how hard they worked to take care of her and her brothers, and how much they wanted her to stay home and get a job, instead of going to the university. She even talked about Ms. Ingram and how much she helped her. She sensed that Dr. Pearson was listening intently and waiting for something specific.

Well, of course she was, I haven't gotten to why I missed the exams yet, Melina thought to herself. Once she started talking, her heart carried her along, but she knew Dr. Pearson didn't care about her family life. She only wanted to know where she was last week.

"Dr. Pearson, I'm so sorry. It's hard to talk about my family in bits and pieces. When I think of us, it's like I see a giant mosaic and it's hard for me to look at the individual pieces. Separately, they don't mean anything. I'm sorry. I'll tell you what happened last week...

Now we wait to see what Mr. Salgado can do for us. He says we all need to help him gather the papers Papá needs for the asylum trial and the U-visa application. In the meantime, Mamá will work her evening shift, come home and find her peace in the kitchen, where she's most comfortable. She'll look after the boys and cook more food than anyone can eat. Papá will keep taking day jobs to make enough money to leave for Mamá in case he's deported. When he works hard like that and gets paid in cash, he hides the money inside the pillow casings on his recliner, so no one knows he has it. They both worry about robbery. They'll pray there's not a knock on the door, and Papá will watch soccer quietly in his recliner. No one will sleep much, but everyone will for sure gain weight."

Margot felt as if she was in a dream. She had never heard a story like this one, and she had never known a family like Melina's. What could she possibly say that would help? With all her training in psychology, she had no idea how to help Melina make sense out of any of this. The most she could muster was, "Melina, thank you for sharing this with me. I had no idea. Your family sounds very loving and warm. You are fortunate they care so deeply for you. I'm sorry for what you are all going through."

Then, without thinking, she leaned across the couch and drew Melina into her arms. They stayed, bound by this hug for a few minutes, just as they connected on the staircase a week earlier. "I don't know what will happen here at the university, Melina, but I can promise you that I'll do whatever I can to help. To do that, I need to go now and call the Dean's Office. Try to get some sleep tonight, and we'll see each other tomorrow. Okay?"

With that, Margot gave the plastic-covered couch a quick pat and left the room as silently as she entered several hours earlier. She'd been so mesmerized by Melina's story that she'd forgotten all about the clay mug full of tea that María made, still sitting on the table.

14
Margot

Walking home, Margot's mind raced, processing everything she'd just heard. She wondered how she could she have been so blind, so insensitive. How could she, a psychologist, not notice how distressed one of her students had been? *Maybe it wasn't just Melina; maybe there were others in her classes who were struggling? It was beyond anything Margot had ever experienced. How was she supposed to know the life stories of all the students who enrolled in her classes when they only looked up to take notes from her PowerPoint?*

She thought back to her own student days: *her professors had never taken a personal interest in her, and certainly never asked if everything was okay at home. The truth was, things weren't always okay at home, but she plunged through her work at school, brushing everything else aside. Or had she simply buried it? Was Melina's way better? She was certainly stressed, but she didn't brush off her family.*

Once this whole situation is resolved, I need to think through how I interact with my students. How I can get to know them, so I'm not this blind if there's a next time.

She avoided going back to the office, even though she recalled the mess of paperwork she left all over the floor. Instead, she went home. As she turned the key in the front door, she heard something on the other side. Assuming that Biko was most likely fast asleep in the bedroom, she was startled to nearly trip over him as she went inside. What a surprise! He brushed up against her leg and stretched out his front paws on her thigh as if he wanted to be picked up.

This cat should be the psychologist, not me, thought Margot. *He knows why I came home. I need a therapy session, and he's the only one who will at least pretend to listen.*

She picked him up with a warm snuggle, and they went to sit on the elegant white couch, to sort out her thoughts. Pulling a well-worn, blue-striped afghan around them, Margot started the session by trying to put her jumbled-up thoughts into words that made sense.

"Well, Biko, I'm in the middle of a very emotional real-life dilemma, and I have no idea how to deal with it."

Looking around her new apartment with her first-ever decent furnishings, she thought about how Melina had described her home as tiny, but full of love and family togetherness. Suddenly, the white couch and the new drapes seemed cold and excessive. *Besides Biko, where was the love and warmth?* She twirled her hair and continued.

"One of my students, Melina, is in trouble. If I stand up for her, I may be ignoring university policy, and my colleagues probably won't support me. I could lose my job. I'm only a first-year, untenured lecturer. If that happens, we'll need to leave our nice, new place and go who-knows-where. I haven't even been here a year, so I really should follow any policy that lays out consequences for students who miss too many classes or exams. The university believes that school comes first, and families need to understand that when they send their kids here. Once enrolled, they become our students rather than their children. If you start making exceptions, no one will ever show up for anything. Students will think they can simply make everything convenient for themselves, and the university schedule will fall into chaos. I never missed an exam. My parents would have killed me! School came first, always…no exceptions. Damn, what am I missing here?"

Biko stirred in Margot's lap and turned to look up at her. He let out a very vocal *Me—oo-w* and stretched out again, putting his head under the afghan. Was he responding to her ramblings, or was he simply giving her permission to continue? Whatever the signal, Margot picked up where she left off and moved to Melina's defense.

"Melina's commitment to family is her foundation. It holds her life together. They all support each other and make sacrifices for one another. She cares very much about that, but she also has a dream of earning a college degree which would give her independence and help improve the family's position and safety. She wants to get her education, so she can give back to her family and community. The fabric holding her family together is being stretched in so many directions that it's beginning to fray around the edges, and she needs to keep it from tearing apart. When she went home during exam week, she didn't think she had a choice. Even though she can't change her father's outcome in court, she provided emotional support to him and her mother. If I can believe Harry, the whole neighborhood came out to welcome her back. How can any institution punish someone like that?"

As Margot mulled over these competing perspectives, she rubbed her hand across the velvety, white couch. *This couch was how her mother rewarded excellence; it was the only way her parents knew to recognize her achievements. If she had been kicked out of college or unable to secure a job, there would be no new couch. She knew her mother wouldn't understand this dilemma; after all, her only daughter had been Phi Beta Kappa, and first in her class. Her advice would be simple and direct.*

"Margot, you have worked hard to get where you are. This student, this Melina girl, she probably shouldn't have gone to college in the first place. She clearly isn't ready to make the sacrifices needed to succeed. Are you going to slow down your career for someone who really doesn't belong there?"

Margot closed her eyes while she rubbed her head, hoping to straighten out some of the mess inside. Of course, Melina was making sacrifices. She was working harder at making her dream a reality than Margot ever had to do. Margot studied hard, but she never had to worry about her parents' well-being. She didn't complete her degrees to give back to her family or anyone else, for that matter. Her family had all the resources they needed, and then some. They never lived with the fear of being sent away. No, Melina was navigating a more difficult path than Margot had ever experienced.

She glanced down at Biko, curled up in a tight ball in her lap under the afghan, purring contentedly. No answers there. Margot closed her eyes, hoping that would help her think better. An hour later, with her thoughts no longer thundering like a raging waterfall against her forehead, Margot knew what she had to do. She would call the Dean's Office. The call could go one of two ways: she could lie for Melina and say she hadn't missed the exam, or she could simply tell the Dean she was excusing the absence.

It didn't seem right to lie when Melina had been so forthright with her story, so she decided to tell them the truth: she was excusing the absence. There, she decided. On second thought, she wouldn't call. She would wait until morning and tell them face to face. That always worked better.

Brrr...rrr! Why was she so cold? Margot brushed the sleep from her eyes and opened them just enough to see that she was still on the couch and that Biko had tumbled to the floor, pulling the afghan with him. The light streaming through the window and the new silky, white drapes signaled that the day started without her, but not Biko; he was angling for attention by rolling around under the afghan. Margot realized that she had slept on the couch all night and forgotten to set an alarm. *What time was it anyway?*

Damn, it was already 9:00!

As she rushed too quickly to get off the couch, she got tangled up in the afghan and fell on top of Biko. He yelped and scurried under the couch, protesting all the way. When she tried to get up, her ankle buckled, and she crumpled to the floor. Biko crawled out to rub against her leg, but she had no time for his attempt at comfort. She batted his efforts aside, used the couch for support, and limped toward the bathroom to hurry through what would need to be an abbreviated morning routine. Margot's head had stopped thundering sometime during the night, and as she brushed her teeth, she felt surprisingly good. She had no more doubts about supporting Melina. Her jumbled thoughts straightened out as she slept and confirmed her decision. She swept her hair back to hide its scraggly, unwashed appearance, and pulled together a presentable outfit. She needed all her credibility for the Dean this morning.

Throwing tuna toward Biko's bowl, she promised him she would be back soon. As Margot reached for the doorknob, ignoring the pain in her ankle, she heard her phone, loud and clear. Rrrr…rrr! God, she didn't have time for this. She grabbed for it and nearly shouted, "Hello!"

The voice on the other end answered with a more formal and serious tone, "Hello. Is this Dr. Pearson?"

"Yes, yes, it is, but I'm in a real hurry. Can I please call you back?"

"No. This is the Dean's Office, and it will just take a minute. We have scheduled a Student Review meeting for tomorrow morning at 9:00 to discuss one of your students, Melina García."

Margot responded quickly, and in a relieved tone.

"Oh, I'm so glad you caught me. I was just on my way to your office. There's been a mistake. I have excused Melina from taking my exam last week. We will schedule a make-up exam later today. No need for a meeting."

"I'm sorry, Dr. Pearson, but Dr. Stakes has already requested the meeting and we invited Melina to come. We will see you tomorrow at 9:00 in the first-floor conference room here in Clawson Hall. Have a nice day."

"Wait! Is this really necessary? I can write out a formal letter excusing Melina and bring it over to you in about ten minutes. Hello?"

The Dean's Office had already hung up. Margot sank to the floor where suddenly she felt the pain in her ankle as it shot like a hot flame up her leg. *What had she done? If only she hadn't fallen asleep on the couch and gotten up so late. If only she had trusted Melina in the first place. How could she help now?* Margot's first thought was to contact Melina and tell her this was all a mistake. She would run over to her dorm now and talk to her. She turned to go, but as soon as her weight landed on her ankle, she tripped and fell to the hardwood floor. Unable to stand, Margot crawled across the kitchen floor toward the couch. Biko scampered over to play this game too, but she pushed him aside, forgetting his role as therapist.

Once on the couch, Margot tried to come up with a solution, but the sharp pain from her ankle dulled her brain. She rolled off and onto the floor once more, crawling toward the bathroom this time, where she kept painkillers for her intermittent headaches. Fortunately, they sat on a low shelf; she grabbed the bottle and shook two into her hand. Since she couldn't reach the water, she managed to grind them into a powder with her teeth and slugged them down her throat. She propped herself against the wall and took a deep breath while she waited for them to do the job and douse the flame licking at her ankle.

Awaking on the floor with blurry eyes and her neck tilted at a weird angle, she heard, from a distance, the blurred roar of her phone. *Damn, where was it?* Margot turned and saw it lying on the floor about 50 feet away by the couch. As she gradually came to her senses, she remembered why she was on the floor. She knew better than to try and get up, but how many pills had she taken, anyway? She noticed that her ankle was no longer on fire, just smoldering a bit.

She reached the phone, but it was too late. She saw a message, left from a university number; she tapped the button and listened.

"Margot, this is Harry. Melina was just in the office looking for you. It looks like Dr. Stakes has been allowed to call a Student Review meeting for tomorrow morning. Melina's embarrassed and really scared. She doesn't know what to do, but she thought you might support her and she wanted to talk to you. I'm worried about her. Give me a call as soon as you can."

Margot called back and Harry picked up right away.

"Harry, I can't believe they're doing this. I talked to the Dean's Office this morning and told them I was excusing Melina, but they said the meeting was already scheduled and Melina was notified. Any ideas on what I can do at this point?"

"Margot, how about heading over to Forbes and talking to Melina. It would help her to know that you're excusing her and that you'll be there for her in the morning. Maybe you can also coach her about how to tell her story. Oh, and you should put in writing that you are excusing her."

"Harry, I can't get there. I twisted my ankle badly, and I can't get off the floor."

"Don't worry about it; I broke my leg last year, and I still have the crutches. They might be a little long for you, but they should do the trick. Give me your address, and I'll bring them right over. I'll even do you one better. I'll drive you to her dorm." Harry signed off abruptly, assuring her he would be there soon.

Margot hung up and realized what a mess she was. Harry was usually disheveled himself, but she really should do something to clean up. She pulled herself up by the back of the couch and rested there for a minute. Inching her way across the floor to the bedroom, Margot managed to find some oversized, comfortable sweats and decided they were better than the too-tight pants she had put on just for the Dean's Office. The simple act of pulling on sweats and brushing out her gnarled-up hair left her sweaty and exhausted. She sat on the bed and tried to map out the safest route back to the couch. Worried that Biko might spring out at any moment and trip her, she waited until she knew exactly where he was and then started on her simple but perilous journey across the room.

As she waited on the couch for Harry, Margot reflected on her current situation. How ironic that her previously unwelcomed office mate was now her ally. She felt kind of funny collaborating with him, but there was no one else she trusted to understand Melina's story. She wondered again how she had misunderstood this part of her job. It was more than simply filling students' heads with academic content. It had to be about helping them learn how to survive in this environment, and that meant developing relationships with students. She had no idea how to do that, but she would try to figure it out. Weirdly, it might just be Harry who could help her with that.

Margot was deep in thought when she heard a brisk rap at the door. As Biko scurried under the couch, she heard, "Anyone home?"

"C'mon in. It's open, Harry." Much to her surprise, she was grateful to hear his cheery voice and looked forward to seeing his absurdly contagious smile. Harry came in carrying the scratched-up hospital crutches over his shoulder. He took a deep breath, threw the crutches aside, and sat down on the couch without an invitation. It was typical Harry with his tousled hair and threadbare corduroy jacket with the torn elbow patches.

"I took the liberty of calling Dr. Stakes before coming here. I hope you don't mind, but I thought maybe I could reason with him and get him to call off this meeting. I reminded him of the approved process where a first-year student simply sits down with the Dean and is assigned to a counselor who provides support going forward. He's a real hard-ass, and I found out that he's applied for a deanship next year. He thinks that adhering to the old, traditional policy that was written by the senior faculty might help him gain their support and get the position. He also came up the hard way, with no breaks, and strongly believes that everybody should do it that way. Oh, and he claims that the process we recommended last year was never formally approved, and he has no respect for the adjunct faculty who wrote it."

"Well, what did he say?"

"He has no sympathy for Melina. Especially since she's a first-year student, he thinks that outside a death in her family, she should have tried harder to take responsibility for her academic obligations and tell her family their emergency had to wait. Even if she didn't do that, her family should have known how important it was for her to put her schoolwork first. He sees it as disrespectful to her professors to miss their exams. End of story."

"Are you kidding? She didn't act responsibly? Does he know that her family never went to college? That she is the first in her family to have this opportunity?"

"No, and he doesn't care. His answer to that would probably be that she doesn't belong here. She isn't prepared to meet the expectations of a university."

Margot twirled her hair furiously and felt the pain in her ankle returning.

"We'll have to help Melina tell her story and remind the Dean of the promise to implement our early intervention process," continued Harry. "Maybe she'll understand. Let's go see Melina now."

Margot hobbled out to Harry's car on the way-too-tall crutches. She felt like she was being hurled up a steep embankment whenever she pulled herself forward. Harry was in such a hurry that he hardly noticed her until they got to his car, and she couldn't figure out how to get in. He grabbed the crutches as she fell into the front seat and off they went. Five minutes later, they arrived at Forbes. Once inside, Margot crutched down the familiar, impeccably clean hallway toward María's apartment because she still had no idea where Melina lived in this oversized glass cube. She hurriedly explained to Harry who María was, and why she was so important to Melina. Harry knocked on the always half-open door.

"Coming!" he heard from the other side along with the quick shuffle of slippers on a wooden floor. Drying her hands with a towel, María opened the door all the way with her foot, expecting to find a student who needed help.

"Hello, María. I'm Dr. Sanders, but please call me Harry. I'm here with Dr. Pearson, to see Melina García. Do you know where we can find her?"

Clearly surprised, María glanced past Harry, as if trying to confirm his story. When she saw Margot and her crutches, she cried out, "Oh no! What happened to you? Come in. Sit down. You want tea?"

Margot gladly accepted the invitation to sit. She awkwardly found her way across the threshold, and nearly knocked over a vase of plastic flowers as she willed herself to make it to the couch. Once she was settled with the crutches carefully balanced on a nearby chair, she looked around, almost expecting to see Melina. Then she focused on María and saw that the gentle, brown eyes had recently been crying.

"What's wrong, María? Where's Melina?"

Staring at her watch as if trying to rewind this day María answered softly, "Melina returned to her family. I give her money for a bus ticket, and I'm not sure she is coming back. She has a suitcase with her. She's afraid about the meeting tomorrow. She wants to go home on her own before the university asks her to leave. I try to help, but she doesn't listen. Maybe it's good for her to be with family for a while."

Margot wanted to jump up and hug María to reassure her that it wasn't her fault, but she couldn't move. It wasn't just her ankle; her whole body was limp and drained of all energy. She was wrestling with what to say when, thankfully, Harry intervened with his usual smile. Margot knew he put it on just for María.

"María, Dr. Pearson and I will try to catch up with Melina. If we can't find her, we'll go to the meeting tomorrow morning and speak for her. We'll tell the Dean what happened and that she is exactly the kind of student this university should be proud to support."

Margot took a deep breath and felt a little better. He was very convincing; maybe they could fix this after all. María looked up at the Virgin and crossed herself.

Then she turned to look at them, her eyes wet with tears, and whispered, "Thank you. You are good people."

María leaned against the door dabbing at her eyes, as Margot and Harry made their way toward the lobby. She noticed that Harry stayed close to Margot's side in case she needed help balancing on the crutches. María could tell that Dr. Pearson was not the type of person to ask for help, even when she needed it. A little like Melina, perhaps? Maybe these two were the lifeline Melina needed. María crossed herself again as she went back inside, this time closing the door all the way.

Melina

Melina slumped back into the sticky, plastic protection of María's couch. She was exhausted after telling her story to Dr. Pearson. She worried that she told her too much. *Would Dr. Pearson report her family to the school...to the government? Would the school report her family and get Mamá and Papá in trouble? Why was she crying at the end? Did that mean she was going to support her or ask Melina to leave school?* Melina was confused and not sure what to do. She should go upstairs to her room and get some sleep, but she felt much safer here, where she could be herself and not have so many secrets. She didn't want to see Theresa and her posse tonight. Instead, she closed her eyes for a minute, then was startled out of sleep by María's soft voice near her shoulder.

"Melina, why don't you go upstairs and get a good night's sleep. Tomorrow will be a busy day for you, and I'm here to help you. I want you to go up, crawl under that warm, blue quilt, and think about your family and how much they love you. I promise you'll feel better in the morning."

Together, they looked imploringly at the Virgin for confirmation, and crossed themselves for insurance. Melina again fingered Mamá's little gold cross as she hoisted her new bookbag onto her tired shoulder and dragged herself, and Rosa, to the front door. As she headed to the elevators, the lobby echoed with the screams of students returning from the long weekend break, so she knew Theresa was probably back in their room. She kept her head down to avoid conversation in the elevator and got off on the fifth floor with several others. Up and down the hall, students were laughing and loudly broadcasting all the fun they had while home. A few called out to her, but Melina stared at the floor pretending not to hear, so no one would ask her about her break. As soon as she opened the door to her room, that all changed.

"Hey, Mel's back! How you doin'?" yelled Theresa from across the room, through the blaring music. Her friends were spread out on both beds but made room for Melina as soon as she walked in.

"You left early last week, and we didn't get to say goodbye. Things okay? Have fun?"

Melina shrugged and dropped onto her rumpled bed that was sprinkled with some of the torn wrappings from the packages they'd all been opening. She tried to unobtrusively smooth out María's blue quilt hoping no one would notice. Clearly, they'd been there a while and weren't about to leave. Their screeching presence, their happiness, and the thumping of their music paralyzed Melina, and she wanted to escape, back to María's quiet bunker. But how would that help? This room was supposed to be her home now, so she should feel like she belonged. But she didn't. She sat on the bed, feeling very much alone. The others hardly noticed. She pulled her knees up to her chin and tried to make herself invisible as she huddled into the quilt. Theresa noticed her new bookbag. "Mel, that's pretty cool. Love the bright colors. Looks a little like mine. It'll make lugging your stuff around so much easier!" The others glanced over but clearly weren't impressed with her very regular-looking bookbag. Melina blushed since everyone else already had one, so she looked down to hide her face that was on fire and pulled the bag a little closer. Theresa quickly turned her attention back to her friends.

The floor was covered with brightly colored tissue paper and empty boxes as they all compared the new clothes they'd bought while on break and how they could share them over the next few weeks.

What a different break they had over the weekend. No fears! No responsibilities! Did their families have any problems? Had they ever held their father up as he entered a courtroom?

"Awesome!" squealed Roxy. "That blue sweater Terry bought will be super cool with my new green skirt." "Oh yeah!" answered Theresa. "I can borrow that crazy yellow scarf you bought to go with my oversized white shirt. I also got some new Lulus that I think will fit all of us. I lucked out at home. My aunt was visiting, and we spent a whole day at the mall! She even let me have a glass of wine and vape a little to celebrate our time together, and after that she paid for us to both get a makeover at Sephora." Sonia trumped that with, "My brother gave me some pot that I stashed under my mattress. Enough to share with all of you later."

Melina was afraid to open her suitcase with its few old, unwashed, and ill-fitting clothes she took home with her. She hadn't had time to take anything out of her suitcase when she was home and didn't want them to see how rumpled everything was. She sat with her arms tightly hugging her knees and twisted her fingers back and forth across the quilt, wishing she could be anywhere but here. As she mentally drifted further and further away from her surroundings, Theresa called out to her.

"Mel, know what? My mom bought another lamp for our room. This way, we both get one by our bed. You won't have to use that flashlight anymore when it gets dark. Awesome, right?" With that, she ripped open the last box and pulled out a huge, expensive-looking lamp that she dragged over and placed by Melina's bed. "I hope you like it."

Then in a sing-songy voice she added, "Aaand…we have more treats for the fridge. My brother slipped me a few six packs of beer along with my mom's nutrition bars!"

Theresa didn't notice Melina's thin smile and quiet thank you, as she and the others went back to trying on each other's clothes and swapping new lipsticks and blushes. Melina was satisfied that she had now become invisible and could nestle into her quilt without anyone noticing.

Interrupting the mania in Room 503 and up and down the entire fifth floor, Abby, the resident advisor, called out, "Welcome back, you guys! Hope you all partied hard over the weekend and got rid of those exam jitters. There's snacks in the lounge, and I'd like to have y'all come down and celebrate being back at Forbes. I brought back some cool new sounds with videos, and we can show off our new moves before classes start up again. How 'bout it?"

"Awesome! Sounds super cool!" screamed the girls. "We're there."

They trampled across the mashed-up boxes and tissue paper kicking them out of the way as they created a twisted path to the door.

"We'll kick this outside the door later, and María can get it in the morning," called out Sonia as she raced out, dismissing any thoughts of cleaning up. The music was still blasting, and the entire room was now simply a receptacle for their leftover stuff and Melina. No one noticed that Melina didn't join them. She was grateful to be left alone hidden underneath it all, and instead of cleaning up or even turning off the music, she pulled the quilt around her and curled into a fetal position, like her nephews did when they were finally exhausted. Maybe when she woke up, it would all go away.

As much as she wanted to, Melina couldn't sleep. She twisted and turned in every possible way but missed the comfort of her form-fitting mattress on the floor back home. She tried some of the Exam Yoga mental exercises she had learned a few days ago, but nothing stopped the tornado of thoughts swirling around inside her head. She wondered how Mamá and Papá were doing. *Were they safe? Were they sleeping tonight?* She remembered how tired Papá seemed when she saw him last. If only she could have helped him! Maybe if she went back home, she could find more ways to help out, to be a better daughter. *Had they talked to Mr. Salgado again? Maybe she could find a way to call him?*

As she held tight to the little gold cross, Melina ached. She remembered how proud Mamá had been when she used the money had hidden away for months to take Melina shopping just before she left for college. They had laughed together that day and shared a real appreciation for each piece they had carefully picked out. *Did these girls appreciate all the new things they had?*

When Melina opened her eyes next, she saw that Theresa was passed out on her bed, on top of the yellow comforter. She was snoring just like Papá did when he fell asleep in his recliner. Also, someone had cleared the floor of the tissue paper rainbow. As she looked around, she noticed an official-looking envelope propped against the desk lamp. *Maybe she should quietly go over to the desk and see if the envelope was for her?* She was careful not to disturb anything in her path to the desk and picked up the envelope that had her name on it. It wasn't sealed. *Had someone else read it? How long had it been there?*

The message she read took her breath away:

> *Dear Ms. García, You are required to attend a meeting in the Dean's Office Wednesday morning at 9:00 a.m. We want to talk to you about the exams you missed last week. The meeting is in the first-floor conference room, Clawson Hall. My name is Sofie. If you have any questions about this meeting, please text me at 800-821-0900. If you have any documents that will help us understand your absences, like a doctor's excuse, please bring them. But you must attend. Thank you.*

Documents? To Melina's ears, this sounded like another version of her father's legal trouble. She grabbed the edge of the desk and willed herself not to collapse as she held back her tears. *Had Theresa read this message? She might have opened the envelope without seeing the name to make sure it wasn't for her when she returned last night. Did the others know about it too?* Melina felt so ashamed. She quickly stuffed the envelope into her bookbag and returned to her bed. Shaken as she was, it only took her a minute to decide. She carefully folded up the quilt, tucked Rosa and the bookbag under her arm, and very quietly tiptoed out of the room leaving the door slightly ajar so as not to wake up Theresa.

It was eerie walking down the hall toward the elevators at this time of day, when it was still dark, and empty of music and laughter. Melina felt a little scared as it reminded her of the streets and alleys at home that Mamá warned her not to walk alone. *Maybe I should go faster* she thought and she looked over her shoulder. Her stomach churned as she reached the elevators, and her legs felt weak. She felt like throwing up, but she needed to keep going. No time to sit down and take a deep breath. She decided to take the stairs. Somehow, they seemed safer. The blue quilt kept escaping her grip, and the edges dragged along the steps. She came close to tripping over it more than once, so she put Rosa down for a minute on the landing and arranged the quilt securely around her shoulders. It was heavy, but the weight and its warmth reminded her that Mamá and María would look out for her.

Melina knew how disheveled she looked when she finally tumbled through the doorway at the bottom of the staircase, holding Rosa tight to her chest. The bright lights of the lobby startled her after the dark stairway, and she had to brace herself against the wall so she wouldn't fall. She took a moment to pull herself together and only then realized that she had the same clothes on from yesterday, and the day before that. Her hair felt greasy and tangled. She had also forgotten to put her shoes on. They were still under her bed, but she didn't want to wake Theresa by going back.

¡Dios mío! She hoped no one else was around as she turned to her right and headed straight to María's apartment. Would she be up yet? Melina didn't have a watch and had no idea what time it was, but it was still dark outside. Since she had her quilt, she decided to curl up with it right outside María's door. Had it been a few minutes? An hour?

She yanked her head up when she heard, "Melina! What are you doing there? Are you okay? Come in, come in. What's going on?"

Melina somehow managed to pull herself up from the smooth, cold floor and wearily stagger into María's apartment. She fell onto the couch, still wrapped in the warm blue quilt. Her neck ached from how she had twisted it when she slept, and she reached up to rub it. It didn't do any good; her neck and head were going to hurt all day. María was concerned, and she tipped her head to the side as she observed Melina trying to rub away her pain. She went to the kitchen, moistened a towel, and gently placed it around Melina's neck while she smoothed her hair. She sat by Melina and leaned in, ready to listen.

"María, I can't stay here. I have to go home. That's where I belong. I don't fit in here, and they really need me at home."

"What's going on, Melina? Is your family okay? Did they call you?"

"No, they haven't called but I know they need me, and I don't belong here."

"Why, Melina? Why this decision, today?"

"The Dean's Office left a note for me that said I'm required to attend a meeting to explain why I missed my exams. They said I should bring documents to show why I wasn't there for them. I don't have any documents, María. I left because I had to. I have nothing in writing like they want. They won't understand about my family. I need to leave before they kick me out! It's just like court...just because Papá doesn't have the documents they want, they can decide to send him away."

Melina shivered and held onto the quilt tighter than ever. María's kind eyes looked into hers and with her arm around her asked, "What about Dr. Pearson? She seems nice. Won't she help you?"

"I don't know...but I do know I don't belong here. Last night when I went upstairs, I sat on my bed while my roommate and her friends hardly noticed I was there. They were screaming about all their new stuff. Stuff they don't need. All I could think about was Mamá and Papá and how they never have any new stuff. It all seemed so wrong."

"I'll make you some breakfast, and we 'll talk. Okay? You go in my bathroom now, while I do that, okay? You'll feel better if you clean up a little and fix your hair, Melina. You don't look so good."

"Okay, thanks, María."

Over a breakfast of eggs, beans and tortillas, Melina described her plan as María listened. "I want to leave today, before they try to find me. I don't want to talk to anyone. I just want to go home."

"How about your job, Melina? What about your roommate and your teachers? Should you tell them before you leave? They'll worry about you, and you have a responsibility to them too."

"No, María, they won't worry about me. They probably don't think I belong here anyway. I don't need to say goodbye. If someone comes looking for me, you can tell them I went home, okay? I do feel bad about Ms. Munson in the Psychology Department. She has been so nice to me, but I'm sure she can find another student helper."

"Are you sure this is a good decision, Melina?"

"Yes, María, absolutely."

"Do you need money for the bus?"

Melina felt the first tear roll down her cheek. She hadn't thought about any of those details. She couldn't look at María, who was being so kind. Instead, she stared at her plate and wondered how she could be so stupid. *How could she confess that she hadn't really thought this through?*

"Melina, I have some money. You take it for the bus, so you can go home. It's okay."

"María, you are so kind to me. I don't know how to repay you."

"Melina, I just want you to be happy like my Dulce. Go home and think about what you want to do. When you're ready, you come back and I'll be waiting for you."

María reached down into her flowered chair by the couch and pulled out some money, which she gave to Melina.

"This should be enough for the bus ticket, and some food. Don't forget to eat, Melina."

Melina reached over and hugged María like she would Mamá. She felt so safe here in this room. She took one last glance around the tiny space that reminded her so much of home and felt sad. But she quickly remembered what she had to do. She slipped into a pair of shoes that María offered her and gathered her things. She picked up Rosa, while leaving the quilt on the couch. As she walked toward the door, María came after her with the quilt.

"Melina, this is yours now. Keep it and remember me. It will keep you warm and safe."

María watched as Melina stumbled down the hall with her head down, and then out into the overcast, drizzly day. She worried about her but knew she would find her way eventually. Melina reminded her of her own daughter, Dulce. Dulce had found her way, but it hadn't been easy.

16
Margot

After a brief, but fiery, exchange about whether Margot should go to the emergency room to check out her ankle, Harry backed off and agreed to a totally unrelated plan: they would go to Crystal's to get some food and brainstorm what to do next. Margot insisted she was fine and that her ankle would eventually take care of itself. What would really make her feel better would be coming up with a plan to find Melina, or to trying to ensure that Melina wouldn't suffer any significant punishment from the university.

They pulled into the parking lot next to Crystal's, and to prove her point, Margot hobbled into the café without the crutches. Her arm pits were worn out from hoisting herself up to inch forward, so they remained awkwardly angled into the backseat of Harry's beater of a car. The crutches and the car seemed made for each other.

Once inside, they found the cafe was packed, probably because so many students, returning from break, needed a place to congregate. They elbowed their way to a corner table, squished behind another that was covered with books and papers. Margot didn't have a chance to check out who was around as she was trying hard to hide the pain in her ankle and keep her balance all at the same time. They made it to the table with only a few bumps along the way, and that is when she realized who was seated behind the books and papers. Too late, she realized it was Jack Stakes. It was as if he had never moved since he confronted her about Melina.

With a gentle elbow into Harry's side, Margot said, "Don't look now, but guess who's right over there. Maybe we should leave. This might not be a good place to work out a strategy to help Melina."

"Don't be silly. This is perfect," said Harry, as he jumped to his feet.

"Dr. Stakes! It's good to see you again. You may not remember me. Harry Sanders, Psychology Department. We spoke earlier on the phone."

At first, Harry wasn't sure Stakes had heard him. His head remained buried so deep in papers that only his bald spot was visible while his hand forcefully punched out words in bright red ink across the top of his students' work.

Suddenly, he waved his pen in the air and exclaimed to anyone within ten feet, "These students! None of them know how to write, and they don't belong here! What a waste of my time!" Several heads turned, and Margot watched slyly from her seat behind them. His fierce tone even scared her.

Harry wondered to himself, *Who uses red ink anymore? It scares the hell out of students, and they never read it.*

Harry was not to be put off but struggled to continue in a most deferential tone, "I'm sorry to interrupt, sir, when I see how busy you are, but I wonder if I could talk to you for a minute?"

With that, Jack Stakes looked up and disparagingly eyed Harry from head to toe.

"Who did you say you were? Do we know each other?"

In as even a voice as Harry could muster, he replied, "We've seen each other at faculty meetings, Dr. Stakes. I presented a proposal at the fall meeting on behalf of the Adjunct Council about an early intervention program for first-year students which I believe the Dean's Office accepted. I'm Harry Sanders and currently assigned to a temporary full-time position with the Psychology Department."

Jack squinted up at Harry and with a grimace said, "Oh, sure I remember you. You're the one who always stands up to tell us the students aren't getting a fair shake, and we don't know what we're doing, right? Part-time, yes? Didn't you call me earlier today?"

"Yes, sir. We spoke on the phone briefly. I'm temporary full-time this year, filling in for Dr. Moore, who's on leave."

Waving his pen more emphatically than ever, Jack Stakes replied, "Well, you can see I'm busy. You know how I feel, and I don't have any more time to talk about why these students need our help. We need help to attract students who are better prepared. Look at these papers...all terrible! I've been working with them for months now, and they still don't know how to write." With that, he grabbed his cup of very dark, steaming coffee and took a large swig, as if to dismiss Harry completely.

"I'm sorry you feel that way, sir, but I really need to talk to you about one of your students, Melina García. She—"

Before he could go on, Stakes cut him off.

"Melina García! She came to my office with some crazy excuse about going home. No sense of responsibility or respect for me or the university! The Dean has agreed to call a meeting for tomorrow morning and ask her to explain herself. I doubt she'll even show up. We'll ask her to leave the university; then she can stay home and help her family all she wants. That leaves an opening for a kid who might understand what it means to be a real student." He slammed his fist on the table.

"Well, I'm glad you remember Melina because that's exactly what I wanted to talk to you about. I drove her home last week, and I know why she missed your exam. She had a real legitimate family emergency and needed to be there to help her father. I met her family and can attend the meeting tomorrow to explain if Melina can't make it herself."

Jack Stakes shook his head before replying, "First, you too flouted university policy by driving a student off campus. It doesn't surprise me, knowing how naïve you are when it comes to our students. I should report you also. Second, I don't need to hear from you that our students' excuses are legitimate. When they are lucky enough to be accepted to this university, they have a responsibility to put their schoolwork ahead of anything else and that includes family and friends. Half of them party all week, and the other half go home to their families when the going gets tough. Those students know they have people like you who will support their choices, so they don't worry. I plan to change that this year with tougher procedures. I'll see her tomorrow morning. Now, please leave me alone. I'm busy and you should be too! Don't you have papers to correct, or do you just give them all A's simply for showing up?"

With that, he once again started marking up the essay in front of him with such force that Harry thought the whole paper would likely be reduced to shreds.

Jack Stakes knew deep down inside that if his wife were still alive, she would have admonished him over that outburst. She was the only one who knew his kind, sensitive side and would have reminded him about their own son and how much they depended on support from others to help him, to tell his story. But she wasn't here, and he was resentful about that. He was also angry that his son with so many physical and emotional challenges hadn't had the opportunity to go to college like these kids he was teaching now. They all took it for granted and felt so entitled. Life wasn't fair, and Jack Stakes had a lot of rage inside him. He vented that on his students and part-time faculty like Harry, but his regular outbursts seemed to be isolating him more than ever. No matter: Once he became a dean, they would listen.

Harry shook his head and, with a deliberately audible sigh, returned to his table where Margot had been straining to pick up the nuances of the deafening rant.

"Well, there's no stopping him," reported Harry. "The meeting with the Dean is on, and he's prepared to shred Melina just like he's shredding those papers he's working on over there. He's a power-hungry asshole who thinks that being tough raises standards and thus his stature. He doesn't give a damn about teaching. Instead, he just wants to work with students who are already proficient, so he can take credit for it."

The more Harry talked, the more his voice could be heard across the café; he had never shied away from letting his feelings be known, especially when it came to supporting students. Heads turned but if Jack Stakes heard the insults aimed at him, he never let on. Meanwhile, Harry worked himself into such a frenzy they could no longer expect to enjoy a relaxing meal. Once again, Margot left the café without eating.

Margot hobbled and Harry walked back to his car as they continued to formulate plans for the next morning. Making things right for Melina wasn't going to be easy, and they realized the need to ask others for help. Harry's idea was to round up his cohort of strident part-time colleagues and stage a protest outside the conference room where the meeting was scheduled. He suggested printing fliers, as well as directly asking faculty for their support. Harry had utilized this approach many times to deliver a message to administrative groups. Public protests made him feel like he was doing something and drawing attention to issues; he didn't see how a small protest could hurt.

Margot listened carefully as she twisted her hands in her lap. She appreciated that Harry cared so much, but she had never been involved with any kind of demonstration and personally felt they were often led by people who were not entirely rational. She had always gone along with things the way they were and left protests to others. Keeping out of the spotlight and staying focused on her future had always worked for her. But this time was different, more personal, not an abstract issue. It had the potential to impact someone's life very significantly. Margot deeply believed that the possible consequences were completely unfair to Melina, but also that it wasn't their story to make public. It was Melina's story, and Margot did not want to add to Melina's difficulties by putting her even more in the spotlight.

Still hunched over in the car, Margot suggested an alternative. "How about if we contact the other faculty members whose exams Melina missed and ask them to attend the meeting to speak on Melina's behalf?"

This seemed like a more rational and much less contentious approach. Melina's story would be shared with just a few, and the Dean's Office would hear the relevant evidence, even without documents, that would, of course, lead it to support her. After all, Melina did reach out to the faculty who were directly involved and asked to be excused from their exams. Except for Dr. Stakes, who unfortunately would also be there, they all agreed to reschedule when she returned. This seemed like a logical and civilized approach to Margot.

But Harry wasn't listening. His face looked like a bright red cranberry about to burst open, and his normally unruly hair was all over the place and plastered to his forehead, covering most of his eyes. His unrestrained anger escalated and made Margot a little nervous; she worried that he might have a stroke right there in his dirty old car. Harry found Margot's plan too naïve, passive, and reliant on others. He believed that making a lot of noise gained attention and eventually brought about change.

"Margot, you just don't know this faculty and its tendency to comply with traditional policies and procedures. They're all afraid of not getting tenured or not getting their contracts extended, and they won't fight the administration over anything, let alone one student. Melina made the right decision, but she did violate the Student Conduct Policy and they'll want her to be an example to others. We need to fight for the new early intervention policy and tell everyone how stories like Melina's are not that unusual. By using Melina's situation, we can let everyone see that policies need to be more student-centered and supportive."

Honestly, Margot didn't understand this kind of thinking. She'd always been afraid to break the rules and never questioned authority. When her dissertation advisor left the university, the department head told Margot this would likely affect her timeline for completion unless she filed an appeal requesting an exception to departmental policy. She didn't appeal; rather, she simply accepted a new advisor following the expected protocol. She didn't want to rock the boat and flout departmental policy. Instead, she just worked harder to please a new advisor so she could complete her work on time. It didn't matter that her research was compromised in the process. In the meantime, her first advisor was asked to repay the dissertation stipend she'd received from the university. If Margot had just taken a stand and supported her original advisor, that wouldn't have happened. But this situation was different. Melina's life and her entire family's life could be turned upside down by an outdated policy based on punishment rather than support. Margot really wanted to fight for Melina.

Harry's anger and frustration were transferred to his accelerator, which he pushed way over the speed limit to get them back to their office. They were uncompromising on their distinctly different strategies, and eventually agreed to disagree. They agreed on one thing: the ultimate goal was to influence the thinking around Melina's case at tomorrow's meeting. They decided that Margot would contact the other two faculty who were directly involved, while Harry would design a flier and assemble a group of demonstrators.

Harry pulled into the parking lot of Anderson, jumped out of the car, and slammed the door, leaving Margot inside. Even though the temperatures were in the 40s, Margot saw sweat trickle past his ears and down his neck; he looked more raggedy than usual, like a terrier left out in a rainstorm. He swept his hand through his hair and dashed off, forgetting all about Margot and her ankle.

Twenty minutes later, Margot reached their office, for once relieved to see the door open and the lights on. She made it down the hallway balancing on one leg and grabbing at the crevices in the wall with her opposite hand. She fell into her chair forcing it backwards and into a 360 wheelie at a 90-degree angle. *Damn!* She squeezed her fingers around the cold, steely arms, and as she fought not to fall onto the floor she dizzily glanced over at Harry. He was clearly in a zombie state, where he noticed nothing but the screen in front of him. As he pounded the keyboard, he called out "How does this sound, Margot?

> *Today's meeting in the Dean's Office is an important one. It will decide the fate of one of our students who missed her exams due to a family emergency. We must end the old Student Conduct Policy that punishes our responsible students with its rigid and inflexible standards of behavior. Speak out now!*

"I'll print it on bright yellow paper, so they can't miss it. I'll distribute these around campus tonight to get lots of people protesting outside the conference room. What do you think? I guess I should add the time and place. Should I add Melina's picture?"

Margot wasn't sure if it was from her spinning chair, her ankle or Harry's flier that roared, but her head throbbed with so many conflicting thoughts. Suddenly, she remembered their promise to María, to try and find Melina before she left campus.

"Harry, do you have any idea where Melina might go before heading to the bus? Did she ever mention to you…?" Harry jumped up in the middle of her question.

"Yes! Brilliant idea, Margot. She told me about a garden by the athletic field where she likes to lie and watch the clouds float by. Let's go."

Harry burst out the door while Margot trailed behind. Ten minutes later, they pulled up to the parking lot closest to the football field. Neither of them knew anything about a garden in this area, and the area around the field stretched out like spokes in all directions. They each headed off to cover a different spoke. Margot, again forgetting the crutches in her eagerness to find Melina, spied a green area surrounded by bushes at the extreme end of the field. She hobbled toward it and was enchanted to find a green space inexplicably surrounded by shrubs and colorful flowers. This would be a perfect spot to be alone and think. As she plopped herself onto a nearby bench, she spotted a bright blue bookbag underneath. Wondering if this might help her find Melina, she reached for it. As she did, a card dropped from the front pocket. She hated to invade someone's privacy, but she read it anyway. *Hang in there, Melina!*

"Harry!" she shouted, "Come back here. I've found something." Harry jogged over to see Margot awkwardly squatting by a bench with a note in her hands.

"Not sure what this means, Harry, but this bookbag has a note to Melina in it. Can you scramble around those shrubs? Maybe Melina lied down and is asleep? I can't really move around too quickly, but she might be here somewhere."

Never one to be quiet, Harry started calling out for Melina.

"Melina! Melina! Are you here? Dr. Pearson and I are here to support you. Help us find you."

This, however, turned out to be futile. She was not there. Harry and Margot sat on the bench on either side of Melina's blue bookbag. Harry's thoughts came pouring out first: "Why did she leave it? How long ago was she here?"

Margot spoke up, "If only we had come here first and not been so rattled about what to do. We are supposed to be the mature ones and act responsibly to help our students. So far, we have failed miserably with Melina. Damn!"

With that, she grabbed the bookbag and with Harry trailing behind, they headed back to the office to start over. She admired Melina for being the rational one here; she had made a decision and thought it through before acting on it. *How much time had she spent alone in the garden? All she and Harry had done was to rile themselves up and argue about whose ideas were better. Hadn't they been trained to think rationally and find solutions to problems?* Margot supposed that was only in the nice, neat world of textbooks and research, not the real world, where things were a bit messier.

Margot tried to contact both Dr. Silverman and Dr. Gregory, and ask them to attend the meeting in the morning. She hoped they might be sympathetic since Melina had told her they both seemed to understand when she told them she had to go home. Dr. Gregory's university mailbox was full, so he probably wasn't back yet from break. She left a message for Dr. Silverman, and hopefully, she was back and picking up her messages. Too bad she didn't have personal numbers for them as a text might have worked faster. She was unable to reach either one.

Thankfully, by this time the chair was no longer spinning, and Margot untangled her thoughts and regained some composure. She couldn't help feeling like she was in the middle of a ping pong match with balls coming at her, fast and hard, from both sides. If she moved at all, she was sure the pain from her ankle and her head would somehow collide in the middle and cause her body to explode. Before that happened, she decided to go home, take an Advil, ice her ankle and order pizza. Of course, Biko would also curl up on her lap, assuming his usual role.

Damn, she'd done it again… With a start, Margot saw the sun peeking through her drapes and not-so-gently nudging her to wake up. As she blinked her eyes open, she saw a pizza box on the floor and a glass of wine, still half-full, on the table. At the same time, she felt something soggy all over her foot. Looking down, she saw the remains of the plastic bag that once held several ice cubes and served as a cold compress for her ankle; it was now simply a wet, empty mess, clawed open and draped sloppily across her foot. The couch was soaking wet, with a water stain that may or may not come out. *Damn!*

Glancing at her watch, Margot saw that she had an hour to get to the Dean's meeting to advocate for Melina. Did she dare test her ankle? The pain had pretty much subsided, but was it capable of giving her the support she desperately needed today? She noticed that she was still in her clothes from yesterday. Worst case scenario, she mused, was to simply wash her face and limp over to the meeting in her wrinkled sweats. No! Of course, that wasn't possible. Her mother's words flashed boldly across her addled brain: *Margot, no one will take you seriously if you look like you just woke up. You need to pay more attention to how you look if you want people to listen to you.*

She looked around to make sure Biko wasn't lying in wait, ready to trip her as soon as she left the couch. She carefully placed her ankle on the floor, raised herself, and breathed a deep sigh of relief as she realized she could at least get as far as the bathroom and make herself presentable.

Forty minutes later, Margot erased the last of Biko's hair from her jacket before she locked the door behind her and started off to a much-dreaded showdown with Jack Stakes and anybody else who showed up. Hopefully, Harry and Melina's other professors would also be there. When she hobbled up the stairs toward the meeting, she was immediately encompassed by a swirl of yellow fliers and voices chanting, "Students First!"

She saw Harry at the entrance to the conference room leading a small, but passionate group of students and a few of his colleagues from the Adjunct Faculty Council. Not wanting to be consigned to this group, she threw a crisp nod in his direction and cautiously walked through the door. Harry raked his hand through his hair to get it out of his eyes, smoothed his jacket and broke away to follow Margot inside.

The room featured a highly polished, dark wooden table, surrounded by even darker paneled walls that made it seem like a fortress. There were no windows, and Margot noticed that the lights had not been turned on. *So, this is what the Dean of Students' conference room looked like? How many times were students subjected to this?* Margot herself was nervous; imagine how a student would feel. Margot was so glad Melina wasn't here to suffer through this intimidating and impersonal experience.

Jack Stakes sat at the far end of the table, rigidly positioned, and seemingly a mile away. He was alone and seemed quite comfortable with that. As always, he was surrounded by a stack of papers and manuals. He never looked up, even when the Dean entered with a smile and turned on the lights. She approached Margot and Harry leaving Jack alone to stew at the far end of the room, and with her hand extended, she introduced herself.

"Hi! I'm Sharon Scott, the new Dean of Students here. It's so nice to meet you both. I really appreciate your coming today. Isn't this a dreary room? Damn, it's one of the first things I plan to change once I feel more settled. I don't think I'll get permission to cut open the walls for windows, but we can brighten it up so that students feel more comfortable in here. And those yellow fliers outside? A nice, colorful touch to get us started this morning. I always love to see students acting on something they feel passionate about."

As soon as Dean Scott took a breath, they heard Stake clear his throat and very officiously attempt to convene the meeting, as if it were his. With great ceremony, as if from a script and no introductions, he began.

"We are here to confirm that Melina García violated the Student Conduct Policy by missing four midterm exams without valid excuses from the faculty." He started to wave a thick document with a dark, glossy cover, when he was interrupted by the Dean.

"Dr. Stakes, this meeting was called by my office to listen to a first-year student, Melina García, tell us why she was not able to take her exams. It is not a meeting of your Faculty Review Board, and I will facilitate how we proceed. Our goal is to first listen, and then provide whatever support she may need to be successful here at Balsam. Do you understand?"

As Margot was going over Melina's story in her head, she vaguely heard Stake's strong, authoritative voice booming out at the Dean, "Let me read the section that outlines very specifically the consequences for missing exams without permission from the faculty. It says that the student will be suspended from all university activities for up to one term, at which time they may appeal to be re-admitted. Now, as you all know, the student in this case, Melina García, was informed that she was required to be here to tell her side of the story. I don't see her here. I consider that insubordination, and a lack of respect for university rules."

After listening as politely as possible, Dean Scott abruptly turned away to face Harry and Margot.

"Dr. Pearson and Dr. Sanders, thank you for joining us today. Dr. Stakes requested this meeting, and I really appreciate your coming to support Ms. García. Will Ms. García be joining us this morning?"

Margot quickly responded, "She is not able to be here today, but Dr. Sanders and I want to tell her story and provide our support for her."

She was abruptly cut off by Stakes, who emphatically barked, "Dr. Pearson, didn't you confirm to me yesterday that Ms. García missed your exam, and that you had not excused her?"

"Yes, that's right. But there were extenuating circumstances, and Melina did leave me a written note that I found when I returned to school. I've also had the opportunity to meet with her, and I believe her reason for going home was a legitimate one. Her family truly needed her, and she plans to make up her exams." Margot was a bit shaken by his tone, but gathered her wits enough to add, "I also know that she met with her two other professors, Dr. Silverman and Dr. Gregory. They both agreed to schedule a make-up exam with her. You seem to be the only holdout, Dr. Stakes."

"Well, where are they, Dr. Pearson? Why aren't they here? Maybe they too need a lesson on the importance of adhering to university policy and respecting their colleagues enough to show up to a meeting in the Dean's Office."

"With all due respect, Dr. Stakes," stammered Margot, "this meeting was called very quickly, and I don't believe they are back on campus yet. Perhaps, we could adjourn until we have the chance to include them also? I'll take responsibility for contacting them if you wish."

Once again, the Dean cut off the discussion.

"Dr. Stakes, perhaps you have forgotten that at the end of last year, we adopted a new, more supportive policy for first years that is not as punitive as the former policy. We now give them the respect of listening to their reasons for missing things like exams or classes. If we find the faculty are willing to excuse them, we assign them to a counselor, who will provide support and direct them to campus resources that will help them succeed. I believe that Dr. Sanders here was one of the faculty who recommended the policy. Am I right?"

Harry vigorously nodded his head. Stakes scowled as he shook his head and reminded them of the importance of upholding standards.

"Why isn't she here?" he repeated. "I move to suspend Ms. García until the end of spring term. If she wants to return, she can appeal to my Faculty Review Board. Do I hear a second?"

Margot was stunned, and the Dean again reminded him she was leading this meeting and that was simply not an option. Instead, she offered, "Drs. Pearson and Sanders, will you please let Melina know that we have met and want to help her. I have counselors and tutors on staff who will work with her. My office can try to call her, but since you both have a personal relationship with her it might be best if she heard from you first. She should come in to see me soon, and we will work out an intervention plan."

Hearing that, Stakes gathered up his papers and outdated policy manual, looked neither left nor right, and stridently left the room with a flourish, only to be caught off balance by a flurry of yellow fliers.

17
Melina

Clutching Rosa tight to her chest and hoisting the corners of the blue quilt carefully so they wouldn't drag, Melina hunched over this scruffy heap of essentials as if her life depended on it. She didn't look back. She wanted to but this time didn't dare. Instead, she leaned into the heavy glass doors of Forbes Hall that stabilized the bubble separating the hundreds of girls inside from the real world. She pushed them open with her right shoulder and began the journey she knew she must take. It wouldn't be easy, but she had to do it. Her feet were already hurting because the shoes she borrowed from María pinched her toes. *How had she forgotten her old, comfy boots under the bed upstairs? Theresa would probably laugh when she found them and saw how worn out they were. She would show them to her girl besties and then would throw them away after agreeing that Melina just didn't fit in. Or maybe, Tracy would take the slightly used boots for her back-of-the closet stash.*

Melina knew that María was watching her just like Mamá would have, but she also knew if she looked back at that kind face with the gentle eyes, she might follow the easier path straight back to María's room where she could curl up under the blue quilt and feel safe. That, however, was just a dream and wouldn't help solve her problem. So alone, she schlepped her stuff out into the drab day that was beginning to take hold on campus. She wanted to move quickly so she wouldn't run into anyone who might recognize her, but Melina really didn't know the best way to the bus station. In fact, she only had a slight idea which way to turn. She should have asked María, but she hadn't been thinking clearly about how to make her plan happen. She remembered Harry advising her to take a problem apart and think through the steps needed to solve it.

With that advice in mind, she hurried toward her secret garden to map out the next steps. No one would see her there, and she could think. She took María's shoes off as she walked and immediately felt the moisture from the evening dew cool her feet and alleviate the pain as the sidewalk led her in the right direction.

As she slipped into the garden a few minutes later, Melina started to assemble her thoughts into something that made sense. She was in trouble, and she knew it. As soon as she read the message from the Dean's Office, she thought about what Harry had told her in the car: She would be judged for a decision she made that she didn't regret and wouldn't apologize for. The best thing she could do at this meeting was to be honest and explain about her family. If she did that though, Melina was afraid her answers would get her family in more trouble. She couldn't take that chance.

She had already disappointed Mamá and Papá enough by coming here in the first place. The university would ask her to leave, and she would go home, ashamed. Everyone would know she failed. Going to that meeting was totally out of the question even though Harry and Dr. Pearson seemed to be on her side. Melina knew she couldn't lie, but she also knew she couldn't tell the truth. The only solution was to leave now when it was her choice. Once she was home, she would go see Ms. Ingram and ask her how to go about formally dropping out of the university and giving up her scholarship. Maybe she could still go to one of the city colleges and not entirely give up her dream of becoming independent. Ms. Ingram would know how to help.

Melina looked up at the clouds and imagined her dream of a college degree floating away on the one that looked a little like a dragon. Lying in the garden, on top of her blue quilt, watching the clouds was oddly comforting, so Melina gave in to her drowsiness and closed her eyes. When she opened them, the sun had broken through the early morning mist and the day was well under way. She spotted one cloud off to the right that was by itself, moving away from the others in an altogether different direction. There was no hesitation to its movements, and its shape somehow became more beautiful as it moved. She knew just what she had to do.

Melina reached inside her bookbag and pulled out the journal that Ms. Ingram had given her months ago. She started to sketch the clouds for a few pages and, unexpectedly, the drawings began to turn into words. At first, it was one or two words: lonely, ashamed, out of place, family, each with a different cloud next to them. Then the words stretched into sentences, and Melina realized she was using words to figure out what to do next.

> *I don't belong here. I'm not like the others. Their music is different, and they have so many things. They don't understand me. They see my worn-out clothes and lack of money as reasons not to hang out with me. My family needs me, and I think I need them. I fit in at home. I don't fit in here, and I never will. If I go to see a counselor, I will be so ashamed that everyone knows I need help. Everybody will laugh at me, and my family will be embarrassed. I need to go home and help take care of them. It was a selfish idea to come here. My family needs me. Amá and Apá always look so tired. I can get a job and make their lives easier. I'll tell them I made a*

mistake. No one here will miss me, so I will leave now. I will never forget María. Maybe I can come back sometime and thank her for being so kind.

Writing this all down helped to lift the fog that had engulfed her ever since she first arrived at Balsam State. Putting her thoughts into words allowed her to see how selfish she had been, and how she had no choice but to return home. Melina gathered her things, damp from the dew, pressed the gold cross between her fingers and after rubbing her still-pinched toes, started off to find the bus station.

℘ ℘ ℘

"I'll be back soon, Amá. Need anything?" Melina called over her shoulder as she hurried past the Virgin and out the front door.

"No, mija, thanks for asking," answered her mother.

Melina tightened her favorite blue scarf around her face against the strong wind and headed down the stairs. She had been home for a month. Running family errands was a given and certainly seemed more normal than living in a half-decorated room with strangers all around her. As she stepped onto the sidewalk and turned toward the nearby neighborhood store, she noticed, out of the corner of her eye, that the yellow curtains above her separated just a little as Mamá watched her go. Mamá's concern gave her a warm, tingly feel against the cold, and she turned to wave. That's funny, she thought, that her roommate's bedspread, symbol of how much of an outsider Melina felt at school, was also yellow. Mamá quickly pulled the curtains shut, hoping that Melina wouldn't see her. She had been overly protective of Melina since her return, and she knew it probably annoyed her only daughter.

"Hi!" Melina smiled at Mrs. Lopez, their next-door neighbor. "How are you today?"

"We're doing very well, Melina, thank you. It's so nice to have you home again!"

Mrs. Lopez had been Mamá's best friend for over 20 years, and it felt good to Melina to watch her as she walked her old and wrinkled terrier, Pedro, down the sidewalk. When Melina was little, Pedro chased after her every morning on her way to school, while Mrs. López called him home from her top step. She walked with a cane now and he could hardly see, but Melina hoped he remembered her voice as she leaned over to scratch his prickly ears.

A few yards further down the familiar block, she saw Mr. Montero as he started down the stairs to retrieve his morning paper that had landed on the sidewalk below. Melina grabbed it and ran up the stairs to hand it to him.

"Thanks, Melina. It's good to see you again."

Melina grinned at him and continued on her way. She inhaled deeply and filled her nostrils with the tantalizing scents from Manuel's cart of grilled chorizo and roasted chiles, which was always planted at the end of their block. And as usual, Manuel thrust a fresh tortilla into her hand, "To keep you warm, Melina," he called out.

She wondered why this all made her so content. *Shouldn't she be angry? Shouldn't she resent that she was no longer living her dream? She was back in the neighborhood that she had struggled to escape. These last few weeks had turned her world inside out. There were so many emotions colliding in her head, all bashing around, seeking some peace and a logical landing place. She no longer lived with others who didn't understand her, and she no longer struggled every day with how to lie to them about why she didn't want to party or go out to eat. Instead, her days were spent drifting into the familiar, comfortable routines of helping her family. Mamá needed help with the boys, as her work shifts were getting longer and longer. Papá needed someone to put a hot meal in front of him when he wearily reached the top of the back stairs after another marathon series of jobs. His faint, tired smile was all she needed when she fluffed the pillow in his recliner as he slumped into it for a much-needed nap.*

When she walked down their street, seeing the same faces that had been there forever made her feel safe and secure. It was certainly not the same as walking the halls at Forbes where she continually got lost, and when she did get where she was going, she wasn't sure why she was there in the first place. One of her brothers had recently moved out of the house, so she was upgraded from a mattress in the hallway, to sharing a bedroom with her nephews. There were no matching comforters or colorful walls, just the cries and laughter of two happy children. She tripped over their trucks every morning, but when they needed help, she understood exactly what to do. It wasn't a guessing game or a trial to see if she got it right.

Her nights were mostly spent on the couch watching telenovelas. Sometimes, Mamá and one of her cousins joined her; that never got old. Melina laughed one minute and cried the next, right along with the familiar actresses. She sometimes fell asleep on the couch and woke up with her skin creased and sticky from the plastic cover. When she woke up in the middle of the night like that, she went to her room and crashed on her old mattress, now mounted on a bedspring, under María's blue quilt and next to the posters that she had re-taped to the wall. If she was too tired, she stayed there on the couch until she heard breakfast sizzling under Mamá's watchful eye.

Some mornings, Gabriela came over, and they walked to the park together. It was weird being with her now; she had a new baby and lived at home with her mother. The baby had finally helped her mamá move on from her grief over Chuy's shooting. Gabriela's boyfriend, Juan, had left for Mexico to help his family, and she wasn't sure when he was coming back. Gabriela had no friends other than Melina and was happy to have someone to talk to, although the baby was all she could talk about. Gabriela worked part-time at the local store to help out at home, and she was always tired, just like Mamá. She seemed so much older now. Gabriela said she felt needed for the first time ever, and that Melina should think about starting a family, too. Melina thought the baby was cute, but she wasn't ready for that kind of commitment at all, so she laughed it off.

"Gabriela, I don't even have a boyfriend! If I did, I'm sure not ready to have a baby."

And it wasn't just Gabriela. Melina's cousins also tried to convince her she was missing something special. Rosita kept bringing boys to the house, hoping that sparks might fly. There was one time when Melina was a little interested; Ignacio, Nacho to his friends, was handsome and had a beautiful smile. They went to the movies a few times and laughed at the same things. He held her hand, and he made her feel special. Mamá invited him to dinner, and later that night on the couch she told Melina he would make a good husband.

"But Amá, I don't want to get married yet. I want to get an education and make you proud. I just haven't figured out how to do it."

"Melina, your grandmother would love another baby in the family, a little girl. She loves the boys, but she really wants to have photos of a little girl that she can show to her friends in Puebla and make clothes for. She's getting older, you know."

"Amá, I'm just not ready. Do you understand?"

"I try to understand. I want you to be happy."

Melina started writing in her journal again.

*I like being back home, but no one here really under-
stands me. Gabriela wants me to be her best friend and
have a baby just like her. ¡Dios mío, that baby is her
entire life! I'm not ready for that. Does that mean there is
something wrong with me? Does everyone want a baby?
And Abuela? Is it fair for me not to give her another
great-grandchild? Am I really being selfish? Then there's
Nacho, a sweet and very handsome guy. I know he likes
me a lot, and I like him. He has a good job, and we have
fun together. Mamá and Papá like him. What's wrong
with me for not knowing what I want?*

Mostly, being back was good. But sometimes, it felt upside down.
She wanted to fit in at home like she always had, but this pressure from
her friends and family to have a baby made her uncomfortable.

And there was the university. She received a letter from the Dean's
Office, asking her to return and meet with the Dean so they could
assign a counselor to work with her. She brushed a few tears from her
eyes that day even though it was not a surprise. She never belonged
there, just ask her roommate, or her teachers. The biggest surprise was
that, right now, she didn't care. Melina took the letter with its attach-
ment, crumpled it up and threw it into a dumpster in the neighboring
alley so Mamá and Papá wouldn't see it. She didn't want them to know
the real reason she came home; she was too ashamed to admit that she
had failed.

Shortly before the letter arrived, she had found a note stuck under
the front door with her name on it. She opened it and read, *Melina, I
just stopped by to see how you're doing. I'd like to talk to you when you
have time. Please stop by school soon. Ms. Ingram.*

Melina had no idea how Ms. Ingram knew she was home. She hadn't told her, and she hadn't stopped by the school. She fell onto the couch and sighed as she thought about how disappointed Ms. Ingram would be. They worked so hard together to make sure Melina got into the university. How could she tell her that she had failed and not lived up to her expectations? How could she tell her that the blue bookbag just wasn't enough?

Margot

The path leading from Clawson to Forbes was affectionately referred to as Slant Walk. It angled across campus, hitting most of the significant buildings along the way. As Margot left the Dark Polished Woods and Yellow Sea of the Dean's Office behind her, she turned left on Slant Walk and headed towards Forbes. The swelling in her ankle had gone down considerably, and she made surprisingly good progress when she almost collided with her department chair, Dr. Berg.

"Oops. I'm so sorry," he said, before realizing who he almost knocked over. "Why, Margot, I haven't seen you in such a long time, and I was about to call you when I got back to the office. Do you have a minute to sit and talk?" He motioned to a nearby bench.

Margot didn't have much personal interaction with Dr. Berg; in fact, she was still reticent to call him Robert. And he had never actually offered that option. This invitation to sit caught her completely off guard, as focused as she was on Melina's situation. But she had no choice, so she nodded and joined him.

"How're things going, Margot? Are you getting the support you need as you settle in here? I know that the first set of exams can be challenging for new faculty, especially when you're teaching freshmen. They get so worried and don't always act appropriately. Have you had any problems?"

Margot hesitated to answer. She had not received the departmental support she had been promised, but she didn't really think that a bench covered with chipped paint and student carvings in the middle of campus was the time or place to air her complaints.

Instead she replied, "Thanks for asking, Dr. Berg. I did notice that the students were nervous about exams, so I made sure they understood our policies about being on time and taking them seriously. I think they understood. I even gave them extra time to prepare by calling off our last class session. I hope that was all right."

"That's fine, Margot," replied Dr. Berg, who still did not invite her to call him Robert. "I'm glad to hear things are going well for you, and I'm sure your students will do just fine. As long as we continue to hold them to the high standards set by the university, we'll all look good. I am troubled, though, by something I just heard in a research committee meeting. Jack Stakes, who loves to stir up trouble, arrived late, complaining about an encounter he had this morning in the Dean's Office. He was alleging that the new Dean of Students was trying to pre-empt a long-held faculty policy around student conduct. He was angry that some student who missed exams without being excused was simply being given a slap on the wrist instead of a harsher punishment. And he didn't stop there; he said that even though the student didn't show up for the meeting, there were two faculty members there to defend her. He saw that as an affront toward senior faculty by two young upstarts, as he called them, who didn't know what they were doing and thought that the university should center its policies around the needs of students, not faculty. Stakes couldn't remember the faculty names but thought they were in our department. Do you know anything about this?"

Margot was stunned that he had heard about this at all, let alone so soon. It must have shown in her reddened face and she turned away to get ahold of herself before answering.

"Yes, Dr. Sanders and I were both there to advocate for Melina. I don't know her well, Dr. Berg, but she is in my Intro class, and as you know, she is our department's student assistant. She came around early last week to tell me she was going home and wouldn't be able to take her exam. I wasn't in my office, but she left me a note about it and when I came back to campus we talked about rescheduling."

As Margot continued, she became aware that Dr. Berg had no idea who Melina was.

"I was there today to offer my support for her and ask them to hear her out. Dean Scott explained to us that her office was implementing a new policy toward students who missed things like exams that was less punitive. Dr. Stakes didn't like that approach and was there to argue against it."

"Well, I know Jack Stakes pretty well, Margot. He's a big player here at Balsam. He brings in lots of research dollars and has the president's ear. He can be difficult, but he does know university policies and procedures. I don't always agree with him, but I do think it's important for us to hold our students to the standards we've created. They're really in place to support them. If we had no procedures, the students would be free to show up whenever they felt like it, and they would lose out on so much. They're so young and without their parents, they need our discipline, and to see there are consequences to their actions. Isn't that our responsibility? What are your thoughts?"

"I think it's complicated, Dr. Berg. We certainly need procedures and support systems in place to help students make the best decisions. It's part of their learning experience and may help them develop good habits, but I also think we need to be flexible. Emergencies come up for all of us, and sometimes we need to set priorities that don't fall neatly in line with a neatly bound manual of policies and procedures. In this case, Melina was troubled by the choices she had, and she chose to go home and help her family, even though she understood there would be consequences. After I talked to her, I could see her struggle and I chose to support her and reschedule her exam. I believe her other professors decided to do the same thing—except for Dr. Stakes."

"I'm sorry to hear there is a rift between Dean Scott and Stakes. I'm also sorry to hear that there was some kind of disruption outside the conference room. I guess it was a pretty vocal demonstration? Do you know anything about it? Was Melina involved?"

"No, Dr. Berg. Melina already went home because she feels so ashamed. There were fliers outside the meeting, and a small group of faculty and students who disagreed with the policy were protesting. It's a bit of an exaggeration to say it was disruptive."

"Well, I hope you weren't part of that group, Margot. I see you as a future leader who understands there are ways to lead change, and demonstrating usually isn't one of them. I think we'll have to investigate that protest more carefully. Thanks for talking to me. I've taken enough of your time. I'm glad you feel supported here, and I hope this gets resolved so this student can return. She sounds like a good person who probably needs a bit more guidance in setting priorities. And you say she's our student assistant? Hmmm."

With that, Dr. Berg abruptly gathered up his papers and continued down Slant Walk in the opposite direction.

Margot felt paralyzed from this odd conversation and stayed on the bench, trying to unravel what she just heard. *Did Dr. Berg support her perspective? If so, why didn't he offer to talk to Stakes? He certainly was respected enough to intervene if he wanted to. Was he disappointed in her for not following protocol? Did he know that Harry was behind the protest, and would this conversation lead to disciplinary action against Harry also? Did he really see her as a future leader?*

Well then, as a leader, and with someone's future at stake, she knew what she needed to do. She wasn't sure how it might affect her career at the university, but she thought it was more important to be able to sleep at night. With that personal confirmation, Margot got up and continued toward Forbes Hall.

Ten minutes later, she shouldered her way past those formidable glass doors and went straight to María's room. As she lifted her hand to knock, the door opened, and she faced a young woman. They were both startled and instinctively took a step back from each other.

As Margot began to introduce herself, she heard María make the introductions.

"Dr. Pearson, is that you? I want you to meet my daughter. This is Dulce. Please come in. How's your ankle?"

Margot smiled and instantly remembered María's gentle warmth, an attribute that was in short supply on campus today. "My ankle is much better, María. Thanks so much for asking. Hi, Dulce. I'm Margot, and it's so nice to meet you." Dulce seemed shy but nodded and smiled.

"Dulce is going out to get something for us to eat. I am so embarrassed. My daughter comes as a surprise, and I have nothing to give her. Will you sit and eat with us, Dr. Pearson?"

What had seemed so urgent only an hour ago in that uncomfortable and sterile conference room, now seemed more controlled in María's warm, quiet space.

"I would love to eat with you two, if that's okay," she answered, surprising herself.

Thirty minutes later, Margot was sitting at the small, vinyl-topped table in María's tiny but tidy kitchen area. The three of them shared chicken and steamed rice while getting to know one another. Margot learned that Dulce graduated last year and lived in her family's house in the city, with her grandmother. She worked as an assistant at an immigration law firm. Things had been tough for them since her father was deported, but she was working hard to help pay off her debts and saving to go back to school. Her dream was to go to law school and help others like her father.

María seemed so proud of her and kept interrupting to add things like, "And she volunteers in the community…she takes Mr. Avila's dog out every morning…she works at a food bank on weekends."

The inevitable topic of Melina was hiding in plain sight, but no one wanted to be the first to bring it up. Finally, Margot thought it was time to lay out her plan to María.

"María, Dr. Sanders and I tried to find Melina this morning before she left for home, but we just missed her. We found her bookbag in a garden where she loves to go and think. Did you know about this special place?"

María shook her head, but Dulce nodded and said, "Oh, wow! I discovered that place when I was here too. It's so peaceful, and no one ever goes there. I wonder how she found it? I so much want to meet her. I made a lot of my own decisions there. It was a perfect hideaway for me when I felt like a stranger in the dorm. I could just be alone and pretend things might be okay someday."

Margot was envious that they had both found this very peaceful place on campus. So far, all she had was a shared office space in a basement. *Where was her secret garden?*

She continued, "This morning, we went to the meeting in the Dean's Office to show our support for Melina. Dean Scott was very understanding and thanked us for coming. She wants to assign a counselor to Melina, who will advise her about resources on campus and provide some guidance on how to balance family and school. Do you think Melina will be open to this idea? Will she come back?"

María wiped a tear from her face and, with a small nod, suggested they move over to the couch to continue their talk. She offered to make tea for everyone and as she went to the stove, Dulce spoke up.

"I'm not sure she'll come back, Dr. Pearson, but we both understand about these meetings. The same thing happened to me at this university five years ago. I was so ashamed and just wanted to go home and never come back. I hated telling Mamá. I thought everyone would be disappointed in me. I went to the meeting in the morning and then straight home that afternoon. When the letter arrived from the university, I threw it away so no one would see it."

"I'm so sorry, Dulce, that you went through that meeting. What happened next for you?"

"Well, I went home and told my parents what happened. I didn't want them to feel guilty, but I wanted them to know just how out of place I felt at the university. They didn't completely understand, but they showed me the love and support I needed. I stayed with my mom for about a year—my dad had already been deported by that point—and they didn't think I was a failure. They just wanted to help me. Everyone wanted to help me. My uncle gave me a part-time job at his store down the street from our house, and I pretended everything was fine. I stocked shelves and helped organize the inventory in the back room. I convinced myself this was a good place to be and that I was helping.

"We didn't really know what to do about the university, so we did nothing for a few months. I got comfortable being back in my old neighborhood. I no longer had to worry about not fitting in. It didn't matter if I wore the same clothes all the time and didn't have a cell phone or a computer. My friends from high school didn't care and were just happy I was back. We went out to the movies, organized parties, and started cooking together. I pushed my dream of a college degree deep down inside, where I kept it locked up.

Then things began to change. My best friends started having serious boyfriends, getting married and having kids. I was happy for them, but I knew I wasn't ready for that. Mamá thought something was wrong because I spent so much time alone in my room, not eating much, talking even less. They wanted me to see a doctor and figure out what was wrong. But it was just that I felt so alone and was thinking about my future. That's when my dream of a college degree came sizzling back up and was in my head all the time. I couldn't sleep, and when I was at the store, I started making mistakes. I couldn't think about anything else, and I knew I had to do something about it. I just didn't know where to start."

The more she listened to Dulce, the more Margot began to understand why Melina had left without trying to explain herself. Just like Dulce, Melina knew the university wouldn't understand her, and she didn't want to expose her family's personal issues to people who really didn't care about that part of her life.

"Dulce, I know you came back and graduated. How did that happen?"

"I was so, so lucky. One morning I was doing inventory at the store, and I heard someone ask for me at the front counter. I hurried over before my cousin could say anything and saw a woman there, not threatening at all but still, an unfamiliar face. Like many of us in the neighborhood, I was suspicious and asked her why she was looking for Dulce. She introduced herself as Dr. Kate Walsh from the university. She went on to tell me that she remembered me from the Review meeting a few months earlier and wanted to check on me, to see how I was doing.

"I was nervous but asked her to come back into the stockroom where we could talk. We sat down on two empty crates as she looked around and asked me how I liked my job. I told her it was okay, a little boring, but it gave me something to do. After listening, she shared that she had never been happy with the outcome of my review. She voted against my suspension, but she was overruled. Since she was new at the university that year, she didn't think there was anything she could do about it. When the semester ended, though, she decided to try and find me and see what I was doing. Dr. Walsh had a friend in Student Affairs who quietly gave her my address."

Margot couldn't believe what she was hearing. She made up her mind to find Kate Walsh and get more information. First, she asked, "Dulce, how did you feel about this? Did you resent her intrusion into your life? Did you think it was any of her business?"

"Dr. Pearson, I was relieved to have someone to talk to who cared about my situation. She didn't judge me or my decision to live at home with a boring job. Instead, she looked around the stockroom and told me how organized it looked and that I should be proud of my work. She told me how she remembered the job her uncle gave her before she really knew what she wanted to do with her life. She said that over semester breaks, she still returns home to relax and spend time with her family on the streets where she grew up. After listening to Dr. Walsh, it was easy to tell her how much I loved being back home where I felt like I fit in. We talked for about an hour before she asked if I might be interested in filing an appeal, to return and work toward my degree. I thought about my dreams of a degree that I had put on hold, and the hours I had been spending alone, trying to figure out my life. She was offering a lifeline, and I decided on the spot that it would be crazy not to accept. I still think of it as the "crate conversation," the one that helped me move forward."

As Dulce finished her story, Margot was barely aware of María, who sat off to the side, sipping her tea and listening quietly. She looked over in time to see her nod and brush away a tear, as Dr. Walsh's kindness once again overwhelmed her.

"She is the kindest person I know, Dr. Pearson. She is not here anymore. I was so sorry when she came to say goodbye last year."

A plan began to percolate in Margot's mind. She turned to Dulce and asked, "Would you work with me to help Melina?"

With no hesitation, Dulce replied, "Of course I would. When do we start?"

Margot gave them both a hug and hurried off to sort things out with Harry. This day might not turn out so badly after all. When she returned to the office, however, she found Harry slumped over his phone.

"Are you sure? How can that be? It just doesn't make sense!" He scratched something out on a small pad just before he abruptly hung up.

"Something wrong, Harry?"

His voice dripping with sarcasm, Harry answered, "Isn't it interesting that this university has no direct contact information for one of its students? There is no way to directly contact Melina. We can only contact her through a high school counselor, a Ms. Ingram. Isn't that just weird?"

Margot had been so caught up with María and Dulce that she had totally forgotten that Dean Scott had asked them to talk to Melina, to prepare her to receive the university's letter.

"That does seem odd. What do you want to do, Harry?"

"Guess I'll give this Ms. Ingram a call and tell her the situation. Ask her to talk to Melina. It seems like an invasion of Melina's privacy, but I don't want her to receive the letter cold. What do you think?"

"Well, we can probably assume Melina and her counselor had a good relationship. I'm sure that's how she ended up at Balsam in the first place. Go ahead and make the call. Then I'll tell you about the master plan that I concocted with María and her daughter, Dulce. I think you'll be pleased."

Melina

"Lina, Lina, watch this!" squealed Berto from the icy sidewalk down below.

Melina shivered as she looked up from her journal to watch him jumping through the middle of a bush in the front yard. Right behind him was Hugo trying to do the same thing, but instead falling flat on his face and laughing all the way.

"This is fun! Watch me too."

She put her pen down and read over this morning's entry.

> *Papá looked so tired this morning. He was slumped way down in his chair. Seems like his head is always resting on his chest, and he doesn't really look at us anymore. I wish he would stop working so many different jobs, but he is really scared. He thinks ICE has been looking around the neighborhood. There are rumors that Mr. Garza from down the street was taken away last week. Papá worries about being deported and leaving us without enough money. He eats dinner in his chair now because he is tired all the time. Mamá and I eat together, but we don't laugh like we used to. I can tell she is worried. I wish I could do more to help them. Just yesterday Gabriela told me how much her*

baby was helping her mother feel better. She said that maybe if I had a baby, Mamá and Papá would not be so sad. Maybe I could have a little girl who would lie across Papá's chest and make him smile. Mamá could make little dresses for her. I tried to tell her that there is no way to know when you get pregnant what sex the baby will be, but she thinks there are ways to make sure it is a boy or girl.

When she talks like that, it is hard for me to listen. Besides, even though I really like Nacho, I do not want a baby. I don't really know what I do want, but it sure isn't a baby. Gabriela also says that if I don't decide soon, Nacho will stop seeing me and find someone else who wants to start a family. That's when I get confused. Does he like me for who I am, or does he just want to have a family? I'm afraid to ask him, so we just don't talk as much as we used to.

Melina closed her journal and smiled as she looked down the stairs toward the boys. Life was so simple for them. This morning routine with them was still her favorite part of the day. It gave her a chance to squeeze into their uncomplicated lives, put her personal worries on hold and temporarily free herself from trying to lighten her parents' load.

Melina scuttled down the stairs to take them to Alicia's, a few doors over, where they played for a few hours with other kids. It wasn't exactly daycare, but it gave the kids in the neighborhood a chance to learn how to share and make new friends. All Alicia asked in return was for each family to take turns bringing a hot lunch once a week. Berto and Hugo loved going there, so they raced each other down the sidewalk as they headed to Alicia's on this very cold morning. Today was their turn to bring lunch, so Melina was balancing a hot dish of macaroni and cheese on top of her journal. She loved how its warmth floated up past her scarf onto her cheeks.

"Have fun! Be good!" Melina told them, as Alicia thanked her and welcomed them inside her home that was already filling up with giggles and overturned toys.

As she turned to leave, Melina decided to stop at the nearby store on her way home. Mamá needed some maseca for the tortillas, and it was always a good idea to have extra snacks for the boys when they came home. She pulled the blue scarf more tightly around her neck and shoulders as she took a left out of Alicia's. She noticed an unfamiliar figure walking in her direction. She knew everyone in the neighborhood and could pretty much call out to them by name based on the color of their winter coats and scarves, but this bright red coat was a new one. And the bulky yellow scarf kept the stranger's face hidden.

As they got closer Melina heard, "Melina? Melina, is that you?"

Suddenly, Melina wanted to draw her head deep into her scarf and become invisible. She recognized the voice.

"Ms. Ingram! Wow, how did you know it was me?"

"I wasn't sure you were still here, but I had a call about a month ago telling me you were home, so I thought I'd stop by and see how you're doing, Melina. I slipped a note under your door a few weeks ago. When I didn't hear from you, I assumed you'd gone back to Balsam, or just needed more time."

"I was planning to come to school and tell you about what happened, but I...well, I..."

"I understand, Melina, and it's okay. Do you have time now to sit and talk? How about I buy you a cup of coffee or hot chocolate down the street? We can warm up together."

Melina felt sheepish, but it was time she figured out what was next in her life, and Ms. Ingram was probably the best person to help her.

She stuttered, "Sure, I'd love that."

The café was empty as the temperatures outside were well below freezing, so they had their choice of tables. They settled into a small round one with two bright yellow chairs in the back corner, and with no one else around Melina felt safe telling Ms. Ingram her story. She was afraid she might break down in the middle of it, and she also didn't want the neighbors to overhear. Thankfully, she didn't recognize the cashier behind the counter, so after ordering their coffee she started to talk about her experiences.

An hour and several cups of coffee later, Melina had told Ms. Ingram why she had to come back home after Papá's removal proceeding. What a relief! Until now, she hadn't realized how much this had weighed on her over the past several months. The journal had been a help, but it wasn't the same as talking to someone. She had pushed her feelings down deeper and deeper, figuring her disappointment at losing her dream of a college degree would eventually go away, but now, everything came out.

She knew her parents wouldn't understand, and her cousins had never gone to college; in fact, they didn't understand why she left home in the first place. They were all just waiting for their kids to have another cousin. For the last several months, she had contented herself by pretending everything was the way it was meant to be. She had tried hanging out with Gabriela but was having trouble relating to her life with the baby and all. Lately, she'd even been turning down Nacho's invitations to go out to movies or concerts because she didn't want him to think they were getting too serious.

Her days had been pretty easy, as they were filled with activities she knew were helping at home. She watched the boys, so her brothers could work more hours. She helped out with the shopping and cooking so Mamá could put her feet up a bit more. Papá didn't say much, but he would sometimes look up at her with a tired smile when she brought him his papers and that made her happy. But the nights were long and lonely; she rarely slept more than a few hours. As she tossed and turned, she alternately blamed herself for making bad decisions, and then her family for not understanding. When morning came, she frequently woke up with the sheet damp and twisted, from her churning through these dark thoughts. Each morning, it took her a few minutes to shake off the guilt she felt for thinking she could blame her family for what happened. On those days, she worked harder than ever to try and hide the resentment that built up inside her at night.

Melina wasn't sure how all this might sound to Ms. Ingram, so she kept her eyes trained on the chipped, blue coffee cup in her hands as she slowly poured out the details. When she finished, she looked up, not knowing what to expect.

"So now you know what I've done, Ms. Ingram. I apologize for not coming to school to tell you, but I was embarrassed. I didn't want to let you down, but I think I need to withdraw from Balsam State. Maybe you can help me?"

Ms. Ingram leaned across the table placing her hand on Melina's arm.

"Melina, you have nothing to be ashamed about. You've had some difficult decisions to make all by yourself. I'm sorry I wasn't there to advise you, but I'd like to help you now. The decisions you've made over the last several months once again confirm for me your strong capacity for empathy and courage. Nothing you experienced at Balsam was easy, yet you continued to try to work it out until your family needed you to come home. Living in a dorm with girls you had nothing in common with was a challenge, but you kept at it even when it didn't make sense to you. You went to class every day and studied hard. You found an emotional resource in María and let her help you when you most needed it. None of those things were easy, yet you persisted. I'm proud of you."

"Thank you, Ms. Ingram. I wanted to stay and do well so you would be proud of me, but now I can't go back."

"Melina, Dr. Sanders called me soon after you came back home. He and another professor, Dr. Pearson I think, tried to find you before you left to tell you about the meeting, but they just missed you. He didn't know how to get in touch with you, but someone at Balsam gave him my number. He told me about the meeting in the Dean's Office. That's why I left a note for you. That meeting ended with the recommendation that you meet with a counselor who can help you with tough decisions, and make sure you find the right resources at Balsam. They want you to know they are there for you and want you to succeed. Of course, returning is your decision, but it sounds like there are people there who understand and really want to help."

"Ms. Ingram, Dr. Sanders is really a nice person. He's the one who drove me home when Papá needed me. I think he does understand, but I'm not sure he can really help. I'm not sure a counselor can help me, either. It's embarrassing to go to a counselor. It makes me feel stupid and even more like I don't belong there. My roommate and her friends would laugh at the whole idea, and I'll never be able to do the things they do."

"I hear what you're saying, Melina. This is not easy. I'd like to help you think it through. Can you come to school tomorrow, so we can look at some choices you might have?"

"Of course, but I don't want Mamá and Papá to know we're talking. They think everything is good now that I'm home."

"Maybe, when the time comes, we can talk to them together. How about you and I meet at 11:00 tomorrow, my office?"

"Sure thing."

Back outside on the sidewalk, they hugged each other against a chilly wind and bundled up as they headed in different directions. Melina felt a little lighter. She had someone who understood her and was able to help her sort it out. That part made her happy, and she noticed how bright the sun was today. Burrowing deeper into her warm scarf, she also worried about her parents, and how any change might affect them. Ms. Ingram said she had courage, and Melina trusted her. She felt pretty fragile and knew that whatever happened next would take lots of courage. She hoped Ms. Ingram would help her find it.

The next day, after dropping the boys off, Melina hurried down the familiar sidewalk that led to her old school. That morning, she had waited for Mamá to leave home first, because she didn't want her to see that she put a dress on, instead of her usual jeans and boots. Melina didn't want to walk into school looking like a failed student; instead, she wanted to confirm Ms. Ingram's faith in her by at least looking confident.

She dropped off the boys, and as she followed that familiar route to her old school, she felt a little lightheaded and knew her stomach was churning a bit. It seemed weird to be returning to Obregon High. *Would the office know she had failed at the university? Would they all be thinking, "Knew she wouldn't make it!" She wondered if the security guard, Mr. Banks, was still there, in his old brown uniform, with his head bouncing between his earbuds. Would he recognize her? Would he even let her in without a school ID?*

She tentatively pushed open the front door and went through the new, scary-looking security scanner, along with some kids she still recognized, who were always late. Moments later, as she turned the corner by the office, she heard, "Hey, it's Melina! How about it? What brings a big shot college student like you back here?"

Mr. Banks now sat on a legitimate chair behind a desk with a shiny surface. She smiled and for once was actually glad to see him.

"Hi, Mr. Banks. I'm here to see Ms. Ingram. We have an appointment today. Do I need a permission slip?"

Just then, Ms. Ingram came around the corner and reached out to take her hand.

"I'll take it from here, Hank. We're headed upstairs to the conference room, Melina. No need to sign a slip today."

Melina didn't know there was a conference room at her old school, but she followed Ms. Ingram up the rough, uncarpeted and well-worn concrete staircase, being careful not to use the wobbly wooden railing for support. She thought it was funny how much more comfortable she felt here than she ever had at her dorm, where the floors and railings were always polished and sparkly. Maybe that was part of the problem; there were no visible blemishes there; if there were, they were covered by polish and cleanser. Here, it was different. Here, in the old, faded building with its cracked windows and peeling paint, it was okay to make mistakes because the bar was low, and there were few expectations. The trouble was that few tried to meet even these low expectations.

Feeling a little conspicuous in her good clothes, Melina kept her head down so the other students wouldn't recognize her. Ms. Ingram stopped at a narrow door and nodded for Melina to join her. As she walked in, Melina immediately recognized the conference room; she remembered it as the long, narrow closet where, rumor had it, some students were sent for punishment. Why was it now called a conference room, she wondered? Although it had a long table with folding chairs leaning against the walls, there was only room for four people at the most.

Ms. Ingram took a seat on one side of the table and motioned to Melina to come and sit next to her facing the door.

"Melina, I'm really glad you agreed to be here today. It may seem odd to you that we're meeting in this room and not my office," she said with a laugh, "but we've been lobbying the principal for a private meeting space for so long that I thought we should use it. I really like the privacy and eventually will make it into a place where students may find it easier to talk to me."

"Good idea, but you'll have to convince kids they're not in trouble when they come here. That's what we all thought it was used for." She took a deep breath. "I hope I'm not in trouble today."

"Not at all, Melina, and I hope you don't mind but I've invited two others to join us. This quiet space will let us all talk openly and honestly, with no interruptions. As you can see, no one remembers this place even exists, except, of course, for the students who were once in trouble!"

She smiled fondly at Melina. Just then, there was a knock at the door, and Mr. Banks ushered in two women who were busy stomping their boots to clean off the snow that immediately melted into the cracked linoleum. Ms. Ingram stood up to greet them as they disentangled themselves from their wrap-around scarves and heavy coats. The first woman was young, a little older than Melina, and had a beautiful smile. Her long dark hair fell over her shoulders as she leaned across the table to say hello. She seemed to know Melina, but who was she? Then the second woman unveiled herself as she shrugged off her puffy down coat and furry hat.

¡Dios mío, it was Dr. Pearson! Melina crossed her arms and hugged herself to stop from trembling while wondering if she really was in trouble. Surely, Ms. Ingram would have told her, right? She could trust her, couldn't she?

"Hi, Melina. It's so good to see you again," said Dr. Pearson, with a smile Melina didn't fully recognize. Even though they had experienced some warm moments a few months ago, Melina was still a little afraid of her. Melina wondered what she was doing here—and who was the other woman? *How much did they know about her family and her own personal failures? Were they here to gang up on her? Report her family?* Melina felt trapped, and her first instinct was to get out of there. She started to push her chair back and grab her coat when Dr. Pearson continued.

"Melina, I want you to meet someone special. This is Dulce, María's daughter."

With that, Dulce leaned into the table and looked over with eyes as kind and warm as her mother's.

"I've been looking forward to meeting you. Mamá told me so many nice things about you."

Sensing Melina's surprise and obvious confusion, Ms. Ingram spoke up to help explain why they were all here in this makeshift room, hidden away from the outside world.

"Melina, I know this might seem like we're ganging up on you, but please give us a chance. We want to help. Don't be angry with me. Yes, I did know most of what happened. Not all the personal details that you shared yesterday, but I knew why you came home. I thought it was important for you to have the chance to tell someone the story. You had kept it hidden deep inside for months with no one to tell. I thought I could help by listening and letting you know that you weren't wrong to feel frustrated and confused. I never judged you. I care about you and want to help you sort things out. Does that make sense?"

Melina pulled herself back to the table but with her arms still crossed to allow herself some distance from the others. She looked up and with her lip trembling stammered, "I guess I trust you, Ms. Ingram, but I'm not sure what I'm supposed to do now."

Dulce could feel Melina's embarrassment and bewilderment, and in her unassuming way, she became the group's voice.

"I understand, Melina. You can trust me; I've been in your situation and didn't have anyone to talk to. I also wasn't sure who to trust. It took me a long time to realize I needed help to figure out what to do next. I couldn't do it alone. In my case, I was suspended from the university, and I contented myself for a while by staying with my family and working for my uncle. I loved all of them, and knew I was helping them just by being there, but there was always something nagging at me. I was letting go of an important dream. If someone hadn't stepped forward to offer their help, I might still be stuck. But a teacher from the university came to see me, by surprise just like this, and offered to help me. I believe you can trust these two incredibly special women who want to help you figure this out. I also want to help if I can. No one is here to tell you what to do or judge you for decisions you've made; we just want to give you a place to think out loud and offer any resources we may have."

Melina was starting to understand and nodded slowly as she began to uncross her arms.

She was surprised to hear Dr. Pearson add, "I want you to know, Melina, that your story has already made me think more about students and teaching than any college course I ever took. Listening to you in María's apartment, I heard a young, very courageous woman with strong values and passion. She filled my head with things I hadn't thought about before. I heard about a decision she was making that could have significant consequences for her, both at home and at the university. She had a tough choice to make, but she did it and didn't look back. That took courage, Melina, and I admire you for it."

"Are you okay with this, Melina?" asked Ms. Ingram. "I know it's a surprise, but we truly do want to give you a place to think out loud and offer ideas to help you move forward."

"Okay! Well then, how do we begin?" Melina felt a smile slowly spreading across her face and was more hopeful than she had been in many weeks. She still didn't know how to move forward or where she wanted to go, and she worried about Mamá and Papá, but at least she was no longer alone.

Suddenly, the dark and narrow room with folding chairs previously used only for punishment took on a new dimension. It virtually lit up as ideas flew around like fireworks on Cinco de Mayo: *How about an internship in Dulce's office downtown? How about returning to the university? How about opening up to her roommate? Maybe going to community college for a year would be a good idea?*

Nothing was out of bounds.

This initial burst of excitement was energizing in a way Melina never experienced. The room pulsated, and there were smiles and laughter all around. As the dynamic grew, Melina and Dulce unconsciously gravitated toward each other, and their shared experiences began to fly back and forth.

Melina noticed that Ms. Ingram had pushed her chair back and was standing up. She worried that she and Dulce were being rude, or that their time together had come to an end. Instead, Ms. Ingram simply announced that she and Dr. Pearson were starving. "We're going out for some food. What can we get for you two? There's a bodega down the street, and we can bring something back to share. Okay?" Melina was relieved, and the girls nodded as they dove right back into their conversation.

"Listen, I hope you don't waste any more time thinking of yourself as a failure. Or being ashamed of anything that has happened to you. You've been brave and made some tough decisions by yourself. I made the same ones, and I haven't regretted them. Family comes first, but we also can't let go of our dreams. Our families won't understand what we are going through at the university, but they do understand dreams. We're here because they followed their dream. They want us to have an easier life than they had, even if they won't always understand what it takes to get there. Make sense?"

Just like that, Dulce clarified Melina's muddled thoughts. Alone, she hadn't been able to put them into words, but here was someone who really got it and could help. She pictured Mamá and Papá as they worked hard every day. *Having jobs, owning a home and providing for family were at the heart of the dream they shared 30 years ago. Now, they owned a small house and put food on the table every day. Did their original dream include stepping up when her brothers' wives went back to Mexico leaving the babies with them? Did it include having a daughter who wanted to leave home for a college education? No, but they accepted it. They accepted it because that's what families do.* Sometimes, Melina had thought her parents were stuck, but she was beginning to understand that wasn't how they felt.

"Thank you, Dulce. You're helping me translate my thoughts into words. I think you're the best one to help me figure out how to move ahead. I'm ready to start."

For the next hour, they used the old blackboard on the wall behind them to scratch out their ideas. Arrows flew all over the board, connecting some ideas and erasing others. They quite forgot about Ms. Ingram and Dr. Pearson, who must have gotten lost on their way to the bodega.

& & &

Acknowledgments

They say it takes a village, and that was certainly true with this debut novel. From the start, I knew the story I wanted to tell. What I didn't know was how much help I needed along the way. It all started with the initial edits of Beth Finke who kept reminding me to show, not tell. I've tried, Beth. Elizabeth DeNoma helped me see the big picture with her developmental edit, and Maura McGurk polished it off with a copy edit. I owe these editors a huge thank you.

As soon as I spoke to Lise Marinelli, I knew that WCP was the right publishing group for me. The team worked as a partner with me as I polished and then polished some more. Many thanks to Dawn McGarrahan Wiebe for guiding me through the process and to Audrey Brock for the final proofread.

I took a chance one summer when I joined the Ludington Writers' Group in Michigan. It was the first time I had ever read my work aloud to other writers I didn't know. Their insights and encouragement gave me confidence and had a significant impact on how I told this story. In addition, I joined an online group, P2P, led by Kathy Ver Eecke where I learned from writers, agents and publishers how the publishing industry works. This group was wonderfully collaborative and helped me clearly articulate the story's focus. The Women's Fiction Writers Association offered the opportunity to enter a competition that resulted in cogent critiques and strong encouragement.

Maria Cabrales and Alen Takhsh verified that my descriptions of deportation hearings, immigration issues and Villacito were on target. I owe them a huge debt of gratitude for the time they took on the phone and in writing. My first two readers, Joanne Daniels and Sharon Silverman, provided me with valuable insights related to character development and story development. Sharon wanted to know more about one character and Joanne told me the ending just didn't work for her. Those two comments led me to major revisions. I sincerely appreciate their honesty. Elaine Kurczewski and Susan Irvings also read the manuscript at important junctures and helped to move me along.

As always, Larry has been there for the entire journey. He has read the manuscript so many times that he could probably recite it for anyone willing to listen. Without his constant support, this story would still be under construction.

I dedicate this book to my father, H. Nord Kitchen, who took me to three libraries every Saturday when I was young. His commitment to reading has been an enduring gift to me and led me to not only read voraciously but to write whenever possible.

About the Author

MARTHA CASAZZA is an educator and author. Her life's work has been dedicated to teaching and learning. She has explored this on a global stage that started in Chicago and stretched to universities in South Africa, Poland, Kazakhstan, Scotland and England and currently to preschoolers in Sayulita, Mexico. She focuses on access and support for underserved populations.

Her work began in 1970 in the Chicago Public School system and moved to National Louis University where she trained teachers to work with previously marginalized adult learners. As a Fulbright Scholar in South Africa, following the end of Apartheid, Martha worked with faculty to introduce strategies for teaching their "new" students from the townships who had been underprepared for university study. As a consultant in Chicago, Martha collaborated with Instituto Progreso to create a college-level educational program to serve local Spanish-speaking residents in Pilsen. Based on this work, she was awarded the "Instituto Spirit Award" in 2018.

Her writings are evolving from nonfiction to fiction, but the theme consistently highlights the importance of educational access and support. Two of her nonfiction writings were cited as classics in the field of developmental education. *Dreaming Forward*, was on the Barnes & Noble bookshelf and the subject of an NPR interview. Please visit www.marthacasazza.com for a link to her interview and professional experience.